ALSO BY ROBERT GAGE EVANS

FICTION

OTHER BOOKS OF THE SOJOURNER SERIES

Book One
YOKUTS WARRIOR
SPRING
1792

Book Three
OMROD SMYTH
A COD FISHERMAN FROM BRISTOL TOWN
1579-1634

Book Four
JAMES CATHCART
SLAVE TO THE DEY OF ALGIERS
1785

NONFICTION

PINE FLAT: A QUICKSILVER BOOMTOWN (2005)
PINE FLAT: FAMILIES OF THE MODINI PRESERVE (2016)

SUTTER'S FORT

ALTA CALIFORNIA

1838

A NOVEL

ROBERT GAGE EVANS

THE SOJOURNER SERIES
BOOK TWO

Sutter's Fort - Alta California, 1838 BY ROBERT GAGE EVANS
Book Two of the Sojourner Series

Copyright 2017 by Robert Gage Evans

Editor, revised edition: Jocelyne Thomas, Branwen Books Editing Services

Cover design and interior layout by Ellie Searl, Publishista®

ISBN-10: 099834253X
ISBN-13: 9780998342535
LCCN: 2017952311

Previously titled JOSÉ JESÚS & JOHN SUTTER, PROPRIETORS, NEW HELVETIA 1838

PINE FLAT EDITIONS
Sebastopol, CA

SUTTER'S FORT
Illustration - 1840s

en.wikipedia.org

CHAPTER ONE

Summer 1838

I WAS one of a dozen Indio slaves following the orders of our Spanish master. The veranda of his large adobe house was cool with a breeze off Monterey Bay, and full of loquacious guests. The general's library was hot and stuffy with only the host and one guest.

"Cider?" I offered. "A canapé?"

Both waved me away.

"I'm not certain where you received such information, sir," the stranger told General Mariano Vallejo, "but it is indeed a fact that I hold the rank of subaltern in the Swiss Guard."

"Ahh, the Swiss Guard." Vallejo, the pretender to diligent interest. "Perhaps you were called to active duty at some time during your military career?"

The visitor stood taller and pulled his stomach inward. "Yes, sir, I was a very young subaltern with a corps of Swiss cavalry against the French."

"The French, you say?"

"It was the famous Battle of Zug."

General Vallejo looked at the ceiling for a long moment, and then back again to his visitor. "I beg your pardon, Señor Sutter, I am unfamiliar with any Battle of Zug."

I moved a step backward, still close enough to offer my tray of delights if required, and close enough to hear every word.

Sutter lowered his head with a brief bow. "Well then, General Vallejo, permit me a brief summary of the battle."

"Proceed as you wish, my friend."

"First, a cup of cider, if I may?"

At the nod from Vallejo I stepped forward, delivered the cider in ritual ceremony, and returned to my former position.

"You may recall, good sir, that in early 1799 our famous Swiss General Alois von Reding organized an army to stop that atheist devil Napoleon from invading our lovely Catholic nation."

"Ah, Napoleon." Vallejo lowered his eyes to study the design of his Persian rug. "He was a powerful opponent, indeed."

"I must admit to you, General Vallejo, that we were horribly outnumbered as we approached the village of Zug. Napoleon's army was entrenched in classic formation, with cannon mounted at the center and infantry on both wings."

"Napoleon's cavalry: what position did they hold in this village of Zug?"

Sutter dithered with his cup of cider for a long moment; first to his lips without drinking, and then examining the depths for inspiration. "You must understand General Vallejo that Zug is a very small village in the very rugged German Alps, and therefore Napoleon was able to use his cavalry only as messengers and spies." Sutter shrugged his shoulders in the European manner. "The French cavalry had no tactical function at the Battle of Zug."

"Yes, certainly," said Vallejo, "cavalry on the plains, infantry in the mountains; every general the world over can make sense of that imperative."

Sutter paused to catch the eyes of his host. "I was, as I mentioned previously, a very young subaltern in von Reding's cavalry."

Mariano Vallejo leaned forward, a skeptical glint to his eye. "Forgive me, sir, although I have no interest in the countless battles of Europe, I am very interested in discussing the maneuvers favored by Swiss cavalrymen in the rugged mountains near the peculiar village of Zug."

Sutter drained his cup of cider. "Well now," he said, "we must get together on some cold and rain-soaked evening and trade our stories. I have heard that you lead a very credible corps of cavalry here in Alta California."

Vallejo snapped his fingers for my attendance, and both men took a smoked salmon canapé from my silver tray. The general leaned toward Sutter. "You must visit my rancho and also you should spend time in my village of Sonoma. We have many cattle on the rancho and some creditable gray stallions for your inspection."

"Your rancho is located on the northern edge of the saltwater bay, I understand."

"Indeed, I can ship my cattle hides and tallow down a creek in a barge, and then transfer the lot onto a seagoing vessel." The general smiled, "The details of life on a remote ranch in Alta California may hold little interest for you, but I'm certain that my stallions, if nothing else, will hold some interest for a cavalry officer."

Sutter nodded his head in the manner of a flustered youngster. "Yes, I'll arrange a visit as soon as possible, but now please excuse me, for I have promised to attend Governor Alvarado and also a few citizens of your lovely..." He stammered for the correct word, "...lovely country," he managed.

"We are currently a province of Mexico," the general said.

"Oh," said Sutter.

"Canapé? Cider?" I offered.

❋ ❋ ❋

Our rigid surveillance of Sutter was into its second month. My team of Yokuts, Miwok, and half-breeds had watched him day and night, yet neither Sutter nor the dons of Alta California had the least inkling of our attention. I was an experienced spy, and held high standards for those who worked under my direction. We were all veterans of the forty-year war, and had learned the depth of stupidity that consumed many leaders of the Spanish invaders. We knew that the mission padres and all those who pretended to own the land of the Yokuts and Miwok and Wappo were fools and tricksters of the lowest sort! Thus it was, when Sutter approached Governor Alvarado upon his arrival in the Presidio of Monterey, I simply joined them as a silent brown post with cider and canapes on a silver tray. Both white men ignored me, as I knew they would.

The preliminaries took some time, as they bowed and smiled one to the other, much in the fashion of two large birds meeting for the first time. The mood changed when Governor Alvarado asked his first question. "Tell me, Captain Sutter—don't you have concerns about your fortune back in Swiss land? What I mean by the question, my friend, is how in the world can your excellent business survive such a prolonged absence without falling apart? Do you have a brother to manage your extensive business operations?"

"I hold not a single concern, esteemed governor, for my wife is a wonderful administrator." Sutter smiled, but his eyes were vacant. "You must understand that her family has sustained the same manufacture of leather goods for three generations, and now the business is mine." The smile disappeared. "My wife, of course, has help from our eldest son and two of her brothers."

The governor of Alta California murmured, "Sir, you are a fortunate man indeed." Alvarado leaned slightly forward at the waist. "Tell me, do you perchance manufacture military saddles with your leather?"

"Alas, good sir, I own a simple business that supplies fine leather bolts to the makers of aprons and dresses, nothing more."

"May I assume that your customers are from your home city of Morgarten?"

"Governor, please, I have no intention of allowing an inflated impression of my wealth." Sutter tilted his head to the left, and with the ingratiating smile of a self-satisfied coyote, continued his conquest of the Spanish don. "But I must admit that we provide to all those who require our fine leather throughout my Swiss country and into France, and also many of the German principalities."

"Captain Sutter, there is no need for false modesty with me. Just tell me, good sir, are you able to maintain a sufficient stream of capital to sustain your far-reaching leather business and also allow some consideration of investment opportunities here in Alta California?"

"A very astute question, Governor Alvarado, for in fact I shall sell the leather business when I see the perfect investment prospect here in your domain. Until that propitious moment, I am at the mercy of every ill wind."

"You have cash at hand, Captain Sutter?"

"My notes of debt are counted as good as gold, governor."

The two white gentlemen traded their unctuous smiles with equal intensity, and then both men silently retreated from the other.

✹ ✹ ✹

I sat on a stool at the end of a wharf that stretched into Monterey Bay. The wind was steady from the northwest while a multitude of birds moved about in noisy search of food. "Good!" I whispered into the wind. "What a lovely partner the man from Morgarten will make."

Sutter reminded me of my Uncle Podnow, with their similar potbellies and misdirection feints. Both were genial gossips and sharp negotiators for any possible prize. When I was a youngster, Podnow could shock me with pulling live scorpions from my ear. Now as a man of some experience, I must admit equal astonishment when I saw Sutter pull from the ear of Alvarado enough land to create an empire. It was the land of the Wintu and Yokuts and Miwok of course, but still, it was all given by one white invader to another with great magnanimity on the one hand, and humble gratitude on the other. The damn sonsabitches.

❄❄❄

I stationed myself on a large red rock cliff on the northeast shore of the huge saltwater bay. My spies were scattered eastward on both sides of the brackish river that flowed into the bay, and each spy was assigned a messenger to run or paddle a canoe until they could whisper into my ear. All was ready.

Sutter's boat made quick work crossing the bay from the Presidio of San Francisco. It was noon when he passed my camp, with sail raised and full from a steady onshore wind. Gulls and ducks filled the water and air. Bald hills on opposite sides of the brackish estuary pinched closer, and when the wind diminished, all forward motion was halted. I could see and hear as Captain Sutter shouted, "Drop the sail!" Then, "Ready with the oars. Now, stroke!"

The invaders moved eastward among flat islands and into heat that increased with each thousand strokes. My spies hid behind rocks and scraggly trees or tule reeds to catch every detail of the crew's behavior. The runners working with the spies described Sutter's red face to me and also told me of two women and six men who were neither Spanish nor Mestizo. Six additional white invaders completed the invasion mob of fifteen. When one invader or another said sharp words to their commander, my clever spies put on their long faces to describe the dismissive gestures or loud voices that went bickering back and forth.

At dusk that first night, I followed the trail of smoke that drifted above a thicket of willow and ash trees. My men surrounded Sutter's encampment and waited for my orders. When most of the crew seemed asleep and Sutter was alone near the fire, I peered through a screen of scrubby willow trees. The sole sentry was slumped against a tree, chin on chest. The fire was cold, and both Sutter and his army slept like rocks on a beach. The planet the invaders called Venus simmered among the lesser stars, and seemed hot as the sun.

I cracked a dry stick over my knee.

Sutter jerked upright. "Who's there?" His voice was slow with sleep.

"Leave!" I shouted. "You are trespassing upon our land!"

Sutter stood and cocked his big horse pistol. The sharp metal crack created a sudden silence for a few heartbeats, then the first bold chorus frog peeped, and a million of his compatriots combined to fill the void. Two hoot owls and mosquitoes without number joined in harmony.

"I am José Jesús, supreme spirit doctor of the Yokuts and also of the Miwok." The tiny turds in my gut settled from their churning. "Who are you?"

"Sutter. Captain John A. Sutter. What the hell you making such a fuss for? Come round in the morning and we'll talk. Go away. I was having a pleasant dream."

"Put the pistol away, white man, and listen to me."

"I detest repeating myself, Indio, so for the last time, I warn that you must go away. Maybe we'll talk in the morning."

"Sutter, you are sleeping on the land of my people. If you wish to wake at the next sunrise, we will talk now."

Two white men readied muskets. Six, whom I decided were Kaneka men, waved huge wooden clubs back and forth. Sutter leaned forward into the dark. "No Indio can tell a civilized gentleman what he should do. Get away from here before I shoot you with this weapon."

"The owls, Sutter—listen to the owls."

"Frogs and owls, that's all I've been hearing on this hot evening," Sutter said.

I gave the horned owl call. *"Hoo hooo, hoot hooo,"* and from each quadrant beyond the shadows came the answering call, *"Hoo hooo, hoot, hooo."* One call joined the next, until the owl chorus built into a crescendo of *hoots* and *hoos* whirling round and round the shadows. Suddenly the song stopped, as if under an orchestra director's baton. Absolute silence continued for two measures, followed by a long solo braying laugh that continued until the frogs reclaimed their domain.

Sutter lowered his pistol. Good, I had his attention. Slowly now, closer, then closer I crept, as patient as Podnow, as clever as my coyote brother.

"Tell me then, Indio, what do you want of me?"

I moved into the moonlight, past the reluctant guards, and sat in front of him.

He continued to stand, and I extended my hand toward the black dirt. "Sit. We have much to talk about, you and I."

Sutter eased back the hammer of his pistol and slowly lowered himself to sit cross-legged on the hard-packed ground. A black blanket humped over his head of frazzled brown hair, and he stared with great intensity at the black-and-white stripes painted on my body.

"Tell me, Indio, what do you have for me that is more important than a night of uninterrupted sleep?" His voice held the practiced arrogance of most white men. There was a hint of padre entitlement in Sutter—the fabricated wisdom they claimed was endowed to them by hairy gods and virgin mothers.

My hand moved faster than his eye to draw a scorpion from his ear. He looked at the quivering creature in my open hand and blinked just one time. I pulled four more—two from each ear—and held the five angry creatures in my cupped hands as if offering a gift. It was an impressive trick, I thought, but Sutter ignored my performance.

"What is your name again, good sir? Speak slowly so that I can remember the correct accent."

"José Jesús."

"Ah! An escaped slave of some mission or other, I imagine." He took a twig to clean his teeth, as if he had nothing better to while away his time. "Have you been following me from the port of the San Francisco Presidio, José?"

"For a much longer time, John. It has been nearly two months that I've been your invisible shadow." I palmed the scorpions. "You're a clever man, and I must say that you have impressed me with your ability to manipulate the Californios."

"Goodness gracious, how can that happen? I find it intolerable that you have been spying on me for two months!" Sutter puffed himself like an ardent toad. "You saw what happened to me in Monterey? Yerba Buena?"

"Every day I have observed your behavior and also every night."

Sutter dropped his twig and leaned toward me. "Why, José Jesús? What do you hope to achieve with such shenanigans?"

I felt more confident now, with this man leaning toward me, listening for possibilities of profit. If he was afraid of me, the lines above his eyes would tell me. If he was bored with me or held me as an ineffectual bother, he would spit the shreds of his twig at my feet. Profit, he smelled. I leaned to meet him with my own gods at hand and my own desire for profit. "You have made a few enemies and a good many friends among the Californios, Captain Sutter. You are about to make the Yokuts and Miwok your deadly enemies. In fact, they will destroy you if you invade their land."

He shrugged. "Governor Alvarado gave me permission to settle this valley of his. I paid the stipulated fee, and he did not place any restrictions that might give rights or privileges to the previous residents of my land."

"Ha! In true fact you gave little Juan Alvarado nothing more than a letter full of empty promises." I moved closer. "Juan was a fool to accept the inventions of your wealth, and you are a double fool to accept a title to land that is not his to offer." A red ball of anger moved from my stomach to my chest. "I'll put Juan's balls into my atole if he ever shows his face in the great valley."

Sutter made his voice very soft, like a clever padre manipulating a rich old white lady. "I've talked with Vallejo also."

I let the frogs sing for a bit before answering. "Vallejo is a warrior of merit—not Alvarado."

Sutter gave a dry cough. "An important person told me that Mariano Vallejo led an army into this valley of mine. I heard that he defeated the Tularaños and burned all their villages."

"It is true that he burned a few villages." The red ball cooled a few degrees. "Vallejo killed some women and children and burned a village or two. It was nothing, nothing much at all."

"I remember now that Mariano said your name to me, José Jesús. He implied that you were a man of noble character."

I laughed, and echoes of my laughter erupted from the darkness. "Mariano is a magnificent liar, and together you make a good pair."

Sutter joined with my laughter. "All good leaders are liars," he said. "The others are fanatics or fools."

We let our chuckles fade, and I leaned forward until our noses nearly touched. "You are surrounded by two hundred of my warriors."

"Ah, very good, José Jesús, I hear a large dose of horse dung dripping from your mouth." He gave me the soul-eating smile that had so befuddled the Californios over the past weeks. "I counted fifty owls," he whispered, "maybe fewer."

I let the smile fade and gave the arrogant white man an opportunity to think about the distance he'd traveled in one single day. "Sutter. You've got just one chance to fulfill your dreams."

"I believe that we have talked enough for this evening, José. Therefore I propose that we continue our discussion tomorrow morning." He inched back from where I could easily touch him and settled the blanket about his shoulders. "My Kaneka lady is waiting for me, and my knees hurt with all this sitting on the dirt."

"Certainly, John. Tomorrow I will divert you from the Miwok land that Alvarado claimed to give you, and instead take you to the land of the Wintu people." I raised my hand to forestall any interruption. "The Wintu are weak and poor and amenable to the work that you will have for them."

"Who are these Wintu people? They're part of your tribe?"

"Don't insult the Yokuts. Listen to me, Captain Sutter, and learn the details that may protect you in the future." I tapped Sutter under the chin with my medicine stick. "The Wintu are not of the People. They're less than nothing, and they serve the Yokuts and Miwok at our pleasure."

Sutter sat with his thoughts for a long moment. "How far away are these people?"

"Not far at all. Just one more tributary river to the north marks their boundary with the Miwok."

"What is it that you want, José Jesús?"

"You must honor the strong nations of the great valley if we are to survive the white man."

"I'm a white man."

"Yes, Sutter, you're a white man, but you listen to your Kaneka people, and you may learn how to listen to me." A coyote joined his song with the frogs and owls. A night-hunting heron croaked and then flapped west toward the river. "You have dreams of a great empire, is that not true?"

"I will call it New Helvetia."

"I prefer the names devised by the elders of each village in the great valley."

"More will come, José Jesús. Many, many whites will come and live in my New Helvetia."

"So it seems." My eyes felt heavy and my stomach empty of even little rabbit turds.

Sutter tapped my knee with his hand. "Why, José Jesús? Why are we having this discussion?"

"The People must survive. That is why you sit here on the black dirt." I held Sutter's eye. "The God of all Spirits seems to have forgotten his favored people, and we must find another way to nourish our strength. We'll work together, Captain Sutter. We'll find a way to diminish our weaknesses and still accomplish our private intentions."

"You'll help me get New Helvetia started?"

"Yes."

"What do I give you?"

"Time, Sutter. You will give my people time. We must join together in plotting the way to protect our land from the white man. We both need time to defeat the white man's tricks."

He was wide-awake now, a trader bargaining for his price. "What do I receive in return?"

"You will have my partnership. I will advise you where to locate your villages, and I will find workers for your fields. I will protect you from death."

Sutter let his eyes blink three times. "Maybe we have a deal," he said.

"We will continue to bargain, John. I will help you accomplish your dreams, and very soon you will do the same for me."

"I need sleep, José Jesús. Tomorrow we must finish this conversation."

"Yes, tomorrow it is. Go to your warm shoulder, Captain Sutter. Sleep well, but leave this land of the Miwok with the sunrise."

"Pretty sure of yourself, aren't you?" Sutter gave me a small smile with his eyes a narrow slit. It was the expression of a thief biding his time.

"We have no choice, you and I. We help each other or we both die."

"Very well then, in the morning, José Jesús—that's when we'll talk."

"Yes." I stood and walked away from Captain John A. Sutter. The horned owl called and I answered. My men joined with their chorus of *hoots* and *hoos* for two rounds of the circle, and then went quiet.

"Very nice," Sutter called into the darkness. "You have a way with the owls, spirit man."

CHAPTER TWO

Summer, 1838

IT WAS PLEASANTLY COOL UNDER the huge white oak tree. Most of my men rested on the soft cushion of duff and leaves or talked in quiet voices, one to the other. Carlos and I sat at the edge of the shade line where we could watch Sutter lead his crew through bramble bushes and poison oak. The white farmers were actually sailors who'd jumped ship from one merchant vessel or another. There was one fellow from Boston, I knew for a fact, but all six had been given a choice between the Presidio jail or signing on with Sutter to plant oats or chase after cows. Now they all yelled vile oaths at Sutter as they pushed ahead on hands and knees to haul themselves up the steep incline of the riverbank. In a final gasp, first there was Sutter trying his best to smile, then his Kanaka warriors and women, and finally the so-called farmers dragging themselves onto a shelf of land full of oak trees and trampled grass.

Sutter's face was flushed red as he walked to stand in front of me. We were both silent, and I gave him the opportunity to stare all around. "Nice view," he finally said. After a few more moments he waved an arm toward the east. "Those mountains over there still have plenty of snow on the top." He stooped to pinch and squeeze and smell a handful of dirt, then smiled at his treasure. "Good little breeze up here." A cavernous smile encompassed his broad nose and every line of his face. "Good dirt, good breeze, and lots of water."

I motioned. "Go ahead, sit down and we'll talk awhile."

"What about my farmers and the Kanaka folks? It's been six or seven hours since they had anything to eat or drink." Sutter pointed a finger at me. "That last stretch after the tributary was a hard haul. More rowing than sailing."

"How'd you figure on feeding your army, Sutter? Do you have some magic seed that grows instant crops?"

"It was my intention to tax my subjects for the goods and services that I needed."

"Yes, tax your subjects." I paused to study the two hundred or so Wintu people and the enormous panorama of flat plain leading to nearby hills and on to enormous snow-capped mountains. "We need to talk about your intentions and mine, so please have a seat."

"Look after my people, will you? They're hungry and tired."

"Don't worry. I've got my people to take care of them, and so now we'll just talk and eat here in the shade and get to know each other for a while."

It was obvious that he had a fine appreciation of the situation because now his eyes were as bold as a prairie falcon's, and the wrinkles over his eyes slanted upward.

"Who are all these people around us?"

I pointed with my chin. "The handsome young warriors over by the first grove of oak trees are Miwok folk from Chief Raphero's village." We looked at the other with steady eyes. "The rest—the pathetic looking characters—are Wintu."

He shrugged his shoulders. "They look fine enough to me."

"They're like children who laugh and cry for no good reason. The men tell silly stories and gamble, while the women feed them what they can."

"Humph," Sutter said. "They sound like our Napoleños, who are also big happy folks but are also very good workers."

"Yes, they are good workers, these Wintu—especially the women."

Sutter motioned toward the oak grove. "What about those six over there—the mounted warriors under the big oak tree? Tell me their story."

"They are my *vaqueros*."

Sutter smiled. "They are fine-looking men indeed." He lifted his nose like a coyote downwind from a bitch in heat. "And tell me, sir, what is that good smell filling my nose—beef or venison?"

"Neither, sir, it is horse—lovely, sweet horse flesh."

"Ah, horse. The French people also enjoy the flesh of horse."

It was my turn to brag, to blind Sutter to my defects. "When I served as alcalde at Mission San Juan Bautista, we served our French visitors the steamed horse. They praised my culinary efforts." I sipped water from a small basket. "I prepared soups and soufflés and three-layered cakes for my French guests, and always they applauded my efforts with loud belches and the most redolent of farts."

"I'm confused," he said. "I thought that you Indios served the padres more as slaves than skilled artisans. Correct me if I am in error."

"I served as a slave at Mission San Juan Batista for three years. I was forced to work from dawn to dusk in the fields or hauling raw cattle hides. We were fed during the short noon break from a wooden trough—a watery gruel that was no different from that served to the Spanish hogs. On one occasion I was confined in a room for seven days and nights with no light or food or water. I was one slave among many."

"What happened after the third year of your slavery, my friend?"

"I learned how to manipulate the padres, and they in turn taught me how to read their ridiculous books and how to cook in the

European fashion. They gave me the opportunity to become a vaquero and to eventually kill a good many of the miserable sonsabitches."

Sutter remained quiet.

"Maybe I will tell you some of my stories in the future," I said

"After you learn to trust me as your partner, I would imagine."

"After you learn to appreciate my power and the beauty of this land. Maybe—and only after I judge the worth of our partnership."

Sutter laughed at my pride. "You and Vallejo sing from the same book, my friend. Mariano tells me that he is the prince of endless tracts of land, and now I hear that you are a remarkable *chef de cuisine*." He winked his right eye. "Others tell me that you are a famous horse thief and a great *tipne* doctor, all in one." Sutter moved closer, as if to tell a special joke. "Tell me, José Jesús, how is it that such a celebrity as you would give notice to a poor farmer like me?"

"It may happen that you are indeed a poor farmer, but it is the land that you pretend to own that holds my interest."

Sutter shrugged. "I was being facetious, Señor Jesús."

"Stop with such nonsense. Humor is for friends to use, not strangers." I looked over his shoulder, away from those strange gray eyes. Humor was often a tool used to control another person; a tool used to injure the reputation of an opponent. "The Wintu are a crude nation, so I have five Yokuts women to direct the cooking. We'll have the young mare steamed under hot rocks, fat elk turned on a spit, and baked salmon. You'll not walk away hungry."

"Shall I send one of my Kanaka boys to retrieve some brandy from my little ship?"

Again! The effort to control me. To mock my people. "No! No brandy! No whiskey!" I grabbed his arm. "You'll destroy your dream with the whiskey—yours and mine both."

Sutter moved away. "Yes! Certainly. I fully understand the problem."

His mouth said, "Yes, I understand what you require," but his eyes looked toward the dirt. My efforts to spy on Sutter revealed time after time that he always sought any advantage he could find—of the Spanish or the Indio, it made no difference. He was a dangerous man, and my flaws were numerous. He would soon discover those flaws of character or circumstance that might help advance his own agenda.

I touched my left ear, and Chief Raphero sent twelve warriors toward us. They screamed at Sutter, danced about him like dogs in a fray. Each painted and feathered squad followed the next, each determined to impress Sutter with their flashing knives and pointed spears. At first he showed some mild apprehension, but after a few blinks, he smiled and applauded the most vicious of feigned attacks.

"Very good, General José Jesús—your men are well trained." He slapped me gently on the knee. "Most of your warriors are well-proportioned and behave in a most virile fashion."

"You have a good eye for detail," I said.

"I'm a farmer and notice the subtleties of nature." Sutter waved his arms with excited animation. "I'm also a captain of the Swiss cavalry and noticed how your troops raced toward me like wolves."

"Coyotes," I said. "Both have yellow eyes and sharp teeth, but coyote are smarter than wolves; they also have a delicate sense of humor that I especially admire."

Sutter sat still, and then looked at me. "I will be honored to serve with soldiers such as you have presented. If we pretend to own a domain as large as many European principalities, then we must have a strong army."

When his silence continued through another attack, I asked, "What else have you noticed today? Other than the good food and virile warriors?"

Sutter again pinched some dirt. "This soil has the luscious sheen of a pregnant woman." He cast his arm in a wide sweep. "I see many oaks gathered in parklike groves near wondrous fields of grasses. I see rivers able to drive huge stones that will grind tons of wheat. I see what an astute businessman can clearly see—profit for my labor and therefore certain wealth and great prestige for my family."

"Enough, Sutter, enough." I was hungry and annoyed—angry that the white man still saw only his visions and not mine. He saw wheat, not clover, and noisy flour mills, not silent fish weirs. "Here we are, on this first day of our partnership, and it is nearly moonrise." I signaled to Chief Raphero to have his people begin with the drums and dancers. Very quickly we had music and dancing and a crew of Wintu women that served us joints of meat from the horse, salmon baked under hot rocks, and grasshopper atole, all on wooden platters. The women gave us manzanita berry cider to drink and water to clean our mouths and fingers, the liquids in beautiful baskets finished with a weave so tight that not a drop was lost on our knees.

Sutter held a mare rib in one hand and dipped into a mashed root concoction with the other. He said nothing, but released a long series of pleasurable groans as grease and mush dripped slowly down his jaw. Each morsel served to stimulate an additional conquest of food. At one moment he seemed satiated, unable to press onward, but a short respite always gave him the necessary vigor to again enter the fray. His stamina was dazzling, and he continued eating even as he joined his clapping with the Wintu villagers. He hummed along with the professional singers as they told of Yokuts victories and the magnificent quality of Yokuts men.

Sutter laughed when I explained the meaning of each song. "So tell me, José Jesús—are such hired troubadours terribly expensive?"

"This crew that performs for us tonight cost twelve cows and two saddle-broke horses for two nights of service."

"What a bargain!" Sutter cackled like one of the padres' pet chickens." He carefully wiped away any trace of grease with a damp rag, and then reached over to put his hand on my shoulder. "We can work together, José Jesús, you and I."

"Partners?"

He squeezed my shoulder in a way that reminded me of my father. "Yes, we are partners. John A. Sutter and José Jesús, partners." He looked into my eyes. "We will grow wheat from the mountains down to this very river. We will cover the hills and gullies with sheep and cattle." Sutter shut his eyes. "Farmers and mechanics will flock to my New Helvetia, and I shall rule a domain larger than most kings of Europe."

"Open your eyes, Sutter."

He squinted through long lashes at me. "What?"

"The People—what of my people?"

"Oh." Sutter fully opened his eyes and smiled with less vigor. "Well, certainly, your people will also prosper in my New Helvetia." He became a bit more animated with his vision for the future. "I will show them how to survive among the whites. I will do my best to give your people the time they need to harmonize their old life with the new. I will teach them the magic of farming and how to use tools and wondrous machines." Sutter dropped his smile and assumed an expression of honest virtue. "Trust me, José Jesús. I will honor you as my partner in all matters."

"Good," I said. "Then tomorrow we shall begin."

"And tonight we shall eat and talk and enjoy these fine people." Sutter drained his basket of cider and held it out into the night air, an imperial gesture.

A Wintu woman poured a full measure and then disappeared.

Sutter turned toward me. "Vallejo says that you are the greatest of all horse thieves. Is he accurate?"

"Vallejo steals rivers and lakes and oak groves! He steals what we have held from beyond memory! Vallejo's cattle steal food from—"

"So! It is true that you are a great horse thief." Sutter nodded. "Good, that is very good, because the Californios are a little bit afraid of you."

I turned away from Sutter to stare at the central fire. Maybe there was an element of honesty in the thief—a glimmer of trust in my ability to help him to his goal. "We do not steal what already belongs to us." I spoke to the flames and smoke. "We return to the People what the white invader has stolen. We return to the People what the God of all Spirits has given to them."

Sutter tapped a rib bone on my foot. "Listen, José Jesús, my partner, you are no longer a horse thief. You are captain of the cavalry and commandant of the New Helvetia Army. Isn't this strategy of mine a better way to help your people and a better way to defeat your enemy?"

"Supreme Tipne of the People is better." I turned away from Sutter to gnaw a rib bone of my own. It was stripped bare of meat, and I stared with blind eyes at the dancers and singers. Smoke suddenly obscured the stars. A child started crying, and Sutter coughed. I tossed the worthless bone toward the fire.

"Tipne Man." He placed his hand on my knee. "Maybe supreme spirit doctor is a better title, but such a profession is no longer possible. The old days are gone, and now we are partners. Now there is my New Helvetia, and there is no more spirit doctor and no more horse thief."

"Partners," I said. The stones were cast, all bets on the table.

"I'm a gentle thief, José Jesús. I'll give your people jobs and some small amount of dignity. I'll give them the time they require."

"Partners," I said.

"Partners." Sutter stood and stretched. "Now we are partners in growing wheat and healthy herds of cattle."

The spirit of Podnow drifted ghostlike among the red clouds of Tipiknits Pahn, but remained quiet as any mouse.

"Partners," I said.

CHAPTER THREE

Summer, 1839

SUTTER WAS SLUMPED AGAINST THE front wall of our shack, arms akimbo, face washed with sweat. Heat devils twirled in frantic vigor. Crickets and cicada churned the air with weak chirps, while a fire-red sun sagged toward the western hills. The first fall, winter, and spring had passed in New Helvetia. We were now working within five hundred paces of our first rendezvous, atop the rise over the huge south-flowing river. In Sutter's vernacular it was now called the Sacramento River, and it met the north-flowing San Joaquin River to go west into the Great Salt Bay.

"Sutter."

"What?"

"We've got to get that sweat house built. My back hurts, and I stink like a white man."

"We both stink. Even my dear wife would admit that I stink." Sutter rubbed an itch against the rough adobe wall, first one shoulder blade, then the next. "Go jump in the river if you want to get clean."

I slapped a handful of mosquitoes off the back of my neck. "Early tomorrow, while there's still a little cool to the air, I'll get a crew on the job."

Sutter stopped moving. "I got another letter from Governor Alvarado."

"Little Juan, my favorite white man. Little-balls Juan."

"This is the third letter now." Sutter let out a long sigh. "He keeps telling me to bring those twelve families out here to settle on our land."

"Little Juan's got cousins to spare. Ask him why he doesn't send us twelve good strong workers from his wife's side of the family, just for a start." I was tired of white men showing up one day looking for work and disappearing with no word after a week or so. Damned white sonsabitches.

Sutter waited until I was finished with mumbling and spitting. "The governor said he'd take all of our New Helvetia back and give it to his cousins if I didn't bring some white people out here before the first hard rain. White people who would stay the course as citizens of New Helvetia. Permanent, hardworking citizens who would increase the prospects of Alta California beyond those of New Helvetia."

I tried to generate a little anger, but it was too hot with this string of sizzling days. In the old days any sensible person would find some deep shade and a few friends to gamble with or to tell some of the old stories. Or again, maybe they'd get a few families together and hike over near the ocean for some cool weather and some soccer games with the Ohlone, or go for a trading expedition with the Pomo up over the saltwater bay.

"Little Juan has lots of fun giving away Yokuts land, doesn't he?"

"Listen to me, José Jesús." Sutter was getting close to his padre voice. "You know perfectly well that I can't get white people out here because they're all afraid of our predatory neighbors. Indio neighbors, that is—not the Vallejo family neighbors or the Pacheco family neighbors who offer perfect protection for any white person that may seek asylum in this part of Alta California."

"Good. It's about time white people showed some fear of the People."

The sun slipped down a few more notches before Sutter picked up again. "If I lose the title of this land to Alvarado, you lose a good partner."

Hot weather ruined the white man's sense of humor. "So, my friend, what's the plan for us to keep the New Helvetia of your dreams?"

Sutter turned to face me, the conniver's smile planted full on his face. "Well, as it happens, and after diligent negotiations with some missionaries on the islands of my Kanaka friends, I've arranged for some Swiss and German farmers to take holdings in my New Helvetia. They're waiting down in San Pedro as we speak."

"Okay." I ruined another batch of mosquitoes with my left hand, squashing them on my knee. "You just go ahead and tell those Swiss and German people to come on ahead to our New Helvetia, and I'll make sure that nothing bad happens to them."

"You're certain of your power over those brigands?"

"Just keep those farmers of yours close to this big-time fort that we're building, and they'll be okay."

Sutter waited until the sun dropped below the horizon and the screech owl started working along the river. "Thank you, partner. I think that we are making fine progress with our endeavor." He slapped his hands together. "I'll send a messenger to Alvarado, and he'll likely have our new immigrants here in two weeks or so."

✻ ✻ ✻

Sutter's first crew of white farmers had lasted exactly three days before they stole his boat and sailed back west. The same six malcontents who had harried Sutter on his first exploration for New

Helvetia hadn't given us a single moment's work. They gave us a bunch of hard looks and hard words and then sailed off with Sutter's nice little scow. During the first fall and winter of working on Sutter's dream, we couldn't get a single white man to take land in the middle of our beautiful tule marsh or even in one of our pretty little valleys full of grass and oaks. The Californios said they weren't interested in moving because they might get lonely for their own kind out among the sinkholes and elk, so they shook their heads at Sutter's offer of Wintu or Yokuts and Miwok land. Sutter knew and I knew that they were more worried about fatal attacks by the Indios in the land of the Tularaños than any lack of neighbors. So the Californios stayed glued to the coast, near the missions and their own pathetic villages, because it was easier for them to steal land close to home than it was to steal land way out in the great valley. Strange and wonderful accidents did in fact occur to white folks in the land of the tules, so why would any sensible citizen of Alta California waste a week sailing or two weeks walking and swimming out into the dangerous land of New Helvetia?

When Sutter unloaded his Swiss and German recruits from his new scow onto our new wharf, located on the river and within sight of our shack, I took one long look and then wandered off to take a good leak. A single glance was enough to tell me that they were the dumbest group of white people I'd ever seen. The entire lot that Sutter imported from his home country was scared of every shadow; ignorant of our grass, trees, and shrubs; and so dumb that they didn't know the first step toward how to get smart. All were helpless nincompoops, but it turned out that the dumbest of the dumb was a German fellow named Nicolaus Allegier.

Wonderful Nick, hopeless Nick—an unmarried man who, if left alone among his own people, would very likely know the evening comfort of only his right hand. Forever until death, his right hand. Dumb is one thing—ugly is another. The man looked like an accident between a small black bear and a big fuzzy spider. He walked crossways and had fur on every part of his body.

Sutter said to me, "Look, you've got to find this simpleton a wife—someone who can manage a man and a farm."

I walked south for two days to sit in the Wukchumni village steam lodge with the tipne and the elders. We talked and haggled for the next three mornings, and the final agreement cost me three bags of wheat flour and two muskets with enough lead for maybe fifty to sixty balls. All this in exchange for a widow who had killed her most recent husband with poison.

I said to Nicolaus Allegier, "This is Munokits. Would you take her as a wife?"

Nicolaus Allegier bent over to grab his bony knees and giggled at the ground.

"She's from a Wukchumni village," I said. "She's a widow with two children."

Nicolaus moved his hands slowly toward his cock. "Wife?" he asked.

"Wife," I said. "But first you must pay bride price to her father, and then we must go to San José Mission for the marriage ceremony."

"Wife?" He peered at Munokits from under his bushy black eyebrows. "For me?"

"Yes," I said.

Nicolaus Allegier smiled.

❊❊❊

I sent a horse loaded with Nicolaus Allegier's iron pots to the Wukchumni village, and after they were accepted, I escorted Nicolaus Allegier and Munokits and her two children all the way to the San José village, where a very old priest joined Nicolaus and Munokits in holy matrimony.

"Until death do you part," the old priest said.

"His death or mine?" Munokits asked me.

"Your choice," I said.

"What about the pots?" Munokits asked.

"They stay with the village, regardless of who dies."

"Good," said Munokits.

It turned out that Munokits was a very smart and very independent person. She was the one who negotiated the iron pots for her father, and then, after I got Nicolaus and Munokits settled on a good spread of land next to Murtossa Creek, she bargained for an additional list of useful white man's gifts for herself. She wrangled the usual cloth and beads, of course, but also a steel knife, a packet of steel needles, and two more metal pots. Nicolaus Allegier smiled at every request from Munokits, and when he thought no one was looking, he smiled and fondled himself.

Munokits did not smile at Nicolaus Allegier. The children who were told to call Nicolaus Allegier their father did not smile either, but held close to the legs of their mother and gave little hiccup sobs whenever the hairy apparition appeared. The look on their faces buckled my knees in disgust, and I tried to remind my stomach how my bargain with Sutter could eventually benefit the People. The churning continued, however, and loose shit most every morning added a more fragrant reminder of my alliance to a white man.

"Good work, partner," Sutter said. "With the three German families and the four Swiss all working hard on their land, we only need another four settlers to get Alvarado off our back." He clapped his hands three times. "Just imagine, Tipne Man, New Helvetia will soon rival the kingdoms of Europe."

"I thought I counted twelve white folks off that scow of yours."

"You know damn well that four of them left the morning after they arrived."

"Vallejo, right?"

"That's the direction they were headed."

"Maybe they got lost or drowned. It took those first six white farmers you hauled up the river at least three months to find Vallejo."

"Don't worry, so much. We've got a solid start now; more and more will arrive to stay. You'll see, my friend."

I shook my head. Sometimes Sutter was like a little child with his dreams, and sometimes he was like Podnow, the smartest tipne of all the People. Both could go from child to genius in the blink of an owl's eye.

"Sutter," I said. "Listen to me."

He blinked. "What?"

"I hate to give you more bad news, but the People usually feed such as Nicolaus Allegier to the gophers. If a child ever showed himself as dumb as your German fellow, the People would lead him off into the deep, deep woods."

"We need every white man we can get." Sutter looked a little embarrassed. "That's the deal with Alvarado—twelve white families settled and working before the next spring. Then, after a full year as residents, they need to become citizens of Alta California."

"So Nick with his wife together make one of your white families? Right? Does Munokits get to become a damn citizen along with her husband?"

Sutter let my trick question mull for moment. "I heard tell that Munokits is Mestizo, so that takes care of her with Nick as head of a white family. No problem that I can see."

"No need to tell Munokits that she just got jumped up to Mestizo status, I guess."

"Nope. And she'll do a good job with Nick. He may be a little touched in the head, but he's a good worker with a back on him like a hickory tree."

"There are lots of nuts on a hickory tree."

Sutter pulled at his ear. "Please, gentle sir, we have agreed that we will have no more of the jokes. You will discover that the German and Swiss people take care of their own, and that everyone has a place in New Helvetia, even our Nicolaus."

"He's got a good wife," I said. "She's handsome and smart, and she'll probably manage poor Nicolaus to his great advantage. That's the way of our people."

Sutter yawned. "Do your people honor these clever women with high office in their villages? Do your men defer to the superior intellect of your women?"

"Our Yokuts women are smart enough to understand the place assigned to them by the God of all Spirits." I coughed. "Well, most of our women are quiet and complacent anyway."

Sutter's silence continued for a stretch.

"In our Tachi village, most women were amenable to the orders of their husbands."

Sutter coughed into his hand, in an obvious effort to control his laughter.

It was a mistake on my part. There had been one winter evening that we shared stories of our mothers, and now he had some inkling of my mother's power. "It wasn't my mother's fault," I said. "Her parents were of the Wappo people, and they held all sorts of foolish notions."

"Your mother's name was Ulati, as I recall?"

"Yes, Ulati."

"Tell me about your mother's mother."

"My grandmother was a spirit doctor in her village, and I was told that my great aunt was the hunt chief of the same village."

"Spirit doctor is the equivalent of tipne doctor?"

"Yes."

"And a hunt chief leads warriors to secure the bounty of elk and deer for the village?"

"Yes."

"Um Gottes willem!"

"Listen to me, Sutter. Don't get yourself all excited by an exception to all other villages that I know. It is only the Wappo that allow their women equality with men. Only the Wappo women have nearly the same power as men."

"My wife suffers the same delusion as your Wappo ladies about making important decisions," said Sutter.

It was my turn to stretch and yawn. "Well, partner, your brash wife is conveniently out of sight, and our Wappo are all dead."

"Dead?"

"Vallejo killed them all."

"Where did these foolish people live?"

"In the hills above Vallejo's Sonoma mission. The Wappo told Mariano to leave their land, and he killed them for their effrontery."

"Your grandmother issued the proclamation to Mariano?"

"Yes."

"Your great aunt led the warriors to their ruin?"

"She was a superb tactician and fought Vallejo's army in the mountains above Sonoma. There was a snowstorm, and she sent small cadres of her warriors to nip at the edges of the Spanish troops until they were forced to retreat."

"My goodness. A veritable Diana of the Hunt."

"Vallejo sent for reinforcements from Monterey and from all the ranchos around San José. In the end, with warmer weather, and many, many Spanish troops from as far removed as Santa Barbara, the Wappo were eliminated."

Sutter was quiet, but I could tell that he was impressed by the audacity of my mother's mother and aunt. Once he moved his shoulder, as if beginning to offer an opinion or a word of solace, but in the end he was silent.

"Maybe Munokits has a little Wappo blood in her veins," Sutter said.

"My guess is that the disease has spread further that we both may imagine. Look at the Wintu with their strong women and silly men." I let my thoughts spin for a moment. "Also, white man, my mother was a prodigious gambler. Only my father could occasionally get the best of her."

Sutter smiled. "And Munokits—have you tried your luck in a game of chance with her?"

"Nope. I'm not that stupid, partner."

CHAPTER FOUR

Fall, 1839

SUTTER SPENT MOST OF HIS time surveying his empire and trying to figure the best places for producing crops, and where to set up mills to grind wheat into flour. He made a list of the best timber lots and then determined where to set up mills to saw logs into planks. Sutter also played host to European visitors and always asked them to send skilled farmers and ranchers to populate our New Helvetia. All to no avail, I must say.

It was Sutter's Kaneka warriors that became our greatest asset. For one thing, they helped build a steam house down near the river. It was a comfortable but ugly edifice, more Sandwich Island style than Yokuts. The island boys also straw-bossed the Wintu at herding cows and sheep and turkey. They were good people, the Kanakas. Hard workers, playful at all times, even with the Wintu women. Especially the Wintu women! Sutter was their chief, and I was both Sutter's partner and their friend.

With all the problems that jumped at us from every direction, we still managed to plant and harvest some beans and squash before the heavy rains of that first winter. Even through the subsequent hard times, Sutter managed to acquire from the dons great quantities of seed for wheat and vegetables, plus assorted farm animals and rough-sawed lumber for our prospective fort. The man always kept his eye on the future of New Helvetia, empty stomachs be damned.

I watched as every few weeks or so, a white trapper or sailor or no-account vagrant would show up at our shack, and we'd give them some work if they were willing. They all moved on after a few days. None could complete the tasks assigned by Sutter to the level of competence that he expected, and none would take a single order from me. Hell's fire—most of those no-account white men looked through my body as if it were shallow water. Damn white men. Sonsabitches.

"They're a useless bunch," I said.

"Some good ones will come along and they'll stay," Sutter said. "The others will drift over to Sonoma and bother Mariano for a while."

"More likely the useless will stay," I said.

Sutter leaned back in his willow-wood chair. "How goes it with our villages?"

"It gets worse every day. I walk up and down the damn valley, back and forth, talking, always talking."

Sutter smiled. "Can't you let me know what's happening in our New Helvetia? I feel like a white beggar trying to get information from you."

I blew a long stream of tobacco smoke toward him. Indio tobacco, not white man's tobacco. "I've just returned from one of the Hoyima villages."

"And where are these Hoyima located, pray tell?"

"If you walk along the east side of the San Joaquin River until it funnels down through the foothills and into the tule swamps, that's their land—and it has been Hoyima land from the beginning of time. It's three or four days south of here when the rivers are low. A month or better during spring flood."

"The Hoyima are also of the Yokuts people?"

"Yes."

"How many souls are there in this Hoyima village?"

A sharp pain stabbed at my throat. "Before the damn invaders and their pox and malaria and fevers, they numbered perhaps six or seven hundred. More likely it's an eighth of that today."

"An eighth!" He nodded toward me the way I'd want a partner to nod, with sad eyes and worry lines all in the right places. "I've seen villages in Europe fall to the plague or an army. I know how difficult it is for people to survive such a catastrophe."

We stayed quiet until two magpie set up a raucous quarrel over a shiny button they'd found.

"Are you sure that you want to hear about my last trip to the Hoyima?"

"Please," Sutter said. "I await your account. Tell me exactly what happened in the same manner as you would receive a report from one of your spies."

"Okay then, just listen to the end. No questions or interruptions."

Sutter gave me a benign smile and pantomimed sewing his lips shut.

✳ ✳ ✳

"It was two weeks ago that I stayed with the Hoyima, so everything is still fresh in my mind.

"On the first afternoon of my visit, the chief invited all of his warriors into their sweat lodge. He waited patiently as the men settled, with the elders near me and their chief, while all the rest, including the very youngest warrior, found space wherever they could. The heat and silence gathered until the chief finally spoke. 'Now, warriors of our Hoyima village, you will hear from our visitor, José Jesús.' He nodded to me. 'Tell my men what you want them to hear.'

"I wiped perspiration from my eyes and slowly scanned the crowded sweat lodge. I said, 'Listen to me, my Hoyima friends. I am José Jesús, Supreme Tipne of the Yokuts and also of your Miwok people.'

"The elders mumbled, 'Yes, we will listen,' but the young men and big boys turned their eyes away from me.

"I raised my voice. 'The spirits whisper a feeble message into my ear. I smoke the *tanai*, and I listen to their voices, but I hear only platitudes from them or silence.'

"The village tipne was an old friend of mine, and he spoke in turn. 'Yes, it is the same with me, José Jesús. Silence, or annoying bits of nonsense from the spirits.'

"The village chief was another old friend of mine. 'I hear nothing from the spirits,' he said.

"'And with me, also,' the village elders chorused.

"'Maybe the spirits are dying,' I said.

"'Maybe,' the old men said.

"'The horse can learn from each new rider,' I said.

"'Enough!' shouted a young man. 'We are warriors, not horses. The Hoyima are best loved by the spirits, and we need no advice from white men or their whores.'

"The elders looked at their bare toes. I stood to my full height. I said, 'I am of the Tachi and you are of the Hoyima, but we are all of the People. We were chosen by the spirits to live in this most bountiful place in all creation.'

"'You're an old woman,' one of the big boys hissed.

"'A whore to that white man of yours,' another whispered.

"The elders continued with their study of small specks on the sweat lodge floor.

"'I am Supreme Tipne of the People and also of the Miwok. You must listen to me or die. You must listen to me, or the Hoyima will disappear from this beautiful valley,' I said.

"'Kill the white invaders,' the young men shouted.

"A squad of boys and young men who stood along the periphery of the sweat lodge began to move toward me in small careful spurts, as wolves around an injured elk. They had bright eyes and hunched shoulders.

"The village chief spoke into the steamy dusk. 'Quiet, you young pups and listen to José Jesús. He remembers the old days when there was always laughter and good jokes in our village. He led the *Lonewis* celebrations when tens of hundreds of the People danced and sang and gambled and grieved for those who died in that particular year. It was José Jesús who led the insurrection against the Spanish at Purisima Mission. It was José Jesús who led the horse gangs against the Californios.' The old man let tears show in his eyes. Now the People are dying and there is no laughter. You must listen to José Jesús. Please, my young warriors, listen to him!'

The young men hissed and farted and shut their ears from the words of their chief.

"My!" Sutter interjected. "I had no idea of the problems in our remote villages. What in the world did you tell those young villains?"

"Sutter! No interruptions."

"Sorry, partner. Very sorry. The thought slipped through my lips. I'll sew them again, but tighter."

"I'll tell you straight out, partner, it is the same everywhere throughout the great valley. It is always the young men that refuse the advice of their elders and thereby contribute to the despondent disposition of every surviving village."

"I'm sorry to hear such news." Sutter waved a hand as if shooing a fly. "Please, José Jesús, continue with your story. Pretend that you are Carlos reporting in his own unique manner."

"I'm tired. I'll take one final piss and then off for bed."

"No! Finish your story. I must hear the denouement of this tragedy."

I wondered how did Sutter manage such trickery? First I'm in charge of telling my story, with his lips promised sewn tight in the bargain, and suddenly I'm the servant of his instructions.

"Will you listen to the very end with no additional interruptions?"

"Why certainly, partner. Please continue."

"Okay. Listen."

Sutter nodded as if he were a silly child.

"Well, now, prowling about the sweat lodge, I needed some time to make my decision, so I sipped tobacco tea from a small basket, cleared my throat, and surveyed the malcontents. It was important to pick the correct victim for my magic. He had to be young and strong and the leader of the defiant fragment from the village. Above all, the young man had to wear pants."

Sutter laughed. "Why the pants?"

"Silence, dammit."

"Okay. Okay."

"Listen, for a change, white man."

I stewed awhile to let my blood settle, and then continued with my narrative.

"I crab-walked through the crowded sweat lodge, and men parted from me with studied distain. One young man did not move for me, and there I stopped, knee to knee with this young stallion.

"'What is your name?' I asked. He spit on my foot. I waited until the silence was complete, and then pulled a scorpion from his left ear. He spit on the same foot, and I pulled a scorpion from his right ear.

He laughed. "My little sister can move her hands faster than you, old man."

I held four scorpions in my left hand and under his nose, then, in one movement, I threw the scorpions into his eyes, reached into his pants with my right hand, and ripped his cock from between his legs.

"No!" Sutter yelled.

"I waved the bloody tool under his nose."

"No!" Sutter said.

"The young man howled with pain, and his friends joined with a chorus of screams. After a moment the young man stopped with his obscene yelling and pulled at the belt of his pants to have a closer look. The other youngsters also shut up and studied their leader."

Sutter dropped his pipe to the ground and leaned forward. "You didn't," he said.

"The sweat lodge became very quiet. The young man released his belt and dropped his pants. His cock hung from the proper mount, slightly shriveled and worried, but nonetheless ready for the next duty.

"The village chief was first with the laughter, and soon the elders and young men were howling and rolling and pointing to the rebel leader with his pants in a wad on the floor and his cock ready to retreat even further into the scrotum. I handed over the cause of his pain, and the young man studied the implement with great intensity. All laughter stuttered to a halt. The young man turned the dismembered cock over and around and finally announced, 'Now I have two cocks. Maybe I'll take another wife.' He waved the dildo over his head. 'Hey, maybe I'll take up with three or four more wives.'

"All the Hoyima joined in laughter. They laughed until pain came into their throats, and then they stopped. 'Tell us, José Jesús,' the young man said, 'what must the Hoyima do to survive the white man? Tell us, Supreme Tipne of the People, what jokes can we make with the white man so that we can all live in peace with the spirits?'"

"You stole that cock from my Kaneka ladies," Sutter said.

"They gave it to me," I said.

"Never would they part with such a comforting tool. I had it carved from the tusk of a narwhal."

"Your ladies prefer flesh to ivory," I said.

Sutter retrieved his pipe and sucked at the stem. "I have made a schedule so that on one night they get my flesh and the next they get my ivory. The Kaneka ladies have learned to share both my vitality and my ivory."

"I think you may be in error, partner."

"You are, most assuredly, a thief of the lowest order!" Sutter sparked his tobacco to life with two sharp clicks of steel. After a moment the pipe glowed red and smoke filled the small shack. "A thief and jokester both," he said.

"My spirit brother is Kiyu, the coyote."

Sutter smiled. "Ha, a thief and a jokester for a partner—I must lock my wives in a tight cage from now on."

"No cage can deny a coyote," I said.

Sutter let the smile hang on his face for a long time. "And the Hoyima, Tipne Man—are they with us or against us?"

"They will follow my orders," I said.

"Did you retrieve my narwhale horn?"

"No."

"Then I must revise in my mind the extent of your duties as my partner."

"I prefer the short Kaneka lady, the chubby one."

"Done," Sutter said.

The arrogance was lost from his voice, the condescension missing from the lines over his eyes. "Are we partners still?" I asked.

"I share my wives with you, and still you beg the question of our partnership? What must I do to prove my fidelity to you?" Sutter shook his head in a morose fashion, but there was a fit of laughter brewing in his throat. "Maybe your new wife will provoke smiles and good humor from her new husband. Then all the citizens of New Helvetia will celebrate the pleasant change in your humor."

"The chubby wife has already given me a decent measure of pleasure during the past few months." I held Sutter's eyes. "Still, I've learned that our partnership is both flexible and solid."

"Is this an example of a Tachi riddle, or what?"

"This shows that you will share with me a spare wife and that I will allow you an occasional interruption of a story that I might tell. A true partnership."

"A true riddle," Sutter said.

CHAPTER FIVE

Spring 1840

IT WAS LATE SPRING OF our second year. There would be no more rain until next winter, and each day was hotter than the one before. We were desperate to get our crops in the ground.

"Sutter," I said. "We've got twelve white families from last year and another batch of white idiots starting crops and cows this year."

"Governor Alvarez is pleased with our progress. Twenty-four families working their own land in New Helvetia, with many more who have written letters to me expressing interest in our land."

"Okay, partner, now is the time for us to put some Yokuts famers in the mix. We've talked about teaching the people how to survive with the white invaders from the beginning. What are we waiting for?"

"Yes, indeed, partner, what are we waiting for? Make it happen."

White men had such simple minds. Sutter flung his challenge at me as if I could instantly invent a complex change in the lives of my people. Indeed, who could ever imagine Indio families working land next to white neighbors? A white woman scooting over to her Indio neighbor to beg a cup of flour? Ha! Indeed. But it was this impossible dream that was the foundation of our partnership. Two witless fools in a world of chaos.

❋ ❋ ❋

Two Hoyima families were willing to work for Nicolaus and Munokits Allegier.

"Look," I said, "this white man will give you a lodge and clothing and food during all of the eight subsequent seasons. You will learn the white magic for growing crops. Then you will return to the home of your ancestors."

The older man of the two families hawked a glob of spit into the dust. "The white man can be tolerated, but how long must we endure the insults of the Wukchumni woman?"

"Two years."

The younger man kicked dirt with his toe. "After two years what do we take back to our village?"

"Two mules and the secrets revealed from seeds and machines."

"Mules are tough and stringy," the older man said. "I prefer the taste of a young mare."

We all laughed at his joke and then stood quietly. When the silence was complete, I spoke again. "As you can see from the short visit, the white man is a simpleton. But if you watch him carefully and learn what you can, then in two years both of you will receive a piece of paper that gives you ownership of two hundred acres near your Hoyima village. Forever and a day, when the white men look at that document, they will leave you in peace."

The older man spit again but remained silent. Our memories of villages burned and old folks killed joined like the smoke from two cook fires. I let my spit join his. "It seems our best hope, my friend."

"Maybe you are correct in your assessment of the situation," the old man said. "Then again, most likely you are dead wrong."

I nodded and smiled and let the sun get a bit hotter. "Give it a try," I said.

"Mule skin makes fine blankets, so I understand." He looked at me for the first time, to show wavy smile lines in deep creases around his eyes. "Mules stink like the white man, but when rain drips through tule thatch, a mule blanket sheds water like a smooth rock."

"They're heavy like a rock," the younger man said. "I'll take an elk or bear blanket any day."

"I fear that my children will inherit a few rocks and a mule or two, but not many elk or bear," the older man said.

I held up both hands. "Okay, my friends, enough with your melancholy thoughts. Let's hold off on blankets and white men. Let's finish our business."

The older man went back to looking at the ground. "What else is there?"

"After you finish your two years with the simpleton, Sutter will sell you tools and seed, and I will provide two families to learn what you have learned from the white man."

"They'll work as our slaves for two years?"

"Yes. Just as you will now work for the Wukchumni woman."

The Yokuts men nodded agreement to the contract while the Yokuts women retrieved their heavy carry baskets and stood blank-faced and ready to move down the road.

"Listen, my friends. Send a message to me if you encounter a difficult problem."

The men nodded again and moved down the trail after their women.

❀ ❀ ❀

The new moon grew twice to full, but into the early fall there was still no retreat from the torrid summer. At sunrise on a particularly hot morning, I looked over the top of a drainage ditch that Sutter and I were digging, and there was Nicolaus Allegier. He was dragging Munokits by both feet, with her head in the dust. Sutter and I clambered out of the mud and waited for some sort of explanation from our loyal citizen of New Helvetia.

At two dozen paces away from us Nicolaus Allegier started yelling at us in his peculiar language. "She *ficker* me not!" Almost upon us, "She no *gebumse*," he cried. "A lesson! You must teach this woman a lesson!" The litany was repeated over and over until the couple stood one pace in front of us.

I took Munokits from the idiot and walked her a dozen paces to some shade. Nicolaus maintained his cascade of scrambled exclamations to Sutter while I asked Munokits to describe the problem to me.

"I'd rather climb under a blanket with ten skunks than with that sack of shit."

I called over to Sutter, "She's holding out on the old man."

"What's on your mind, Nicolaus?" Sutter put hands to hips. "You want me to throw her in the New Helvetia jail?"

"Yes!" Nicolaus Allegier yelled. "Into the jail until she learns to ficker with me."

"Okay." Sutter stroked his moustache and beard. "Tell you what, Nic. We'll teach that wife of yours a good lesson." He pulled Nic over to us and took Munokits by the arm. "She's been spoiled, Nic, so it'll take some time to teach her what she needs to know."

Nicolaus Allegier narrowed his eyes and leaned closer to Sutter. "How long you teach?"

Sutter shooed Nicolaus away, like a chicken out of a garden. "Back to work, my friend. Get along now, and come back with the next new moon. Check with me then, and we'll see if Munokits is ready to serve as your wife."

Nicolaus Allegier looked up into the sun-blasted sky, and then joined us in the shade to go nose to nose with Sutter. "No, that is too long for no wife."

"Now, now, Nic. This is a difficult situation. The woman needs a good lesson." Sutter took a step backward and held up both hands, palms forward. "A lesson, Nic. I will teach her a good lesson."

"Yes! A lesson! A lesson!" Nicolaus Allegier made an about-face and marched quickstep down the trail and out of sight.

"Sutter," I said. "You are a lowdown skunk."

"Partner," he said. "You've got to stop talking with those trapper fellows. Somebody will mistake you for an Americano and shoot you dead."

"You're still a lowdown skunk."

Sutter jumped into the ditch and gave his new prisoner a broad smile and quick wink of his left eye. "Munokits," he said, "how about you grab a spade from that pile over there and then pull some dirt back from this ditch."

She studied her prison warden for an instant, then, "How far back you want the dirt spread?"

"Double the length of your spade."

Sutter started throwing dirt up from the ditch like six hungry badgers. Munokits cleared space away from the ditch with steady persistence, and I stood watching the two fools.

"Hey! Partner!" Sutter yelled. "Grab that fine new spade we just got from Vallejo and move some dirt."

I ambled slowly to the high end of the ditch to throw the beautiful black dirt toward the surface. Each strike and pull motion became easier, and soon there was no pain, just the red mountains to the west that stretched across the horizon of my eyes.

✳✳✳

Sutter was a conscientious man. After a full day in the ditch and spending the twilight hours writing letters, he still remembered his obligation to Nicolaus Allegier. On the first evening he whispered through the fragile tule-thatch wall of our hoosegow to Munokits, "Come here, my lovely one."

Munokits peeked out the open door. "What for?"

Sutter shrugged. "Well, first to the sweat lodge, and then for your gebumse lessons, of course."

Munokits looked at Sutter and shrugged. "You giving or taking the lessons?"

Sutter and Munokits and I twittered along with the multitudinous bats, and then teacher and student disappeared down toward the sweat lodge. It was near noon the next day before they reappeared, hand in hand. They spoke in confidential whispers and giggled at nothing. Sutter found a small tin of maple syrup and poured a liberal portion on her morning mush. When she finished licking the last speck of sweetness from her bowl, Munokits took Sutter by the arm and pulled him back to the New Helvetia hoosegow.

There was no ditch digging that day. I spoke to the Kanaka warriors, and they chased off after their Wintu girlfriends. The few Wintu men who were around disappeared in a blink, so I spent most of the day in our new sweat lodge. There was no bean planting by the New Helvetia workers that day either. Or chopping weeds, or making adobe bricks or any of that white man's nonsense—just some pleasant talk with a few of my Yokuts vaqueros and lots of good steamy silence.

✳✳✳

The jail was a joke, of course. Munokits quickly made our Swiss shack more comfortable with her good humor and decent cooking. During the day we three conspirators worked as laborers, and after the sweat lodge we sat on the dirt or on primitive chairs to watch the dusk grow dark. Assorted friends joined us, and we all sipped hot tea until one or the other broke the silence. On our third night of fellowship, Munokits spoke first. "Tipne Man, why don't you find yourself some nice widow lady to keep you company at night?"

"More better you should pay better attention to my sister," a skinny Kaneka lady said. "She's complaining all the time about missing Sutter or his narwhal."

Sutter reached down to put his hand on my arm. "Get up, partner." His voice was soft. "Let's all of us move over to our little hill and talk for a while."

I struggled to my feet, and Sutter gathered us to move away from our lodge and toward a small rise that offered a breeze and fewer mosquitoes. We sat with Munokits to my back and the skinny Kaneka lady to his. The chubby Kanaka lady was close by, and Chief Raphero as well. The stars were dim near the moon, but low and huge toward the western sky. I was tired through to my bones, but it was a comfortable spot to sit, especially with good people on every hand.

"José Jesús?" We were silent while a covey of dead spirits flashed overhead, then Munokits cleared her throat. "Tell us about the old days, José Jesús."

She turned to massage my neck and shoulders and whispered so that only I could hear, "Tell us, Tipne Man. We need to remember the old days."

My throat and mind remained quiet. I listened to the Poor-will flitting through the night. My friends waited patiently until Munokits whispered again. "Please. I must tell my children about the old days."

"My wife was Sedit."

"What a lovely name," Sutter said.

"She was tall and quiet, like the brown crane of our great valley." My voice settled and I shut my eyes. "Sedit."

"It is the same tall bird that spends the winter with us," Munokits said. "It is the one with a red splash on its head."

"Yes." I watched as Sedit took one careful step down the dream path. "I stole her from the Maidu when I was sixteen—maybe even fifteen." Sedit stopped and looked up into the night sky, as if alert for a passing owl, and then she took another step closer to me. The scent of oak leaves and tule reed filled the night.

"She was soft to my touch, but I pushed her away. I did not hold her or listen to her. But always she remained my Sedit, my beautiful wife."

"We are all stupid in our youth, partner," Sutter said. "All young men are blind to any gift of kindness."

I inhaled a deep breath of night air and expelled it slowly past my teeth. "The God of all Spirits selected me to spy on the white others." I opened my eyes to see Munokits and Sutter lean forward to listen, while the skinny Kaneka lady feigned sleep. "My cousin Hineh was also selected for the job. Podnow, spirit doctor of the Tachi village, was my uncle and Hineh's father. Podnow told the Tachi people that Kiyu and Hineh together must learn how to destroy the white invaders—that together Kiyu and Hineh must learn how to cure the sickness that was beginning to destroy all of the Yokuts villages."

Munokits moved against me again, her arms over my shoulders. She whispered to Sutter and the others, "My grandfather used your name in many of his stories. He called you Kiyu, and said that you were a famous tipne doctor from the Tachi village." She rubbed my shoulders and arms and let her breasts rest against my back. "Maybe we can hear more about the life of a spy on another evening." Her right hand slithered upward from my knee. "What about Sedit?"

I shut my eyes again. "She was a dutiful wife and very gentle with our son." I tried not to remember, but my beautiful crane took three quick steps toward me and opened her wings. "Sedit was thoughtful with both kin and neighbors, and she always honored me as her husband."

"A fine, fine woman, I imagine," Sutter murmured.

I dropped my chin. "But they died, Sedit and my son."

Munokits now rubbed into my thin hair with her strong fingers, and the fat Kaneka lady moved over to massage my feet. "Shush, now. Shhhh," Munokits said.

"Many of the People and Miwok and strangers among us have died, and I failed to help them." My eyes fluttered as Sedit stepped upon a hummock of tule reed. Sharp nettles stirred my stomach with the pain of her absence.

Sutter stood to make a sharp shadow against the moon. "Well now, enough with your happy stories, partner. Tomorrow is almost here, and I must get some rest." He pulled the skinny Kaneka lady to her feet, and Munokits joined them. "I'm sorry for the sadness you feel about your family. I'm sorry for the empty villages." Sutter stopped for a few heartbeats. "But listen. Hard work will erase all your grief. Hard work and soft women will carry us to happiness." The three walked a dozen paces. "Come on then, tipne man, find a soft shoulder, get some sleep, and wake tomorrow with a smile."

I held my silence and waved the threesome away.

Sutter checked the position of the half-moon. "Ah well, I'll write some letters before taking my ease. We need a dozen iron pots from Alvarado and six muskets from Vallejo."

"What about my lessons?" Munokits asked.

"Go on ahead, both of you. I'll be along in just a few moments."

Sutter gave me a careless salute. "Give a fond good night to your Sedit, will you?"

"Yes," I said.

Sedit moved her wings faster, and with six little steps flew up and over the red mountains and into the heaven of Tipiknits Pahn. The moon dipped beneath the horizon, and the last owl called *"hoo hooo."*

CHAPTER SIX

Summer, 1841

WE KEPT OUR BARGAIN, SUTTER and me.

I warned him every time Nicolaus Allegier came down the road.

I found him survivors of the smallpox and malaria in the villages to work his fields. I encouraged those who were confused by the silence from the God of all Spirits to make candles for Sutter, and led others down from the hills to work in his rope factory. When the wheat crop was ready for planting or harvesting, I took my cowboys—my vaqueros—to herd Wintu and sometimes even Miwok into the hot valley. I gave them sickles made from barrel hoops or willow branches and made them work for Sutter even though it was the season for harvesting acorns. I made them plant the seeds and hoe the weeds even though it was the season to capture salmon. When the rains failed and there was no wheat, I found orphan children and hill country widows for Sutter to sell to the Californios. When my old enemy Mariano Vallejo made little probing jabs toward the great valley with his Suisun allies, my vaqueros burned Vallejo's fields and stole his cattle and killed the warriors of his ally, Chief Solano. All these things I did for Sutter and for the People.

The People.

Sutter gave the People time.

He tried to keep the Vallejo clan away with letters full of pompous threats, and he kept Governor Alvarado tangled in a snare of letters full of flowery compliments and vague promises. Sutter encouraged me to train Yokuts families in the operation of independent farms. He gave Miwok warriors metal traps and then quickly repaid his most pressing debts with lovely beaver pelts. The Wintu women, of course, did the drudgework in New Helvetia, while the Miwok and Yokuts men were trained as the mechanics and farmers and administrators that were necessary to maintain a country larger than most kingdoms of Europe. My Miwok and Yokuts and Wintu all worked hard to help Sutter achieve his dream.

And mine.

After the planting of wheat or selling of children to the Californios, my balls hovered upward through my stomach and chest until they were lodged like sharp pebbles in my throat.

My spirit brother Coyote whispered, "Listen, Brother. Look for the tasty leaves on every plant, but always expect the poisonous roots. Keep moving, Kiyu, and keep a watch over your shoulder for trouble. Never let the white men know what you're doing, and of greatest importance in this scheme with Sutter, you must never, never show any sign of weakness to the white people. Endure their insults so that you can secure time for the People. Learn to survive the good times and bad in New Helvetia. If you can endure the hard times, my brother, then the People will survive."

The pebbles of my balls dropped in slow progression to their rightful place, but sleep remained elusive. Coyote snickered at my weak disposition. Owl ignored my trespass upon his territory.

Sutter nagged, "Stop with your stubbornness. I keep telling you to drink warm milk just before you climb into bed, and then you will sleep like the angels in heaven."

The damn white sonofabitch, with his constant presumption of superiority. His posturing of military knowledge, and blatant façade of empathy toward the people, stirred my stomach to a boil.

"Time," Brother Coyote whispered. "Return the bastard's deceit in kind. Show patience with the enemy, because I foresee Sutter's demise as inevitable."

"Sutter is not the only enemy. What do you see for all the other invaders of our land?"

"One at a time, my brother. First Sutter, and then the others will perish."

"Your record as a soothsayer is somewhat tarnished, my furry brother."

Coyote winked at me, first with his red eye and then with a bright yellow orb. "Patience," he counseled.

✳✳✳

Gusts of cold wind slammed against the log wall of the abandoned Russian fort with the force of a large hawk on a small rabbit. Two wavering candle flames made small effort to illuminate Sutter's ledger. It was late summer, 1841, and already four years into the history of New Helvetia.

"Stop sulking, José Jesús. Get up and help me with this inventory." Sutter dipped the quill and pointed toward the western side of the large room. "Open that closet door in the far corner and tell me what you see."

"This corner of Alta California must be the white man's idea of heaven." The weather was a perfect match for my sour mood. Our partnership was frazzled by our constant disagreements over any subject, large or small. The possibility that Sutter's New Helvetia would increase the odds of survival for the People seemed increasingly remote. Nothing was good—all was disturbed by the arrival of more and more American invaders. On top of everything else, Sutter had dragged me by boat and foot to this land of constant wind and fog. The entire building rocked with another blow from the frigid wind. "There's not a damn thing in this damn fort that's worth putting in your damn ledger. No Indio would live near this damn place."

"The Russian ambassador wrote a lovely letter inviting me to visit their Fort Ross."

"The damn Russians pulled out of here last summer, after they'd killed off all the otter. There's nothing left to kill or salvage around this damn place."

"The ambassador included the keys for every lock in the fort so that I could make an inventory of every asset that they left behind."

"A few rusty cannon and piles of shit scattered around—that's what they left. Let's go home to the valley and get warm."

Sutter scribbled in the ledger and then pointed again toward the closet. "The ambassador guaranteed the very lowest price for any items that I could take from the fort." He glanced toward the ceiling. "He even suggested that I may wish to buy the land and fort as my own."

"Yes, indeed, a fabulous idea. Maybe you could get old Nic to take over as commander of your new fort. General Nic of Sutter's Fort. How's that sound, partner?"

Sutter remained unruffled by my senseless comments. "I've given some thought to the possibility of this western of my two forts as a rival with the Presidio of San Francisco."

I pulled the two blankets around my ears. Wool blankets, a pathetic swap for nice, soft rabbit blankets. "Let's get back to where it's warm."

"I know for a fact that the Pomo people live here, so stop with your constant whining. You remind me of the wife I left in Swiss land."

"Just so you know the actual facts, Captain Sutter, the Pomo are a damn sight smarter than the Russians. They hunt and fish around this place in the proper season, but the Pomo people make their homes to the east, over the next range of mountains and away from this perpetual fog."

"How do you know so much about these Pomo?"

"The Tachi came to visit the Pomo every other summer or so." I smiled at the memories. "We traded our best tanai for their beautiful baskets and held our own with the daily soccer matches and with the constant gambling and singing."

"A pleasant group of people, it seems."

"Their summer territory was benign enough, and they were accommodating hosts, but it was my observation that each extended family of the Pomo quarreled with the other families like petulant children."

Sutter placed his pen next to the ledger and walked around the room with a slow pace and thin annoying whistle. "Ah, well, none of us are perfect in every way." He stopped and opened the closet door. *"Lieber Gott im Himmeln!"* he shouted.

I dropped both itchy blankets to the floor.

Sutter stood in front of the open door and hissed. "Partner," he said, "what have we discovered?"

The jackets were blue with red trim and gold braid. The trousers green with the same red trim. All were neatly folded and stored on closet shelves.

"How many do you count?"

Sutter ran his fingers up and down the shelves. "Better than a hundred, I'd say."

I reached over his shoulder and felt the heavy wool fabric between thumb and fingers. "Looks like you can put ten Russian cannon and a hundred Russian uniforms in your ledger."

Sutter whispered, "The New Helvetia Army." He put his arm over my shoulders and pulled me close. "Can you do this, José Jesús? Can you make us an army?"

I shook out two jackets. The sleeves of one held three gold stripes, the other jacket but one. "We've got to be careful, partner. Vallejo and Alvarado might turn from your best of friends into your worst nightmare."

His arm left my shoulder, and he stepped back two paces. "I'm not worried about the Californios, my friend—it is the Americanos that churn my gut. We need an army that can slow the Americanos from taking our great valley."

I shook my head. "We shouldn't worry about a few trappers and a couple of sorry-looking farmers that come over the mountains. The farmers seem willing to sign on as citizens in exchange for a small bit of New Helvetia, and the trappers move on after they've purchased our stock of pelts." I swallowed my spit. "We most emphatically do need an army to keep the Californios in hand, not the Americanos."

Sutter turned and looked deep into the redwood closet. His head and upper body moved in a slight bobbing motion, like a willow tree submerged in a spring flood. "Give me a strong army, José Jesús, and we will make a rich nation. The royalty of Europe will send ambassadors to bow at my feet. The Americans of the East Coast will honor me with secure treaties. We will have both our ocean and river ports to accommodate ships from Boston or London or Tokyo."

"Sure, partner. Ten cannon and a hundred wool uniforms—that's a good start, all right." I gave a backward kick at Coyote. "But just keep in mind that it is Vallejo and the dons that are the immediate threat to your dream, not the Americans or English or Japanese."

Sutter turned from the closet. "Imagine! General José Jesús and his horse thieves in gold braid! I can see you leading troops down the streets of New Helvetia, with sword in hand and beautiful women throwing flowers!"

"Tell you what, partner, you work on getting a ship to move the cannon, and I'll hire a bunch of Pomo to hump our uniforms over to the valley. With any luck, we can walk from here to our place in five to six days. We'll have to avoid Vallejo's land and stick to hills north of Petaluma and Sonoma, then whistle for the scow to give us a ride across the Sacramento River."

"Yes! Certainly! You handle the Pomo, and I'll write a letter to Governor Alvarado, my patron." He paused, hand to chin. "Tell me, partner, would you prefer service as my ambassador to England or to France? Both have many beautiful women."

Wasn't Sutter a wonder to behold? The man conjured a few dreams in his head, and immediately ambassadors were required to give substance to his fantasies. "Give me the French title, Chief Sutter. I'm partial to their soup and soufflé."

❄ ❄ ❄

My vaqueros, plus various agile Yokuts and Miwok warriors, became Sutter's horse troopers and served as the New Helvetia Light Brigade. They quickly mastered two orders—"Charge!" and "Retreat!" But for the rest, they rode like a herd of elk.

The infantry was another matter altogether.

Sutter had the uniform of a general, of course, and my old friend Chief Raphero wore the six stripes of a master sergeant.

"You must speak German words for the drill," said the general.

"Teach me the words and the drill," said the sergeant.

So it was that every evening after supper a routine was established. First Sutter pumped his right arm twice in the air, then thumped a large bell with a wooden mallet. Next Raphero screamed across the parade ground in his best German language, "Company! Fall into ranks!"

Raphero drilled his men to march with each foot and leg stiff from the hip and the opposite arm out in a similar fashion. His assortment of Miwok, Yokuts, and a few Wintu troopers moved from one formation to the next with the precision of band-tailed pigeons coming into an evening roost. They were smooth and precise and ferocious.

"Now lookee there, will you?" the few wretched Americans hanging around our fort said, one to the other. "Damned monkeys is trying to march around like civilized men."

"Imagine! Digger Indians! Ignorant savages marching like the soldiers of Europe," exclaimed the French and German and English visitors. "Imagine!"

The Americans were similar in their ignorant, brutish manners, but the Europeans were different, according to the language they spoke. The English visiting Fort Sutter were mostly military officers, and were obviously scouting Alta California for possible invasion. The French and German contingents frequently included women, and they behaved more as tourists than potential invaders. All the European visitors behaved as if they were attending social events in their home countries. Yet, even with the fluff and bold colors, I perceived a common dedication for one and all to stealing our land and merchandise.

Damn white sonsabitches.

I do have to admit that our flashy uniforms caught the attention of folks from every nation, but it was the perfect execution of an occasional "Right! About-face!" that got the New Helvetia army boys talking among themselves.

Sergeant Raphero pulled me down to a grove of willow trees near the river.

"We need some action, tipne man. The boys are tired of all this marching. They want some blood."

"Patience," I said.

"C'mon, tipne man. Let's go clear out Vallejo and his clan. There's a bunch of Americans between here and him, so let's whip their asses too. Two nests of yellow-jacket wasps in one sweep."

"Not yet, Raphero. We need time to gain our strength and time to learn the white man's secrets. Patience," I said.

Raphero was older than I was by a year or so, a skinny gray-headed Miwok. "Not much longer, tipne man. Your army needs some white man's blood. Soon, tipne man, and very, very soon."

He was my friend of longest acquaintance. I had been sixteen and on my sojourn with Uncle Shup and spent about half a moon in Raphero's village. In those long-past days, it was only Raphero who took me fishing and showed me secret caves and sat with me to hear my childish lies and laugh at my pathetic jokes.

"Patience, old man," I said. "Let's not go killing white men if Sutter can talk them to death."

CHAPTER SEVEN

Fall, 1841

SUTTER'S EARS GOT RED WHEN he was angry.

"I want the walls on our fort at least four feet higher than anything in Alta California, nothing less."

I could tell that he was comparing the old Russian fort in mind with this latest enterprise of ours. "Sutter," I yelled back at him. "Listen to me before we do something stupid." He looked at me the way a padre would at a bare-ass Indio. "I can tell you from my own experience that wood walls burn real fast, even very tall walls. So let's just put up some little barrier that's quick and easy and then get back to planting more wheat fields."

Now the subaltern of the Swiss cavalry puffed himself up another size and proclaimed: "This fort is not merely a decoration; it is a proclamation to all nations that New Helvetia has no peer in all of Alta California. The walls will be tall and straight and strong."

"You are not listening to me, partner."

"Tell me something that I do not know, partner."

"There was a time when I led all the villages of the great valley against the white invaders. We built a large fort not a day's walk from where we now stand. A fort with tall wooden walls."

Sutter puffed himself one size larger, into his grand personage persona. "Oh, yes, I've certainly heard numerous reports of that silly adventure of yours. Vallejo told me of the encounter, and though he admits that it took his army three separate attacks on the fort over three separate seasons, still he finally burned the muddle of logs and sticks to the ground."

"He followed that bloody victory with burning a few Miwok villages and killing a few old men and boys." I swallowed some air. "Listen, partner, I contend that small or large, a wooden fort is not only vulnerable to fire but it also forces us to give up the power and mobility that we have developed with our army. A fort may serve as a pleasant symbol, the foreign nations recognize the fact of our abundant military power."

Now both Sutter's nose and ears were beet red. "And I contend, my Indio friend, that my fort must be the symbol of that abundant military power. These visitors to our fort are constantly calculating in their minds what can steal from us at the least possible price. They all speculate if they can buy land or trade goods to their advantage with New Helvetia or with the dons of Alta California. Certainly we must plant more wheat and prepare more cow hides, but a magnificent fort will keep the dons at bay until the leaders of all foreign nations recognize General A. Sutter as their political and military peer."

I made my voice softer, as if we were having a comfortable conversation. "Well, now, my partner, it seems to me that the Europeans mostly want to purchase our cattle hides in large numbers and as quickly as possible. Then there's a good market for our flour in old Mexico. Let's improve our farms and ranches and just use my infantry to rustle a few lost cattle while you go ahead and build a nice, tidy little fort."

"Damn stubborn fool," Sutter said. "Big mucky-muck tipne doctor—that's what I've got for a partner."

"Supreme spirit doctor to all the People and—"

Sutter turned a bronze color. Liver spots puffed his skin like mole tracks. "Stop! Enough! No more with this lying around the swear lodge and pontificating as if you were a Roman senator! Now is the time for the hard work!"

"I am the—"

"Stop at this moment! Get to work!"

So I worked. I learned white man's tricks from before sunrise until well into the darkness. Sutter and I shoveled adobe mud into wooden forms and swirled bits of straw and manure into the mixture to create strong bricks. We worked with the Wintu people to set the plumb line and build a wall higher than two men. At the end of our fourth summer at New Helvetia, we had a fort stronger than any presidio held by the Californios. The outer wall was three hundred feet long and one hundred sixty feet wide. It was reinforced with redwood trees shipped from the Russian fort, and it reached a final height of eighteen feet. The fireproof walls were three feet thick with adobe bricks around the entire perimeter.

Visitors walked in wonder around our edifice. They stretched arms to measure thickness, then leaned back to study the breastworks and gun turrets. "It's good. Very impressive," the English and French and Germans always said.

My soldiers stood guard at the main gate and inspected all visitors. My sentries patrolled the catwalk built around the outer wall and shouted, "All is well," with every turn of the hourglass. When any of the Missouri men got too drunk or insulted one of my soldiers or got Sutter angry, I'd give them hard looks and forced them to leave our fort. I knew that Raphero and his two corporals and six privates were standing on the wall, all with big coyote smiles and shiny muskets. Whenever Sutter called, "Hey, tipne man!" my men brushed dust from their beautiful uniforms and stood ready. Raphero waved from the catwalk, and I smiled at those fools, the Missouri men, and shouted, "Out! Out of our fort, or I'll feed your little balls to the dogs."

Outside the fort and up a willow-filled gully about two hundred paces, I retained my small sweat lodge. It was big enough for five or six people, but mostly it held just three, plus a youngster to throw water on the fire. One evening into the late fall, I sat between Sutter and Raphero.

"Sutter," I said. "Those damn Americans are robbing you blind. They take your horses, food, and workers. You've told me more than once that you're the general of this place, the king of New Helvetia, so you've got to make them stop their constant plunder of our land."

Sutter shook his head, like an old horse with a stomach full of worms. "Stop the nagging, partner. I keep telling you, but it's true—you're worse than the wife I left in Swiss land."

I moved around to face him. "Those American boys will swallow you like a grape, Sutter. They'll shit your seed down a deep hole and use your bones for fertilizer."

"I can't touch the Americans." Sutter dropped both hands into his lap. "Whoever comes to the fort I must accept as a friend. Some are good men with the skills we need, and some are not." He stared up into the steam. "In the end, we will survive this plague of Americans."

Raphero opened his mouth to speak, but I held my hand toward him for silence. We sat quietly for a long time until I started again, but with Ulati's comforting voice. "Sutter, you've got to act for your own good." I lowered my voice to a whisper. "The People need your help. You must get rid of the American vermin. We've got the troops. We've got the guns. Let's destroy them now."

Sutter's eyes fluttered. From the new rope factory, located on the eastern side of the fort, I could hear the *tick, tick, tick* of a bobbin unreeling skeins of thread, and the sound made me think of an elder clapping while he told a story.

"Don't worry," Sutter said. "I'll figure something out for the Americans. They mean no special harm. They're ignorant children, and we must teach them how to live in a civilized country. You must show then some patience, José Jesús. We need the Americans as allies if we are to defeat Vallejo and the Californios." He looked at his toes. "Everything is working according to my plans, partner. First we defeat Vallejo and the dons, and then we destroy the white rabble from Missouri. Our fort is impregnable. Our army is stronger than all who might oppose us."

"Sutter, I'll tell you how it has always been with the People here in our great valley." I moved closer until we sat knee to knee. "When a person in any village lives only for his stomach and gives no thought for the People, the elders meet with him for a long discussion. Do you understand me so far?"

"My name isn't Nicolaus Allegier."

"The tipne of the village will also study this greedy person, and if he continues to ignore the needs of his family and village, the tipne doctor must escort him far into the wilderness and say, 'Go! You will die if we see you again.' Do you understand, Sutter? This is the way of the People, and you will do well to implement a similar strategy with the damn greedy, mindless Americans. The sonsabitches."

"I can't," he said.

"You're dumber than Nicolaus Allegier. Do you know why?"

"No, but I'm certain that you will tell me, tipne man."

"Nicolaus knows enough to follow my advice, and you don't."

Sutter sat straight in the steam. "Where is Nicolaus, by the way? I haven't seen him around here for months."

"His wife paid old Nic a visit a while back."

"Really? Munokits went down to their farm?"

"Yes."

The youngster saw my signal and he poured a full basket of water onto the fire. Steam filled every cranny of the lodge.

"He's dead. Old Nick's dead, isn't he?"

"They gave him a good funeral. Munokits even cut her hair short for the mourning period." I tapped Sutter on the knee. "Didn't you notice her short hair?"

"No, partner, I can't say that I did."

"In the future you may want to consider not eating or drinking in the company of Munokits, partner."

"Well, now, I will make sure that Munokits gains title to that nice bottomland she has." Sutter made an effort to display a smile, but failed. "Evidently she got rid of a hairy spider, but I have no concern for my safety with her under my blanket."

Raphero finally interrupted our chatter. "Listen, you two. My boys tell me that they'd like a good funeral real soon, Real soon, and they're not at all choosy, my boys. They'll be happy to bury any American idiot, one or all, whether from Missouri, Boston, or Tennessee."

❋ ❋ ❋

The very next day I rode my horse eastward at a slow walk, and Sergeant Raphero rode at my side. All his soldiers followed, some in uniform, but most wore comfortable cotton shirts and trousers. A few were shirtless with deerskin aprons hung from a belt, but none were naked as in the old days. Meadowlarks sang in erratic bursts of irritated alarm. Poppy and lupine were in seed and limp with the heat. No one spoke. We followed cattle and deer trails until we reached the first hills to the northeast, and then I signaled a halt in a sheltered cove of trees.

The men gathered dry oak branches, built a smokeless fire, and settled down to stare at the tiny flames. A few of the soldiers smoked short clay pipes, and others mixed tobacco with fresh water in small drinking baskets, let the tea soak for a bit, and then consumed the beverage with tiny, pensive sips. All remained silent.

My back and knees ached as I stood and looked slowly about the circle. The soldiers tapped pipes empty and drained their tea.

"We are of different villages, yet we are all cousins of a sort." This was a difficult moment for all of us. They were good warriors—good men with a common vision for restoring their villages to an approximate image of the old days.

"Yes," they murmured.

"I was a small child when my dead father first spoke to me from the spirit world. He warned the Tachi village of the white people and their evil medicine. He promised the People many problems before a final victory over the invaders." A few men coughed, and others spit tobacco juice onto the grass. "Brother Coyote was my close companion in those bygone times, and he often warned me of traps concealed by the white people. I've lost a toe here and there to their metal jaws, but I am still here to lead you in this world. I am José Jesús, supreme tipne doctor of the Yokuts and the Miwok."

Some of the older Miwok men and all of the Yokuts thumped hands on the dirt in recognition of my position.

"I have listened to the words of people from distant villages—from the Walla Walla people far to the north, the Paiute people of the eastern desert, and people who live along the Colorado River. They all say that many Americans are coming to their lands, and we, of course, see the same situation here at the fort of Sutter." All eyes were upon me. "These American invaders are different from the Spanish and Californios. The Americans have been expelled from the villages of their ancestors, and they owe allegiance to no one. They refuse to share what they steal even with one of their own village." I lowered my voice to a hiss. "The Americans are mindless killers of all who would restrain their greed."

Raphero led the chorus: "Killers! Thieves! Killers! Thieves!"

"Beware the Americans, my warriors. They are not constrained by the padres. These Americans are evil demons who claim that we are as less than a rabbit. They are evil demons who will deliver you into the mud of mindless stupidity with their brandy. They will bury you with the vomit-stained dirt of your own land if you give them comfort or shelter."

No one smoked or swallowed or spit. I held my arms to include the entire New Helvetia Army and spoke with sharp, crisp words. "None of my soldiers will drink brandy with the Americans. None of my soldiers will sleep with women who have known the Americans. You will stand tall before these Americans and give them your warrior countenance. They are outcasts and deserve only your hatred. Remember your ancestors and honor them during every moment of the day." I lowered my voice. "If you ignore my admonitions, I will take your uniform and your musket and will escort you to the end of Sutter's land. I will kill any who return after I have sent them away."

A woodpecker drilled, hesitated, and then repeated his attack a few times before flying toward a distant grove of oak. Raphero stood.

"You are the greatest tipne of our people. You are my friend. I know that the dead ancestors of our villages speak clearly to your heart. The God of all Spirits loves you, José Jesús. We honor your every word." He struggled for the precise words. "What do the spirits say, tipne man? Can we destroy the white invaders and reclaim our land? Tell us the purpose of playing soldier for Sutter if not to learn the white man's tricks and to use them to our advantage? What do the spirits say of our future, tipne doctor?"

"We will never defeat the whites," I said. "We will never again know the life of our ancestors. The Americans will come in great numbers, and the People will die in great numbers."

The warriors stared at me but remained silent.

The cords on Raphero's throat pulled tight in his jaw. "What is the sense in playing the fool? Let us end this game and join with the horse thieves and those who would die fighting for their land. The

Chemehuevi people and the Klamath people do not turn their bare bottoms to the Americans, so why should we?"

"What do you suggest, my friend?"

"Better a quick, honorable death than this slow death of yours."

I turned slowly about the circle and gave each man a nod of recognition. "I will not stop any of you who choose Raphero's path, but you must stay away from Sutter's land."

A young Miwok private stood in regal calm. "If a white man dies by my hand, his allies with fear. It seems obvious to me that we must kill the American farmers that compete with our Indio farmers. We stop feeding the white beggars who frequent the fort of Sutter and José Jesús." He shuffled his feet, looked around the circle for support, and then sat down.

When the muttering and whispers stopped, I said, "My brother Coyote advises that we watch the white man with cunning patience. He suggests that we seize each small morsel that falls into our reach and avoid the white man's snares and poisons as best we can. Coyote says that we must endure the white man, protect our women, and remember the stories from the elders. We must wait. We must endure."

"It's easier to fight and die," Raphero said.

"Yes, my friend."

Raphero's body shook, as if suffering from malaria. "Am I truly your enemy, José Jesús? Will one of us die at our next meeting if my boys do not follow your explicit directions?"

"Yes," I said.

Raphero brushed a strand of gray hair from his face. "I predict that most of the young soldiers will ride at my side, and soon many others will join us. It seems possible that if you stand with us, then we may find a victory of some sort before we die."

I looked at my friend and felt tears move from my clogged throat. "I need you, Raphero." I made an effort to see each of my soldiers through the mist. "All of you. I need you. The ancestors need you. Follow me and give the Yokuts and Miwok and lesser villages the time they need to survive the white others."

"No!" the young Miwok private yelled. "You are wrong and Raphero is correct."

Raphero studied my red eyes and touched me lightly on the shoulder. After a moment he struck me on the face, forehead, and back, as light as any butterfly, and walked over to face the pugnacious Miwok warrior. "Give us another moon or two, young brother, maybe even a season or two. In the end we'll all die, so what's the difference?"

The young man dropped his eyes and spoke to his toes. "Many more Americanos could be dead—that is the difference." He looked up with slow, painful increments. "I apologize for my impudence, Sergeant. Tell me when you are ready, and I will follow."

Raphero turned to face me from across the circle. "Let's get back to your damn fort, tipne man. I'm hungry."

"Thank you, Sergeant," I said.

"We're getting old, tipne man. Soft in the head and soft in the belly."

Raphero yelled in German, like the Swiss man who first drilled the New Helvetia infantry into order. "Attention! Line up, you fools! No talking! Follow me!"

I followed my army from the little hill to the gate of Sutter's Fort. There was no victory that day—only a small pause toward the inevitable end of New Helvetia.

CHAPTER EIGHT

Winter, 1842

T HE ARRIVAL OF A NEW governor for Alta California on the last day of the year 1842 was a shock. Until now, Sutter and I had been comfortable with the perpetually dull-witted Governor Juan Alvarado. His feuds with nearly all the Californio families had served to distract him from our goals and debts. Poor dumb Juan was easily manipulated to our advantage; but then, with the suddenness of a snake bite, there on the throne of power was Governor Manuel Micheltorena. He was everything to us and nothing in the same instant.

The dons of our province saw him as Mestizo foreigner who was miraculously proclaimed governor of Alta California by the hopeless collection of charlatans, weaklings, and penniless incompetents that called themselves the government of Mexico. This stranger in our midst became our governor under Mexican law. This intruder was designated the military commander and inspector of Alta California and under the law of Mexico, was given the right to assign jobs, collect the tariff on imports, and accept friendly gratuities from petitioners.

My spies told me how the deposed Juan Alvarado scurried about the ranchos and pueblos of coastal Alta California to chatter garbled nonsense. "God ordained me as governor, not this atheist from Mexico," told his recent enemies. "Arise, good Christians! Arise!" he shouted to the inhabitants of small villages. "Together we must defeat the Devil!"

Sutter switched allegiance from Governor Juan Alvarado to Governor Manuel Micheltorena with supple ease. "Good!" he said. "Now maybe we can get something done around here in the great valley of this country."

"Your debts still stand," I said.

"Yes, of course they do; but now the Californios must show more patience with me." Sutter winked his right eye at me. "I have an understanding with Governor Micheltorena." Another wink in my direction. "He will give me protection from my debts, and I will give him command of my New Helvetia army." Sutter managed a magnificent shrug from his royal shoulders. "It is the beginning of a grand alliance."

"Remember the story of Father Quail, partner."

"Remind me of your simple parable."

"In sum, the story simply reminds us what happened when Father Quail became so immersed in eating sweet grubs that he ignored the threat of Coyote."

"Bah!" Sutter stood and walked away from me.

A month later, when Governor Micheltorena appointed Sutter the commander of all troops in the great valley, he gave Sutter a new steel sword and a new sergeant. The sword was fragile, but Jacob Düerr was tough. On the morning that General Sutter introduced Sergeant Düerr to his troops, Raphero ripped gold buttons from his beautiful green jacket and threw buttons and jacket onto the ground. As he passed within a pace of me I could hear him practicing his Missouri words: "Bastard! Shit! Sonofabitch!"

Later in the day I met Raphero under an elm tree near the river. His jaw bulged, and his eyes looked past me toward a big patch of tule reeds.

"How many chevron on my arm?" I asked.

"One," he mumbled.

"Who is partner to Sutter?"

"You, and no other."

"Does it matter if the whites see Düerr as sergeant of our army?"

Raphero remained silent.

"Listen, old friend, we'll continue to hide our power from the mushroom people, and they will walk blindly into our snare." I punched him on the shoulder. "I'm the Tipne Man, and you're the sergeant. The People know the truth of the matter."

Raphero continued to look at the tule reeds and spoke without inflection to his voice. "I'll follow you until the winter floods begin. Not a day longer."

"Good enough," I said. "Maybe this Düerr fellow can make the Americans swallow some of their own poison."

Raphero spit into the dirt. "I guess we'd better pay real close attention to this Swiss sergeant fellow." He fondled his holstered pistol. "Maybe he can teach us how to plant bullets better than we plant wheat."

"Sure. That's what we need—bullets and wheat both."

I had spies everywhere.

They told me when Vallejo received a shipment of guns from an American ship and where the Bernal brothers were training troops. Sutter ignored every bit of information that I gave him. He kept watching for grubs and worms and juicy insects and remained blind to the coyote's big teeth. I warned him that José Castro, one of the young and ambitious dons, was collecting money from the Californio families and parceling out jobs in his future government.

"Don't you worry," Sutter admonished. "Castro is a young fool. I know what I do. Don't worry."

"Micheltorena is doomed," I said. "They'll send him back to Mexico, and you'll end up dead or a pauper."

"Pauper?" Sutter put his English cup full of Brazilian coffee on his French table. "What do they say, Castro and the others?"

"They say Micheltorena is a Mexican mestizo and not a proper Californio."

"Pah!"

"They say he's a thief among thieves who would use convicts and foreigners to steal the Christian blood of all Californios."

"Psh!" He retrieved his cup and drained the dregs of his coffee. "We've had enough of this old woman's gossip. Let's get to work. Laziness is the certain ruin of New Helvetia, not Castro and his crybabies."

❄❄❄

I worried through the days and nights. The People were not ready. Raphero was ready to bolt at any moment, thus destroying the one last hope for saving a few scraps for the People. In one memorable dream, Brother Coyote called from the top of a small hill. "I'll be busy for a while," he said. "Unavailable."

In another dream my dead father appeared on his winged sorrel horse and whispered, "I'll be busy for a while, unavailable."

Everyone was deserting me. The end seemed very near.

My teeth hurt, especially at night.

"Stop with the silence," Sutter demanded. "We're too busy with big problems to suffer your little-boy tantrums."

"You are still searching for the grubs and bugs, Father Quail," I said. "Look to the teeth of the coyote and see the danger."

"Nonsense, José. Why don't you go and find yourself a woman and leave me alone. In fact, go and find two women and stop your constant caterwauling."

The tanai root needed to be steeped in a basket of hot water for a good hour. The first sip always moved from my mouth to the tips of my fingers and toes, as if a dozen spiders were pulling thin gray webs through my veins. Once the tanai was comfortably in place, Brother Coyote usually came jogging down the dream trail to flop at my feet and match my grin with his. Even when he was on the trail of an injured fawn or cavorting with camp dogs, Brother Coyote usually showed up after a big basket of tanai tea. Not always, but usually he appeared in those days of memory.

Occasionally the tanai would be contaminated with deer piss or mildew and Brother Coyote would not get my message. Then there are also times when he had problems of his own and ignored me. Brother Coyote's problems were usually horny problems. He'd hump anything that stood still for a moment or two. When he was feeling especially randy, no amount of calling could pull him through the fog of my dreams. A tree stump, a dead deer, a village dog—almost anything would serve his mindless ejaculations. Anything except badger, that is. Badger would bite Coyote's penis clean off and never even smile about it.

A week after Coyote disappeared, he returned to sit on the little hill of my dreams. I could tell he was in an ornery mood from the way he moved his nose and from how the ruff on his neck stood up. His first words were smart-assed. "That Podnow fellow was a pretty smart tipne doctor in his day, but he wasn't always right." Coyote turned one eye to show red while the other he kept bright yellow. "Not by a long shot."

I sipped the last dregs of my tanai and took exception to the scrawny mutt. "Podnow's always right. Even when he's dead wrong, Podnow's always right."

"Your dead father wasn't so hot either. A good enough *antu* doctor, but that's about all." Coyote scratched at his ear, then flopped back onto the dust. "Broken bones—that's what your dead father could fix."

"I don't remember much about my father."

"He died a little before your name day. You were still hanging near your mother's teat, for that matter."

"How'd he die? Tell me again," I said.

"The People stoned him to death."

The tanai drifted on the wind of my mind. Long, thin webs dangled from tall trees and slipped in diaphanous threads through the clean air. "Why?" I asked.

"Why! Well, your dead father promised to cure the village chief of his fever and blisters. Your dead father promised the Tachi people that the chief would live, but the chief died."

"Therefore, I imagine that the people were correct in killing my father."

"He wasn't much of a loss. Nobody could cure the fever anyway. Certainly not a simple antu doctor like your father."

Gray cobwebs coiled about my eyes. Once in a while Brother Coyote got mean. Sometimes he was as mean as my cousin Hineh. Not often, but sometimes.

Cobwebs appeared in ordered hexagons over each clump of dewy grass—quiet, complex, strong cobwebs. My father was dead. His spirit could never tell me about the soul of any white, nor could my dead father understand their machines or medicine. Podnow was just as dumb. Both were long dead and ignorant of the empty villages and the Missouri men, but Brother Coyote was alive. Together my brother and I could talk about the white men and red men and exchange information without concern for filial constraints or family judgments. We could tell each other beautiful lies and still appreciate the crucial truth from each falsehood. In this element of our lives, we were as the white man—unable to determine the difference between what we desired and what we were capable of achieving.

My spirit father never told a lie. Podnow tried to stretch the truth, but he had fast hands and slow lips. Lies slipped from Coyote's tongue like water over little pebbles, in the same fashion as the white man.

"I see that you're feeling sorry for yourself today." Coyote poked his nose onto mine. "I'll bet you're juicing up with that green tanai again."

I didn't answer.

"Hey! I get to ignore you, not the other way around. I've got better things to do than put up with your tantrums. I've got fleas to scratch and dreams to dream."

I scraped at my cheek to remove the resident spider. There was a question floating near my left ear, a problem for Coyote to unravel.

Coyote sniffed my nose and eyes. "I've got to tell you something."

"What?"

"It's simply that you and Sutter are nothing but ground squirrels, and those Californio folks are going to eat you two for breakfast." He leered at me. "If there's anything left, the Americans will eat you for lunch."

I pulled my head back from the smell of dead deer. "Damn," I whispered. "This tanai must be full of mustard seeds."

Coyote stood and peered through the growing fog in my mind. "Your father made promises to the People, and they killed him. What silly promises are you making to the People?"

Quiet cobwebs, long skeins of delicate cobwebs, were floating on the wind of my mind. Coyote disappeared and in his stead stood Sutter. First one, then the other—it was Podnow's old scorpion trick.

I blinked three times.

Sutter leaned at the waist until his nose nearly touched mine. "So, partner," he said, "are you talking with me today? Do you have some troubles for us to discuss? Not too much trouble, I hope. It's hot today, and trouble always makes me hotter." He stood straight but kept his eyes on mine. Both remained the same gray color. "Tell me what you know from your spirit world and all the juicy gossip you've collected from the world of my enemies. Tell me, greatest tipne of the People, why did you call for me?"

"Call? When did I call for my esteemed partner?"

"Two of my wives heard the same cry and encouraged me to fly to your side. Together we decided that the tone of your call—the distinct sense of urgency that it displayed—indicated that you were removed from your melancholy state and ready to grace us with your thoughtful advice."

"You talk too much, Sutter. You sound like a damn Californio politician." I rubbed cobwebs from my eyes. "You screw too much and you talk too much."

Sutter smiled. He moved his body forward to catch a small breeze floating up from the river. November hot spells always seemed more onerous than the inevitable furnace of summer. "I'll admit to talking too much, José Jesús—only that." He sat in the dust. "Go ahead. Tell me what I must know."

"This war coming up between the Californios and Micheltorena is a trap designed to destroy you. Each step is planned for the sole purpose of your death, and nothing else."

"No, no, no. You are very wrong in this matter, my friend. The governor has promised me more land and more power if I support his cause against Castro and the others. The settlers of the great valley are my dependents and will support me with their lives. They will follow me into this war, and we will eliminate the Californio parasites."

"If you follow Micheltorena, you are dead."

"No, no, no. You have it all wrong."

"Sutter. Listen. You must stand back and maintain a position of neutrality between the factions. The Californios are not a threat—it is the Americans you must fear. You must work toward uniting the Californio dons so that they may destroy the Americans."

"You must think for a change, José Jesús! Think of the army that I offer Micheltorena—plus the one hundred American trappers, another one hundred American and European settlers, and you, José Jesús. The governor will have the services of my partner with his trained cavalry and sturdy infantry. There is nothing that the Bernal brothers or Vallejo or Little Juan have that can stand up against such a multitude. A victory over the old-time Californio dons will eliminate my debts and entrench me as the ruler of New Helvetia."

"You have only my men, Sutter. Only me, no others."

Sutter dropped his chin to his chest. He poked a small twig among the curled-brown willow leaves. Finally he spoke. "Tell me what you know."

"There are Americans on both sides of this war. My spies have listened to many conversations, and they tell me that the Americans will not fight for you and Micheltorena." I leaned forward and lowered my voice. "They will not fight for the rebels either. The Americans laugh at both sides in this war. The Americans will play at your war, but their intention is to diminish any authority of the dons that may impede their own greed."

I took the twig from Sutter's hand and forced him to look into my eyes. "You must think about the situation, Sutter. You hold deed to most of the great valley. With every new moon more Americans spill over the mountains and follow the rivers to your fort. They smell the richness of our soil. They see the water and trees and wild horses, and they lust for your land in the same manner that you and Brother Coyote lust for a female in heat. It is only a matter of time, Sutter. Soon you will need to bend over and pick something up from the dust. You will feel a sharp prod entering your ass. It will not be Brother Coyote—it will be the Americans satisfying themselves at your expense."

"How come you're so damn smart?" Sutter said.

"I'm the greatest tipne of the great valley."

"You got any advice, partner?"

"Go along with the joke, but wear strong leather pants."

"I see no joke." Sutter wiped globs of sweat from his face. "Just tell me—one, two, three—what I must do."

"You must get written orders from Micheltorena, and therefore you will have documented proof of loyalty to the government. When this phony pageant is complete, you must smile and show the written evidence as your dedication of loyalty to the then-legally designated governor. You must bend your knee and declare a willingness to follow Castro when he declares the new government. You must hope that his distorted sense of honor will keep you from the gallows."

"Okay. What next?"

"Beware of the Americans, especially that Frémont fellow. Smile into their eyes and give them whatever they want. Expect them to steal what they can. Expect them to deceive you and betray you. These Americans have no ancestors to control their contemptible urges. You are nothing in their eyes. Nothing!"

"Okay. Okay. What next?"

"You must realize that the Americans hold all of us as worthless."

The cobwebs of my mind seemed to dissolve as a single beam of sun penetrated a crack in our sweat-lodge roof.

"Listen, Sutter, for here is the order of their contempt—you, Sutter, are a small bird, probing for insects in the dust, while the Californios are small insects, and we red men are dust. It is our land— we of the dust—but the Americans proclaim that our land is a gift graciously given to them by their great hairy god."

"You have a bitter tongue, José Jesús."

"Will you follow my advice?"

"Yes." Sutter touched me on my big toe. "You are the greatest tipne doctor in the known world."

"Good, get ready then. Follow my advice—one, two, three."

CHAPTER NINE

Fall, 1843

EVERY DAY AFTER THE DAY I warned Sutter of his impending death was the same, with me standing and him behind his large empty black French desk. "Tell me, José Jesús," he always said, "what is the most recent information from your spies?"

So it was through the interminable dregs of 1843 and into the summer of 1844. With the first killing frost and the first heavy rain, my reports changed from fitful bits of bad news to a persistent deluge of impending disaster.

"Governor Micheltorena whispers to one and all that he wants to return to Mexico."

"Never! He's the governor! My true friend!" Sutter held tight to both padded arms of his willow chair. The man looked a year older than yesterday. His cheeks were hollow pits and his dark gray eyes a shade lighter than the day before.

I leaned forward at the waist. "His wife misses the theater, Sutter, and she dreams of the social life in the cosmopolitan labyrinth of Mexico City. Manuel suffers from the piles and needs his favorite surgeon."

"Impossible! The governor has promised me yet another land grant and the freedom to sell any parcel in the great valley to the person of my choice. My debts will evaporate like the summer fog with our inevitable victory over the dons." Sutter expelled a long sigh. "Manuel constantly takes me into his confidence, and he speaks only of the need to punish the insurgents." Sutter smiled. "Your spies are in error, my friend."

I pulled up a stool to rest my bones and raised my voice in both volume and tone. From my previous near-whisper I now gave a full-voiced baritone lecture. "My spies tell me that in this latter part of the year 1844, your governor Micheltorena and the infamous José Castro have joined to author a melodrama in which you play an important role." I let Sutter squirm for a moment. "The script will have you lead troops loyal to the current government against the rebels, but it is José Castro who will portray the final hero."

Sutter's head flopped against the padded surface of his willow-wood chair. His eyes blinked in a rapid dance. "Nonsense," he said in a ragged whisper. "Your spies are drunk with brandy. Castro is the leader against the governor, and soon Castro will suffer the ignominy of defeat."

I held my voice at the same emphatic level. "My spies claim that you will lead a long chase after the rebels, with the beginning skirmishes performed in the north of California, but the unfortunate dénouement will occur far to the south."

"Enough." Sutter waved his left hand in a weak flutter. It was his apparent signal that I should cease my attack on his knowledge of reality. "Manuel Micheltorena and I are good friends. We have common goals for our land, and he has granted executive power to me throughout the entire great valley. He will never leave California. He will never betray me to those who lust for his position."

"You are flawless in your role, General Sutter. In fact, you are word perfect from the script devised by your friend, Micheltorena, and your enemy, Don Castro."

Sutter squirmed and twitched, trying to find a more comfortable position in his chair. "What is the status of the Americans?"

"Castro has promised the Americans land and his protection, and you have promised the Americans land and your protection, plus you have added numerous barrels of brandy and free slaves as reward for their loyal support of your army."

Sutter dropped his quill on the desk. "All three? I've promised land, brandy, and slaves?"

"They're stubborn sonsabitches," I said.

"How many of those smelly Americans do I have at my service?"

"They're split in half—you and Castro each get about two hundred Americans."

"It is of little matter." Sutter brushed imaginary dust from his blue uniform, flounced his gold epaulets, and touched his Mexican sword. "Only Sergeant Düerr and I have experience with leading troops into battle. Castro is a politician. Vallejo has only encountered savages with arrows, never Europeans with cannon. There is nothing that I should worry about."

I stood in silent contemplation while Sutter pulled the top letter from his pile. He flayed it open with a rapid slash of the letter opener and then smiled at me with what seemed benign affection.

"Forget your foolish stories from incompetent spies," he said. "This situation will develop into a magnificent war!" He waved the silver letter opener over his head and spoke with his old confident voice. "My grenadiers will attack the center of their army; my horse brigade will sweep both flanks; and my artillerymen will pound Castro and his pathetic army into a glorious surrender." He placed the letter opener carefully in the upper right-hand corner of his desk and picked up his pen as the favored tool for a general of the army.

"Students of military science will study my tactics until the end of time. Mark my words, José Jesús."

"The elders always fought their wars in the late fall," I said.

Sutter kept writing. "There is no season for war. Astute generals find advantages in all seasons and in any climate. Think of Caesar Augustus at the battle of Pharsalia, where he defeated Pompey and chased him—"

"Late fall is best. After the acorn harvest and before the cold winter fog."

Sutter sprinkled blotting sand on the paper and leaned back on his favorite willow-wood chair. "Fall? Tell me, Private José Jesús, why is late fall the best season for war?"

"The young men are always sassy in the fall. They're impudent toward their parents in ways that disturb the spirits, so the elders start a war during the fall season."

Sutter leaned back against the chair and shut his eyes. "Civilized nations do not invent absurd reasons for starting wars." After a long moment of silence he cleared his throat. "Okay. Tell me how savages conduct a war."

I leaned against the wall of Sutter's office. "This is the way of war with the Yokuts and Miwok and Pomo villages. First the elders from two villages send their messengers back and forth with threats and counter threats until everyone is filled with noble indignation. Then the elders from each village organize meetings with speeches and food and dancing, and they pay professional singers to lead the village through songs that describe spectacular victories of their village from the past."

"Thus far I see no difference between European and Indio strategies."

"The elders always smile at the lustful youngsters and clap their hands in time with the foot drum. They drink their tobacco tea and keep the young men busy practicing with sling and arrow for weeks on end until the final meeting on the field of battle."

"Finally!" Sutter said. "Tell me how your generals order their troops."

"The young men stand in opposite rows and from across the meadow, yell at the others. They beat their chests with vigor and eventually exchanged a flight of arrows or spears or rocks."

Sutter sat straight in his chair. "Rocks!"

"As soon as a single warrior is killed or seriously injured, the war is terminated."

Sutter stood and pulled his Mexican sword from the scabbard. "Never!" he said. "Where is the honor of victory if the field is not soaked in blood?"

I smiled at him, and he lowered the sword. "Then, of course, the victorious village must pay indemnity for the loss of life and—"

"Senseless! Stupid!" Sutter sat quickly in the chair, jabbing the sword handle into his ribs.

"Such is the way of the People. What could better serve the spirits?"

Sutter rubbed his ribs and refused to answer my question, so I continued. "The celebration of the peace must be held in the village of the victors, and at their expense. In this manner the former enemy becomes a friendly village, and the constantly engorged young men from both sides are able to meet exotic women from the former enemy's village." I shrugged in the European fashion. "Is it not true in your villages that cousins and sisters and neighbors always have vivid memories of youthful mistakes? Is it not equally true that foreign women are always fresh and lovely and listen with rapt attention to tales of heroic sacrifice?"

I stood, but continued to lean against the wall. "Of course the young men and young women quickly come together to dance and sing and eat and copulate, just as the elders did in their day, and the youngsters remain engrossed in those blissful activities until the rain and fog of winter cover every thought of anger."

Sutter remained silent for a long time, and then cleared his throat. "Very interesting, partner." He smoothed his moustache in a slow caress, a half-dozen strokes on either side. "I have every order from Governor Micheltorena in writing here in my desk, just as you suggested."

"Good, keep them near at hand as we move to the south," I said.

"Castro has stationed most of his troops near Los Angeles Pueblo."

"Yes. The Californios call the place Cahuenga."

"My troops are ready," Sutter said.

"Yes," I said.

"We will soon see if this war is fought in the manner of civilized nations or not."

"Yes." I smiled at my partner. "I predict a short and harmless war that is quickly followed by a wild celebration on the land of the victor. The sequence of this war will mimic that of the civilized nations of Alta California in the olden days. The days before the invasion of our land by savages from the villages of Europe."

It was January 1845, and a month after our discussion of a civilized war. General Sutter had the remnants of his army sprawled within sight of Cahuenga Pass. We were about ten miles northeast of Los Angeles Pueblo and on the road from Santa Barbara Mission, high above the valley floor. Sutter and I were slumped against a large stone wall. A few soldiers worked to erect their tent among the vines of an ancient vineyard, but a gritty wind leveled their shelter and drove the soldiers to take refuge in the lee of our wall.

"How many of my soldiers remain?" Sutter asked.

"We lost a good number while departing Santa Barbara, so you have maybe thirty of the Americans and a dozen or so of Micheltorena's convicts and the New Helvetia army still under your command." I hacked a cough into the wind. "The three cannon are ready to move into action at your orders."

Sutter pulled the red and blue cape up over his head and tight around his ears. "The priest from Mission San Antonio told me that the dons will nail me to a large cross if they catch me."

"I doubt they will carry out the threat." The wind-churned dust erased all except Sutter from my sight. Each word skipped from my mouth like flat stones over a pond. "It was the same with the elders in the old days. Lots of talk, but killing lots of people was not part of their scheme."

"Ach! Enough with the sad talk. The forces of our enemy are now twice that of ours, but we still have our New Helvetia army. They are well-trained soldiers, and I will not fail in my duty as their general. At dawn tomorrow we will attack the enemy." Sutter turned to face me. "Listen, José Jesús, if I do not survive tomorrow, hurry back to New Helvetia and tell my Kanaka wife of my death."

"Manuiki? The skinny one?"

"Yes, my true and faithful wife, from the time of your owls."

"What shall I tell her?"

Tell her to take the money we have buried together, and return to her island." Sutter moved closer to my ear. "Tell her to stay away from that American fellow. You know the one—the cook that I hired a few months back. Tell her to take the money and sail back to the island of Kauai."

"Yes, General, I'll tell her."

The wind diminished, and almost immediately snow turned stone walls and vineyard into a frozen tableau of soft contours.

Sutter coughed. "Now you can see why I left my Swiss land. It is always cold like this— cold and snow, from early fall to late spring."

"Get some sleep," I said. "Tomorrow is the battle."

"Move closer, Tipne Man. I'm too cold to sleep."

"There's no warmth in these old bones, partner. The rocks on this wall will warm you faster than me."

"Move closer anyway, partner. There's no sleep for us tonight, so we'll just talk about the old days, you and me."

"Sure, partner. Sure."

The New Helvetia fifer, a bass drummer, and three snare drummers led Sutter's army up toward the final crest of Cahuenga Pass. General Castro waited with six hundred men and two cannon. When our three cannon were within range, Raphero ordered his artillerymen to unhook them from their mule teams, then swab and load and fire— all within the time of a thrush's song. I saw the first cloud of smoke and cheered with the rest of my army as the wheel of Castro's largest cannon was shattered into tiny windblown fragments. The two sides exchanged cannon balls until Castro's side was without ammunition. Raphero continued his onslaught but seemed to cause no further damage. The enemy disappeared from sight with our last cannon salvo.

"Charge!" General Sutter yelled. "Victory is ours!"

"Charge!"

No one moved. A group of Micheltorena's convicts scuttled past large boulders and disappeared toward the north, away from the enemy and away from us. Sutter ran to a group of Americans squatting in a circle.

"What are you doing here?" His voice matched the high-pitched wail of the wind. "Why do you not advance? Why are you not obeying my orders?"

"Well now," one said. "We is voting which of us want to go on one side and which want to go onto the other side." The others nodded, as if their friend's common sense could offer no better strategy for fighting a war.

"Traitor!" Sutter exploded. "This is the time to fight, not to vote!"

The Americans stood. "Well now," the tall, skinny spokesman said. "If that's the way you're going to talk to us folks, then I'm going to vote with my feet. I'm heading over yonder."

"Wait!" Sutter followed after the men. "Wait. We will win. They have no cannon." He stopped to look around and saw me waving. "What is it, Tipne Man?" he yelled.

"Look! Over near the big boulder!"

Sutter glanced over his left shoulder, then fell to the ground as if shot. Thirty Californios, a few on horseback with long, thin lances probing the air, but most on foot, moved quickly to surround the prostrate General Sutter.

There was only the flap of many flags to disturb the silence. Castro rode up to the circle of his men. His large gray horse spun three times in a tight circle before stopping. Castro shouted, "I shall take charge of the prisoner." He bent forward to salute. "I am very glad to see you, General Sutter."

Sutter sat up, like a child from his nap. "I surrender, General Castro. You have won a magnificent victory." He stood and pulled awkwardly at his sword. "Here is my sword, my Swiss sword."

"No! No! Keep your sword, General Sutter." Castro looked around the circle of his troops. "Quickly! Bring a horse for General Sutter. The war is finished, and now we shall have peace."

The wind-swirled dust covered victors and vanquished alike while I moved toward my men. Up on the hilltops, villagers from Los Angeles surrounded the field of Cahuenga. Many of the civilian men pointed this way and that, talked of military strategy as if they were all generals of great experience. Their children played at hide and seek, while the women told their rosaries.

"What shall we do?" Raphero said. "Run for the tules and hide?"

"Wait for a while. The white men are saluting and hugging their enemies. Maybe the war is like the old days, and we shall celebrate together with dancing and food and drums."

Raphero maintained his stoic expression. "Where shall we wait?"

"Take our army down the hill among the trees and near water. I'll find you in a day or two."

"What will you do, Tipne Man? Hug General Castro? Share a meal with Governor Micheltorena? Salute the Bernal brothers?"

"I'll watch and listen." I looked over my friend's shoulder. The hills were nearly empty of spectators, and the wind remained cold. "Keep your men alert and ready to run."

"Nothing has changed, Private Jesús."

The battlefield was turned into a riotous picnic, with jugs of brandy passing from one hand to the other. No one paid attention to me as I followed Sutter from a distance. First there was the little cell with villagers crowded around the single barred window, whispering and pointing at my partner. Then there was the comfortable room in the home of a wealthy Californio, where he was given a razor and orange juice and a clean shirt. Eventually there was the invitation for General Sutter to play billiards and walk the garden with important men. All on the same day of a battle destined to be studied by military tacticians throughout the civilized world.

The newly appointed secretary of state for Castro's government lowered his voice and made each word as soft as a newborn chick. "Now, please tell me, General Sutter, how was it that you came to join forces with the traitor Micheltorena? Did you come of your own free will, or did you receive specific orders to march with him?"

Sutter allowed just a hint of indignation to coat his response. "Your name, Señor? I'm sorry, but I do not recall a previous introduction."

"It is Alvesio, General Sutter."

"Well, then, Don Alvesio, you must record that I received very specific and written orders from Governor Micheltorena to march against those who declared themselves against his office as governor of Alta California."

"Ah. And you have those orders? Can you show them to me?"

"No, sir, I cannot. I believe that they are with my baggage in San Fernando." Sutter managed a feeble smile. "I could certainly get the papers if I was able to send servants to retrieve them."

"I must have the papers today, my friend, or you will have the gallows tomorrow." The secretary gave a short bow. "I will provide the horses."

Sutter turned and waved me to his side. "Did you hear everything?"

"Yes."

"Then hurry. Waste not a moment."

✳✳✳

When I returned near dusk, Sutter gave the papers to the secretary of state. He read them quickly and smiled.

"Now you are saved!" he said. "Governor Castro will be very pleased with the news."

"It is my pleasure to serve the new governor." Sutter gave the new secretary of state his famous smile. "And what about my troops and horses and all of my military equipment?"

The secretary of state waved his hand to dismiss an awkward condition. "The white men, of course, are granted parole, but not the Indios."

"But, sir! The New Helvetia Army served with distinction throughout the entire campaign. Many of the white men deserted our cause. Only my Indios remained loyal."

The secretary of state looked embarrassed. "Ah. There is the problem, General Sutter. We have two problems, actually."

Sutter took a step backward. "Please, sir, please do not harm my New Helvetia Army. Please!"

"You must understand, General Sutter, we cannot tolerate an army of Indios armed with muskets and cannon in our midst. No, no, no. The civil tranquility of our nation would suffer a serious blow if such an aberration were permitted." He held his hand at arm's length to silence Sutter's rebuttal. "There is also the matter of a severe labor shortage here in the southern portion of our country. We need porters to haul and carry those items of our former governor, and such an ugly activity would demean a Califorñio if he were required to take on a servant's job." The secretary of state shrugged. "What else can we do?"

"Yes," Sutter said. "What else can we do?"

We carried heavy burdens from Los Angeles village to the port of San Pedro. My infantry was stripped of their lovely uniforms and powerful weapons. My cavalry was robbed of every gray horse and steel-tipped lance. We were whipped down the streets to carry baskets full of Micheltorena's provisions to the Mexican ships anchored in the harbor.

The American soldiers from both sides were hired by the Castro government to oversee our labor. "No talking there, you diggers. Keep moving, you damn diggers."

From dawn to dusk, with wheat gruel at night as our only food, we submitted to Sutter's defeat. Raphero and his army, my beautiful cavalry of loyal vaqueros—we all became slaves. Not so with Sergeant Düerr or those American trappers who voted to oppose the insurgents under Castro, just those of the New Helvetia Army who were caught among the trees below Cahuenga Pass. A few got away to the marshes of the great valley, but most were caught and made to serve their new masters.

"I told you to stand ready,'" I said.

"The men were tired," Raphero answered. "They had three months of marching. Three months of feeding all those damn no-good Americans."

"Damn sonsabitches!" I said.

"Damn sonsabitches!" Raphero said.

CHAPTER TEN

Spring 1844

THE SWEAT LODGE WAS NICE and hot. There was me and Sutter and Raphero sitting one next to the other with no conversation but lots of heavy thoughts. It was mid-March; we'd had a full month to chew on the famous battle and digest our week of slavery to the dons.

I was thinking that Sutter had done his best to keep the army together during that chaotic period, and that he pulled some kind of miracle to get us out of San Pedro in such a short time. Those American sonsabitches were especially enjoying themselves with tormenting us diggers, so I guess we had some dumb luck getting out of that mess after such a short spell. Then there were the three weeks straggling up the great valley full of mud and across six different rivers at flood stage, with every portage from one side to the other a nightmare of frozen water.

This was our first full day back at New Helvetia in more than four months. No horses or uniforms or weapons, just a defeated army of hungry and exhausted warriors putting one foot in front of the other until given the order to collapse. Even Sutter had to walk or swim with the rest of us and let Raphero lead us home.

Raphero was first to break the thick silence. "You and your damn Coyote friend talk about Cahuenga?"

"Sure."

"Big joke for the sonofabitch. Right?"

"He thought you looked real good with the pack of women's dresses on your back."

Raphero moved closer. "I've been thinking about the battle most every day," he said.

Sutter and me kept our mouths shut.

"I believe that if Düerr would've held back his infantry, and let me harass Castro with our cavalry, then we'd maybe give up useless ground and gained the time we needed."

"Time?" Sutter whispered.

Raphero raised his voice toward Sutter. "Duerr would have waited till the Californios were drunk and tired and scared after the first long day. Düerr would've attacked the sonsabitches just before dawn. None of that toy cannon stuff, just a bunch of wild Indios hollering and shooting and stabbing. In the end, the old sergeant would've killed Castro himself and let us ruin a big bunch of mushroom-faced white men." Raphero spilled a dipper full of water on the fire, and waited until the cloud of steam settled. "That old German fellow would have been the first to laugh at the big pile of spilled guts we'd churned out, and been the first to bring us back to our right minds of what came next for the New Helvetia Army."

I tapped Raphero on his knee. "Good! You learned a whole bunch from that sour-faced old white man. Real good."

Raphero made the hot rocks hiss with his spit. "Maybe that Coyote spirit of yours is worse than any white man. Damn no-good coyotes. Sneaky, useless critters."

"It's too hot in here." Sutter waved his left arm. "Open the door a bit. Let out some of this steam."

"You toadstools do hate hot weather, and that's a fact," Raphero said.

I sipped at the basket of tanai, hummed a buzzing kind of tune for a while, and then whispered, "Raphero. Don't run off on me." The tanai webs strained to reach the very end of my toes. I whispered again. "I need you more than ever, Raphero. The People need you. Even Sutter needs you."

Sutter matched my whisper. "Raphero, you're the best damn sergeant I ever saw. Better than Düerr and better than I ever saw in the whole Swiss army."

"We've got to stick together, Raphero—the three of us. You know what happens when one village fights another. You know what happens when brothers fight." I gave the basket of tanai over to Raphero, and after a small sip, he passed it on to Sutter. "The People will die if you leave."

Sutter spoke with his usual big voice. "Listen, Raphero, I'll make you a captain in the New Helvetia Army. Two gold bars on your shoulder, just like that sonofabitch Frémont."

Raphero poured more water on the hot rocks. Steam filled the lodge, and after a long while Raphero leaned toward me. "You keep telling me that the God of all Spirits loves us and that we need to keep fighting the white man until we're no different from the white man." Raphero took a gentle sip of the tanai. "You want the red man and the white man to act the same way. To hold the same notions." Raphero moved so close I could count the beads of sweat on his face. "What's the sense in making slaves out of a bunch of Wintu so Sutter can call himself king?" He took another sip of tanai tea. "No sense at all, right?"

Sutter sipped water from a small basket, but kept his mouth shut after a few swallows.

I knew it was a waste of time, but I made another plea to Raphero. "All three of us know that Sutter's a good talker. He'll keep

Castro under control and give us some time to get better organized. We've made some mistakes, but there's still time save the great valley for the people."

"Sure. Talk, talk, talk, and look what happened at Cahuenga. The whites made us slaves. The Miwok and Yokuts are the best loved of all God's creatures, and yet here we are, nothing but slaves to the whites." Raphero let the steam swirl about his face. "There's no hope for anything better." He stood at a crouch under the low ceiling. "I promised that I'd hang with you until the first heavy rain, and I've gone far beyond that time. My warriors are waiting for me out there in the mud, so now I'm going for good."

Raphero kicked the door open, and steam dissipated like fog from sunlight.

"We'll meet again," I called.

"Sure, Tipne Man. In the white man's Hell."

"No." I felt empty of all substance. "In Tipiknits Pahn, with all our ancestors and the God of all Spirits. We'll laugh with Uncle Shup and tell jokes about the white man."

"Don't go stealing any of my horses," Sutter said.

Raphero spat at Sutter's feet and walked through the open door at a half-crouch. Sutter held his hands toward me. "No yelling! Please."

I felt like some old leaf that had managed to hang on a branch through a winter of hard rain. The veins in my arms bumped through the skin. My fingers shook. "C'mon, Sutter, let's go to work. You've got women to screw and letters to write."

❉ ❉ ❉

Raphero looked real handsome when he left Sutter's fort. A Miwok seamstress had set him up with a blue jacket that had red piping and six red master sergeant's stripes on each sleeve. The old man sat as straight as a stick on a gray gelding that was seventeen hands at the shoulder. He never waved as he rode through the gate.

During the first three months after he deserted from Sutter's army, Raphero and his men stole over forty horses from the rancheros near San José and sold them to Sutter. "Good horses," Sutter said to his former master sergeant. "The Americans will pay top dollar for saddle-broke horses like these."

When the rains continued for days on end and mud mired horses hock deep, Raphero and his men stole thirty-six horses from Sutter and sold them to Vallejo. Sutter got the information from a couple American fellows who wandered into the fort from Sonoma.

"Damn traitor!" Sutter turned from those two no-account white men and yelled, "Tipne Man! Get on over here!"

Me and Sutter stood near the flagpole, out in the open with a big crowd listening to what we said. The two American boys stayed close to Sutter and kept shouting, like two old roosters, "Damn diggers stole the man's horses. Him that took care of 'em for years and years." They had narrow eyes and narrow smiles, and the lines over their eyes were all scrunched together.

I looked Sutter up and down with my angry coyote face until everyone was settled down. "What's up, Sutter? You got some trouble for the Tipne Man?"

"Your Judas friend. He stole my horses. I told him not to steal my horses, and he went right ahead anyway." Sutter stopped for a breath and looked me in the eye. "Are we still partners or not?"

"You tell me," I said.

"If we let Raphero steal my horses, every hot blood in every village will take his chance stealing my horses until we're all walking from one place to the next."

"That's right," I said.

"You've got to stop him." It got very quiet around the fort, with only the steady drip from the eaves into a large barrel. "You've got to bring Raphero back to the fort so that we can court-martial him in the proper manner. That's the only way."

I didn't look at Sutter but spoke into the mud. "I'll get some men together. We'll leave before the next storm moves through the valley."

Sutter spoke to me but looked at the two informers. "There're some Americans hanging about the fort. Go ahead and take them along. They're good men in a fight."

I shook my head. "There won't be any trouble. I've got men enough."

"Take a dozen or so of the white men." A bunch of American fellows gave me their snarky smiles. "That's an order," said Sutter.

✳ ✳ ✳

I had the white men break up into groups of four and keep Raphero moving night and day. It was the old elk-surround strategy. On the fifth night clouds broke free, and there was a nearly full moon. Raphero was asleep in a cave on the backside of the big mountain on the Bolbones rancho.

When I woke him, he said, "Kill me now, Tipne Man. Don't let those white bastards see me die."

"Tie him to the saddle of his horse," I said to four white fellows.

They jumped to the task and kept saying "Yes, sir. Yes sir" one to the other and rolling their eyes, in between bouts of laughter.

We brought Raphero back to the fort, and Sutter was waiting. "Thief! Liar! Is it your intention to destroy my entire life? Do you have no regard for the many Yokuts and Miwok who enjoy the prosperity they have achieved on my land?"

Raphero spit at Sutter's foot.

"Insolent traitor!" Purple veins bulged in Sutter's neck. "Beg for my mercy if you wish to live."

Raphero studied a passing flight of sparrows with great interest.

"Take him!" Sutter yelled. "Put him against the stockade wall!"

"Is this what you call a court-martial?" I asked.

"You have my orders, Private. Move!"

Five of my men held rifles pointed at their sergeant's heart, but just at the moment of Sutter's command to fire, a mule walked calmly in front of Raphero.

"Out of the way!" Raphero shouted to the mule. "A chief is about to die." He looked first at Sutter, then at me. "This sergeant doesn't want to hang around any old mule. This sergeant prefers death to the life of a mule."

"Fire!" Sutter said.

Raphero collapsed in violent spasms against the adobe wall. He twitched in the dust, my friend. Once, twice, he twitched, then nothing. The God of all Spirits was quiet, and Pokook, the little burrowing owl, the guide to Tipiknits Pahn, was also quiet. I was a hollow shell. Empty and fragile, unable to move. I had killed my friend and let Sutter live. What could this Swiss invader offer the people that could be worth the murder of such a noble and honest man?

Sutter walked to his office. The Americans drifted away through the gates of our fort, and then they hunkered down in their shacks with women from the lesser tribes. Over the next few days all Miwok and Yokuts people drifted away from New Helvetia and back to whatever villages they could find. In my dreams the great hairy god of the white invaders roamed the darkness. He tore at my eyes. He laughed at me. He peed on the face of my dead friend Raphero.

I slept, but infrequently. The god's hysterical laughter filled my head from one sunrise to the next and through every subsequent phase of the moon.

The People were still dying of the diseases introduced by the white invaders.

The God of all Spirits was still asleep.

Raphero was dead.

Chapter Eleven

Spring, 1845

Lupine rolled down each hill like wind-blown froth. It was the spring season of 1845 in the great valley, and green and gold covered the huge expanse of land from the Tehachapi Mountains in the south to the base of Mt. Shasta in the north. In the old days, the spring season was the time for villagers to harvest the first green vegetables. It was time to catch spring-run salmon, gather tasty army worms, and harvest tender sweet tubers. It was a time to laugh and play and watch youngsters learn to walk and talk. The old days.

"Listen, vaqueros." I waved my hat to gain attention from a few youngsters toward the back. There were a dozen old men and a dozen children who sat on horses and let me call them vaqueros. "Sutter's going to open up some new land for wheat, so we need a couple hundred more workers."

"Padre Sutter!" one of the youngsters yelled.

"Padre José Jesús!" another yelled.

"You boys better keep quiet—I'm going to start throwing holy water into your mush."

The boys tittered and looked around to see who was watching them. The old men smiled, with eyes on the dirt, as if they remembered an innocent joke.

"I want you vaqueros to work together, one village at a time. If the chief won't give you a fair share of his people, then you will have to rope up twenty-five and haul them down to the fort." I settled the Spanish hat down on my ears. "No elders and no little children."

"What shall we tell the chief as we take his people into slavery?" The oldest vaquero asked.

"Tell him we are sorry for stealing his people and that Sutter will return his villagers in the fall."

The horses under my vaqueros shuffled about like dancers at a celebration for the dead. The Lonewis.

"Get going, now. I want two hundred good workers at the fort by sunset tomorrow."

They did their job, my old men and boys. They brought people from Yokuts, Wintu, and Miwok villages, and all of Sutter's slaves worked side by side to replace bunch grass and flowers with the seed of the invaders' wheat. There were no priests in brown robes directing the slaves. More likely it was a white man from Missouri, up on one of Sutter's gray horses and dressed in rags or fur or whatever the damn white sonofabitch could find or steal.

During the hot months of summer, the villagers from the great valley used sharpened barrel hoops and the sharp edges of split willow branches to harvest the grain. They loaded wheat into two wheeled *carretas* and pulled the vehicles with teams of twenty warriors hauling against the harness. The carts screamed like a thousand hawks from field to fort.

There was no laughter from my workers or vaqueros and none from me. Raphero was dead, and our army of proud warriors was a bitter memory. I saw red people die of starvation and from diseases carried by the invaders. I saw red people shot by white invaders because they were diggers and of no account. The people died in great torrents, like fields of clover after a heavy frost. The mushroom people grew in clumps throughout the great valley and multiplied once again with every change in season.

Yet I continued as Sutter's shadow partner. I had no plan for myself and only a slight twitch of hope that I could help some few of the surviving red people. There was certainly no substance to my relationship with Sutter. No jokes, laughter, or quarrels. Sutter usually delegated one of his white men to give me various jobs, and the tasks always required my diligent labor from false dawn to black night.

All the nights were black during this period of my life. The moon and stars disappeared from my eyes. All the nights were filled by a niggling twitter from the hairy-faced god who stared at me from the roof thatch or from beneath my sleeping mat. There was no sleep during the dark nights. The slobbering, fat-lipped god laughed at me, and I laughed back at the fiend. I spit in his face. I drowned his laughter with mine, for it was the great valley people who were doing the work of New Helvetia, not the whites. I saw my managers getting tougher and smarter and more independent of Sutter's advice. Some of my workers were beginning to perceive the rhythm and worth of the white man's crops. Many of the Yokuts and Miwok and the lesser tribes were learning to endure their losses and live with the new way. They were surviving. I laughed at the hairy god. I shit on his face. But I never slept.

The god of the white others was clever and very patient. He finally stopped his laughing, yet I still remained awake in anticipation of his first giggle. I felt his hot breath on my neck. I saw shit dripping from his beard, but he was very quiet. I knew that he was merely waiting. I knew that he was waiting to see if I would accept his assignment of me to his fiery Hell. I knew, of course, that if I displayed even the vaguest notion of another mission designed by

Podnow or brother Coyote or Sedit, then the hairy god would renew his assault upon my soul and continue through eternity and beyond.

Every morning, row upon row of sweet-smelling bread cooled on wooden racks. The aroma drifted over the adobe walls of Sutter's Fort, and through the neighborhood's tule-thatched roofs, to draw saliva to every tongue. The bread, baked by Wintu women from wheat and honey and water produced by the labor of Yokuts, Miwok, and Wintu, was not the bread eaten by the workers, however, but by the guests of John A. Sutter. His mushroom-faced leeches increased with every sunset, as did the number of loaves. When the white others ate the bread of our sweat, they laughed like donkeys. When they sat with Sutter at his long table and stuffed themselves with his meat and whiskey, they laughed like gulls fighting over fish guts. When the white invaders rode horses in the fields around the fort, they mocked my workers with the laughter of little girls. "Dig, you diggers, dig!" they chortled.

Their hairy god was quiet, but they laughed in his stead.

"Sutter," I said. "What in damn hell are you smiling about? Are you some idiot-child that can't see what all these white people are doing to you?"

Sutter sipped coffee from a white cup and maintained his smile in my general direction.

"You can't feed every damn white person who walks through the stockade gate and expect to watch our dream come alive. We've got to sell the wheat, not give it away. We've got to take better care of our workers because they'll never understand why they should hang around New Helvetia and act like slaves."

I lowered my voice a notch. "Sutter, I must tell you that I can't for the life of me figure why in hell I'm sitting here pretending that I'm your partner in any manner at all." I swallowed and coughed while his expression remained the same. "It appears to me that I'm more slave than partner around here."

Sutter filled his cup to the brim from a silver urn. "Now, now, José. None of your dour tipne talk today." He poured me a glass of apple cider from a clay pot and handed it over. "Today is an auspicious day." He held his cup up in a salute. "Today a Russian brig cleared the Golden Gate. It has in her hold our wheat as the final payment for Fort Ross. My debts are paid, and I own more land than many kings of Europe." He displayed most of his teeth. "I smile because I'm a happy man."

"You are a stupid, happy man," I said. "Your crop of Americans nearly matches your crop of wheat. They descend from the mountains and from Oregon Territory like hungry grasshoppers. They eat your bread and your land as if you owed each of them a large debt."

Sutter put his English cup onto his large desk, looked vacantly about his office, then back at me. "Stop with your silly talk, José Jesús. It is an uncontested fact that many of the Americans are good family men and hard workers. Men that I can use—here at the fort or at the farms. Those of good character will receive some of my land for their farms. They will become my loyal dependents. A ruler must have loyal supplicants."

"How about if you stop this invasion of fish-belly people? Maybe you can listen to me instead of those white robbers." I slammed the glass of cider on his fancy desk. "Who said you could give Wintu and Miwok land to people who look upon them as dirt? 'Diggers' they call us. 'Diggers' they yell at those whose ancestors lived upon this land for generations beyond number."

Sutter mopped cider with a rag until the desk was dry and polished. "I've done my best to keep our bargain, José Jesús." There were lines straight across his forehead. "You wanted time to reconcile the behavior of white men with your people. You wanted time for the people of the great valley to learn the tricks and skills that I could teach them. You wanted time for your ancestors to find some comfort in the new medicine, to find a new path to Tipiknits Pahn. I've done my best."

I nodded. "We have both failed, partner. We were both dumb fools, and now our dreams have vanished."

"Look, Tipne Doctor, you smoke too much tanai, and you spend too much time with that damned coyote friend of yours. The old ways are gone. Your land is gone. Look at Raphero—he was unwilling to change, and he's dead."

"I killed my friend."

"He was a good man who could not change. He was stuck in the old ways." Sutter paused to sip his cold coffee. "Here's some advice for you, José Jesús. Some advice from a dumb white man to the greatest tipne of the People." Sutter stared into my eyes for a long time. "Instead of honoring those who dream of the old times, you must look at the many that are willing to change. Look at the red women who will bear children of white men, for their children will walk in both camps. It seems likely that half-breeds will prosper to a certain extent, and the dreamers will remain slaves."

"Nonsense! Everybody hates the half-breeds and quarter-breeds and any damn breed at all. They're doomed to wander about in the purgatory of life until they die. Only death can allow the breeds the comfort of hell."

"Okay. Forget the breeds. Think about the vaqueros and barrel makers and weavers and farmers. These are the people who will find peace in my great domain. I promise that all the colors and races will find space to grow strong as farmers and mechanics and ranchers in my empire."

"Fat chance," I said. "Slaves—that's all we'll ever amount to in your New Helvetia. The smart Miwok women will always take orders from dumb German men, filthy Americans who—"

"Stop. Please. You're ruining my day."

"I've killed my friends, Sutter, and the People still die like grasshoppers on a fire. Every time I shut my eyes, I hear that hairy god of yours laughing at me."

"I'm sorry. I've done my best."

"The hairy god and his evil spirits will destroy the People."

"Enough of this twaddle." Sutter stood, hands on his desk, and spoke with even-tempered control. "I want you to take a crew of workers and tag along after my new foreman."

"What's his name, this new man of yours?"

"Marshall. He's looking for a good sawmill site, and you can straw-boss the construction work."

"With Marshall as my boss?"

"Sure, he's a good mechanic. Best man around for the job."

"I know for a fact that he's dumber than sin."

"Marshall knows how to set up a mill, and I want you to follow his orders. Just do what he tells you and learn a little something. Stop complaining all the time." Sutter looked down at the rumpled pile of papers. "Go ahead and report to him right now."

"Good luck, Sutter," I said.

His eyes remained downcast. "You too, José Jesús."

Chapter Twelve

Summer, 1845

Ames Savage showed up at the fort about dusk on the same day that Sutter gave me my marching orders. He had blotchy oilcloth skin that barely covered his pointy bones. I gave him a basket of water, but he just stared at it and mumbled.

"Damn," he said. "She was one good woman!" His eyes looked at me like a dog with worms in its stomach. "I buried her in a hole east of Steamboat Springs." He sipped some water as if it were thick, hot soup. "There's lots of rocks mounded up around her so's the varmints can't get at her. I made sure of that."

Even while he was working on his first bowl of water and gnawing his first hunk of bread, Savage kept talking about this dead wife of his. "Damn," he told me. "All the way from Missouri she walked. Nicest little gal you'd ever want to meet, with her big smiles and the easy way she could listen. Everybody liked her." Savage swallowed his last bite and stared up at a gathering thunderhead. "We was almost to the mountains and some sweet water when she just up and died on me." Tears bubbled and fell from his eyes. "Damn, here's the Truckee River not but a few steps away, and she falls down dead as a doornail. Sweetest, nicest woman you'd ever want to meet."

"Tough luck," I said.

Savage didn't say much more. He thanked me for the food and then begged a couple horses and supplies from Sutter to carry back up into the mountains for his band of white folks. I didn't give a thought to one more of those sonsofbitches Missouri fellows who came down to the fort, always begging for food and sympathy.

Sutter poked his head out the office door. "Hey, Tipne Man!" he shouted.

I almost smiled. The call brought me in mind of the old days, back when we were partners. Back when each decision about Sutter's fort was mine as much as his. Those were the old days, so instead of answering the sonofabitch, I walked out the fort gate to take a pee in a latrine that me and a bunch of Indios had dug. I talked with a couple of Miwok fellows who were standing around, and finally I sauntered into Sutter's office. He looked almost like his old self, washing his hands in the air and talking about big schemes.

"Frémont needs my help," he said.

"Don't lay your troubles on me, white man. We're not partners anymore, and I'm real busy with helping my new boss dig a ditch."

Sutter tried to smile and then turned to talk at the wall. "I volunteered my New Helvetia troopers to Captain Frémont." Now he turned to me and spoke at a faster pace. "That bunch of Walla Walla fellows that have been hanging around the fort—I threw them into my army too."

I got up from the chair and turned to leave. "That sonofabitch Frémont and his soldiers killed a bunch of Wintu and Maidu up in the north end of the valley—burned their villages, raped the women."

"Wait! Think about the situation, José Jesús."

"What?" I spoke to the closed door.

"If this Frémont fellow had an accident, or if he got lost somewhere and fell off a cliff with this map he has in his back pocket, we'd both lose an enemy."

I stood still for a moment. "What's going on?"

"There's a bunch of Mexican hotheads down around Los Angeles Pueblo, and they killed a few Americans down there with their lances."

"Good," I said.

"Now Frémont's running around trying to play the hero. He wants to take an army down south and conquer all of Alta California for himself."

"King Frémont," I said.

"Governor," Sutter said. "The Americans don't have kings."

"Either way, he's still a sonofabitch."

Sutter leaned forward over the pile of papers on his desk. "I'll admit that Frémont encouraged a gang of ruffians to steal Mariano Vallejo's property in the Sonoma Village." He dropped his voice to a whisper. "I also know that the next thing you know, he'll steal my New Helvetia." His voice was soft and crackly, like a big snake over dry leaves. "We've got to kill this invader of our land."

"Go ahead," I said. "You've got a bunch of lazy white men hanging around your fort. Give them some nice bottomland and a few mules in exchange for Frémont's scalp."

Sutter sat back against his new plush velvet chair. "You, Tipne Man, you are the only one who can stop this snake. There's still a bunch of your New Helvetia Army boys hanging around the fort." Sutter winked at me. "I sure that they'd rather follow you on the warpath than dig latrines for me."

"What's Frémont pay?"

"He'll provide hay for your horses and five dollars a month for each soldier."

"When do we get the money?"

"After the campaign is over, I guess."

"Who pays if the sonofabitch does in fact have a fatal accident?"

"I'll work something out." Sutter picked up a pen from his desk and twirled it in his fingers. "Don't worry—I'll have some cash-money work for you and the boys when this adventure is over."

"What about Marshall?"

"I've got another job for him. You and Marshall can work on the saw mill later in the year."

"You'll pay for me and the boys to kill Frémont?"

"Certainly, my friend."

"Cash money?"

"Don't worry for a single moment." Sutter placed the pen carefully beside his glass ink pot. "Maybe I won't give such a good deal for the Walla Walla boys, but you and the New Helvetia troopers can have jobs here at the fort and back pay, both. Don't worry—just find a way to kill our Captain Frémont."

"Okay—my boys get the army pay, the Walla Walla boys get hay for their horses, that's all fine and good. But what about you just put me down for ten dollars gold money per month that I'm following Frémont around the country, plus two dollars per month for the army boys."

"Certainly. Certainly; I agree to your terms, José Jesús, so consider everything we've agreed to as a very good investment for both of us."

I admit to walking away from Sutter with a smile on my face. First smile in a month of Sundays, probably. Killing white sonsabitches was a whole lot better than digging ditches for that dumb-ass Marshall. One thing, though, I damn well should've called for ten dollars gold money up front from that slippery sonofabitch Sutter. Maybe even twenty dollars up front.

❋ ❋ ❋

Company H in Frémont's combined army had him as captain of course, but there was also a white lieutenant and two white sergeants assigned to command my warriors. Not a one of those white boys ever came anywhere near my troopers. Never. It was Private José Jesús, who was commander of Company H—the combined New Helvetia Army and Walla Walla bandits. It was Private José Jesús who decided what was what with my portion of Frémont's army, and all the white men understood the situation. Every morning they'd yell at us to go steal some cattle or beans, but I ignored them and took my time to do what I wanted to do. My only problem in the beginning of our march south to Los Angeles was Private James Savage. He was the only American who actually rode with my Company H.

Jim couldn't tolerate any part of Frémont's army. "I do declare," Jim said, "that captain of yours looks at hisself in the mirror more often than ten pretty whores."

Frémont and his officers started calling us the "forty-two thieves" instead of "old José and his forty digger thieves." Those white fleas on Frémont's back always curled their lips, spit in the dust, and sneered, "The damned diggers—nothing but forty-two phony thieves."

Frémont and his toadies called Savage "Squaw Man," and since Savage didn't care what the other Americans said, the men in my Company H—even the Walla Walla folks—figured that he was our friend. In fact they all took some time to train Savage on the proper ways of getting along, and eventually he developed a decent sense of humor and a fair way with a horse. Savage was never a vaquero, but he could follow along in our dust and never complain.

"Listen, Savage," I said, "you are the lowest-down creature in the world." I pointed to a big half-breed kid. "Carlos, over there, is the next-to-the-lowest-down creature. If you see Carlos talking to somebody in Company H, then you can follow after him if you've got something important to say. Otherwise, keep your damn mouth shut."

"Sure, I understand," he said.

Company H followed me to rob Califorñio ranches as we moved from Sonoma Village down to Monterey Bay. We took anything with four legs, or anything edible, and Private Savage followed every order that I yelled in his direction. Every evening when we roared into camp with a few dozen cows or a carreta loaded with corn, Captain Frémont turned his head from us and mumbled, "Thieves, all forty-two. Nothing but goddamned thieves."

✳ ✳ ✳

The first time I made a try at killing Frémont was in the hills east of San Luis Obispo. It was a standard ambush situation, with me and Carlos and a young Tachi warrior holding behind some big red rocks, while the rest of my Company H troopers continued on down the trail. The white boys followed along the dry creek bed a good deal later, with Frémont packed in the middle of about forty men. I remember a red-tailed hawk screaming up over my right shoulder and a scrub jay screeching, but didn't think much of it at the time. It was a long downhill shot, and I wanted us to fire our bullets all at the same time before the horses started stirring dust and bucking and chasing off downstream.

I heard the noise of sand on rock. The birds were quiet now. Frémont came around a bend, and all his troops moved slowly underneath our perch. The gritty whisper sounded again, and my Tachi warrior turned to face into the sun. Explosions suddenly erupted from a thicket of small madrona trees above us. Sharp, angry clicking wasps tore into our red-rock fortress as a small group above us began firing down at us, and then Frémont's troops began firing up from below.

"They're onto us," I shouted. We were catching a load of lead from both directions.

We had big boulders between us and Frémont's troops below, so I yelled, "Get those bastards above us." By the time we had fired four shots each, there was silence from both sides of Frémont's troopers. The red-tailed hawk called again from down the canyon, and Frémont's small squad of troopers disappeared into the willow trees and red rock. The trail below was empty and quiet of Frémont's main body of troopers.

Nobody said anything for a while, and then Carlos started tittering. "You full-blood Indio fellows are kinda dangerous to hang around. A body could get hisself serious hurt."

The Tachi warrior looked at Carlos as if he were a small black bug. I ignored the half-breed and listened for further problems. After the birds sounded as if they didn't care if we ever moved again, I stood and led the way downhill and followed a good distance behind the trail of Captain Frémont. The sonofabitch.

The second time I had a shot at Frémont was during the so-called Battle of Rancho Natividad. My Company H boys were in heavy timber a few miles northeast of Monterey, and Frémont had his boys spread to our left. A contingent of Califorñio lancers came riding down a bushy draw toward the middle of the American army. I figured that the dons were trying to turn Frémont around and maybe chase him back up toward Sutter. It also seemed likely that at least my Walla Walla hot bloods and some of Frémont's hot bloods would dash out to meet the lancers, and with everybody yelling and shooting and stirring up dust, I could find a way to put a couple of shots into the back of Frémont's head. That's what I figured, anyway.

My Walla Walla boys were decked out in feathers and paint, so when they broke out of the woods with whoops and screams, those Califorñio boys took one quick look and beat a fast retreat. Frémont kept his troops under control and maintained a considerable distance from both me and the Califorñio boys through the entire so-called battle. I never got off a single shot. The sonofabitch.

Later that night I said to Savage, "What do you think about killing Frémont?"

He looked over at the Americans, all gathered around a huge bonfire. "You'll never get a shot off at him. He's got at least ten people on guard around him, and he's got another ten watching you all the time you are anywhere near the sonofabitch."

"Well, why in hell doesn't the sonofabitch just go ahead and kill me if he knows what I'm up to?"

Savage handed me a cup of coffee. "He'd starve to death without you. If the Tipne Man ends up dead, Company H will disappear without a trace."

"Damn right."

"Why don't you just give up the whole idea of killing the fool?" Savage sucked cold coffee through his teeth. "Even if you got lucky and killed the sonofabitch, there's always somebody else to take his place."

"If they kill me, Company H disappears. If I kill Captain Frémont, the American army disappears."

Savage nodded his head a few times. "Maybe so."

"I'm going to try a little poison on the sonofabitch, and I need your help." When Savage didn't say anything for a while, I asked, "Are you with me or against me in this plan?"

"Tell me what you want, Tipne Man. I'm all yours."

Savage set up the diversion by complaining to Frémont that Company H was always stuck with the dirty work. Savage talked loud and ticked off his fingers right in the captain's face. "It's always us that gets all the food to feed this damn army, and we never get paid a single penny for our work. Everybody else here gets three square meals a day, and they all gets paid three American dollars every month—everybody except Company H, that is."

Frémont stepped back a half pace. "Colonel Sutter made arrangements to pay you fellows at the end of the campaign, and not a day sooner," he said.

Savage put up another finger. "We bring in the dried beans, and your troopers get two cups for our one."

"Listen here, Squaw Man, you fellows can go dig up some roots, or whatever you diggers like to eat. A white man rides on beef and beans, not like you diggers." Frémont smiled at his wit, and those around him giggled like springtime geese.

I circled around the crowd while Savage kept talking and finally managed to drop a handful of stone-black crystals into Frémont's large white coffee cup. It appeared that no one was watching me, so I eased on back to watch Savage finish his playacting.

Frémont stood his ground and yelled, "Hey, Squaw Man!" His nose wiggled like a little bush rabbit. "You can shut your goddamn mouth and walk away, or you can suffer a bad case of lead poison. You just go on ahead right now and choose one or t'other."

Savage shrugged his shoulders, smiled, and walked away.

Frémont reached for his coffee mug that was sitting cold and lonely on a camp table. He smiled and yelled, "Damned squaw-lovers, I do believe that they're worse than the diggers or niggers." He moved the cup toward his lips. "I'm certain sure that they're lower than a gnat's ass."

One of Frémont's longhaired soldiers bumped his elbow and spilled coffee all over the captain's fancy uniform. There was yelling from the captain and many hands mopping with greasy rags and white handkerchiefs, so Savage and I moved away from the crowd. We didn't run but moved straight to our horses and spent the next few days burning driftwood under the dunes south of Monterey Bay.

We returned to duty on the fourth evening, and the next morning Frémont circled his troopers all around my troopers and then stared everyone on both sides to utter quiet. When there was only squirrel chatter that could be heard, he curled his lip and yelled, "You diggers got a count of ten before my boys start with a little target practice."

We all moved real fast, not having much to carry or horses to settle. I heard a few shots fired into the air, but nobody got killed. Especially Frémont didn't get killed.

The sonofabitch.

※ ※ ※

We all hightailed it to the north and east, back toward New Helvetia. After a full day of easy going through mostly chaparral and small oak trees, Savage moved up beside me for a long stretch of time. Toward dusk he started talking as if we'd been in friendly conversation the entire day.

"You've got time," Savage said. "Show some patience. Eventually you'll get the bastard."

"Right," Carlos added. "We've got plenty of time for the likes of Frémont and his pals."

Savage kept on pace and looked over to me and right into my eyes with a comfortable stare. "I want to thank you, Tipne Man. You and the rest of Company H has taught me some good manners. I sure hope that I didn't slow you boys down too much."

"You moving on, Jim?" I kept my eyes on his. "You can stay with me if you want."

Savage looked down at the dust. "Well, thank you, José Jesús, but I've got to get me some cash money, so I'm going to look around for a job."

"You got anyplace special in mind?"

"Nope. I'll just keep my eyes open. It seems that Frémont gave us a tour of all that counts for anything hereabout, so I'll check a few of the best places."

Carlos coughed and added his piece. "I've got to say, Jim, it sure was fun to have a little brother to kick around."

"I'll serve as your brother anytime, Carlos. Just pucker your lips and give me a whistle. I'll come at a run."

Carlos moved off to where he couldn't hear what was said.

"I want to warn you to be real careful around white men," I said. "They'll shoot you dead in a blink."

"Sonsabitches," Savage said.

✳︎✳︎✳︎

Savage crossed my path again about a year later—early December of 1847. I had a bunch of Wintu and Yokuts workers digging a second millrace for the new sawmill up in the hills near Sutter's grape farm. The Hock Farm, he called the grape farm, for no reason that I could understand. I saw this yellow-haired American watching us from behind a stand of white oak, but I was too far away to make out his features. He sat up there for a good part of the morning, and I was about to send a couple boys over to sneak around and scare the shit out of him, when he walked the distance to stand two paces away.

We were about the same height, Savage and I, but now he had a chest like a grizzly. "You want some advice, Tipne Man?" He spoke in the Tachi language, not American or Spanish.

"Advice about digging this ditch, or what?"

"You've got this ditch all wrong."

"Marshall's the boss, and I just try and keep these lazy diggers moving."

"This millrace is for Sutter's sawmill, right?"

"Where'd you learn the Tachi language?" I asked.

"From a woman who knew your name, José Jesús. Every night for near on a year she's been teaching me the beautiful Tachi words."

"Were you kind to this woman?"

"Yes sir, for every minute of the day and night. She brought to mind the wife I buried under the rocks, and we had great fun teaching each other a bunch of songs."

"Tachi women are known for skills beyond cooking and singing."

"Well now, Mr. Jesús, I'll admit to learning a few moves that my wife never offered."

"What've you got in mind for this job?" I asked.

Jim waved his arm upstream. "You need to start farther upstream to get a better drop. That wheel of Marshall's is going to be a big sucker, with driving a saw through some big timber and all."

"Marshall figured the fall on his own, and he said start where we started."

"He's wrong and I'm right."

My band of workers gathered around us, and one of the Yokuts spoke up. "This dandelion head talks like he has some good sense."

I looked around at my crew, then to Savage. "Okay. Let's you and me go talk with Marshall."

"Lead the way," Savage said.

I turned to my gang of loafers. "Back to work, you no-good diggers."

The men laughed and punched each other and drifted back to the shallow ditch. One Wintu warrior even stuck his shovel into the muck, but the rest stood in a loose circle and joked about the invariable stupidity of white men.

Jim followed me up the riverbank, through a tangle of willow and alder, and along a path into the yellow pine forest.

"I've got me a twist or two of Yankee tobacco," Savage said.

"Let's sit for a bit," I said.

We leaned against a tree wider than two men and nipped off two bites of tobacco. Savage chewed and spit. I chewed and swallowed.

"You still supreme tipne doctor for the Miwok and Yokuts?"

"That's right," I said.

"I hear nothing much happens around here without your say-so. I hear you and Sutter kind of run this place together."

"You've been hearing wrong, white man. I'm just another one of Sutter's tame diggers."

"I guess things have changed," Savage said. "More than a few have told me that not so long ago Sutter wouldn't take a crap without your say-so. At least that's what I hear from at least one very reliable woman."

"What do you want?"

"I guess you and Sutter are moving off in different directions." Savage smoothed down his tobacco-soaked mustaches. "I'd like to go partners with you."

"I've got problems enough with my Miwok and Yokuts partners—I don't need more trouble."

"I might have some magic tricks to show you, Tipne Man. Some other stuff also, where we can laugh at each other and sit in the shade on hot days and do nothing. I'm looking to move in the Tachi direction of life, not the damn white man direction. I think that we'd make good partners, you and me."

I swallowed the sweet brown juice. My stomach didn't even twitch on the Yankee tobacco, not like it did for the great valley tobacco. "We don't need any name for sitting around like two old men with a day of gossip and a night of gambling, so let's just look out for the other over the seasons as they pass, and we'll find a way to get together, once in a while."

"Good enough." Savage stood and stared down at me for a long time. He was a very ugly man with blue-gray eyes and a jutting forehead, but he was a good talker when the situation called for it. "I did a passel of survey work when I was in Missouri land, so you can take me at my word when I say Marshall should start digging upstream another hundred paces." He put a beautiful smile on his ugly white face. "You've got to have more drop on your water or you and Marshall will be back to cutting his timber in a whipsaw pit."

"I hate that whipsaw," I said.

"Me too." Savage squatted on his heels. "If you ever try Missouri hickory trees in a whipsaw pit, you forever always will favor a good sturdy mill saw."

We sat squatted while a busy little brown bird worked the bark of a big pine tree for bugs. Savage eventually started up again with his soft talking.

"Yesterday I happened to overhear some of those trapper fellows that hang around the fort."

"Zeke and that bunch?"

"Yeah. Zeke Merritt and his cronies—they've got their eyes on some of Sutter's horses."

"Sutter's got horses all over his empire."

"The herd between the fort and the second stream coming into the Sacramento. They're mostly grays."

"I know the herd."

"There's a good moon in a few nights," Savage said.

"A horse-thief moon," I said.

Savage stood again. "Well, I've got to get going. Oregon sounds good, so maybe I'll try up there for a while."

"Watch out for those Klamath fellows—they'll cut your hair real short."

"I'm not worried about the men, but I hear those Klamath women are real nasty."

"Give me the rest of your Yankee tobacco, Savage. You won't be chewing much after a night with those Klamath folks."

Savage smiled and dropped a twist in my lap. "I'll look for you when I get back, Tipne Man. Maybe you'll have some ideas for us getting together."

"I'll think on it."

"Good enough."

CHAPTER THIRTEEN

Spring, 1848

SNOW WAS STILL KNEE DEEP along the upper reach of the American River, yet it seemed to me that every sailor, poker dealer, and rancher from Alta California was waist-deep panning in the freezing water. Half the fools got drowned or laid out with pneumonia, but a few happened on a sizeable nugget or two. By mid-April, the mob was still unable to work the main channels, so they tried for bits of gold by prying away at icy crevices along the shore with knives or pickaxes. Then there was a pack of folks shaking dry-bed gravel back and forth in Indian baskets. Maybe one in twenty picked up any gold of consequence, but the fever kept all desperate for dawn and oblivious of dusk. I purchased baskets from women of various villages at one colored bead each, and sold each one to white men for an ounce of gold dust. I sold one metal needle and ten glass beads to the Indio miners for the same ounce of dust.

In early May, a few miles beyond the south fork of the river, a hook-nosed Georgian named Humphrey set up a machine he called a rocker. "The Georgia goldfields was full of 'em," he told me.

"Do tell," I said.

"Yup, the buggers are simple to make. Plus you just cain't beat a rocker for shaking the damn gold loose."

These rockers had a trough with a handle for jostling and a hopper at the upper end to sort out the big rocks. Within a couple of weeks, rockers were set up along the river and in every tributary. The miners shoveled gravel into their rockers and sluiced water along the trough to flush out the debris. More often than not, the diggers were valley Indios, and it was white men that picked up the gold trapped in the cleats and filled one leather bag after another. The rocker created such a huge demand for cheap labor that suddenly all the white folks were asking me to fetch them a crew of diggers. Some of those Missouri sonsabitches wanted two or three of my men to shovel rocks, and a couple others from Chile and Australia wanted up to a hundred workers. Men or women—they weren't at all fussy.

Of course nobody was left at the fort of Sutter, so I had a constant stream of vaqueros ,and Miwok farmers and Yokuts trappers who came looking for the Tipne Man to give advice or find them a job. By mid-May, miners of every color and country were up along the Rubicon and Bear Rivers, and they found gold everywhere. About one in five were finding enough gold to keep them in food and supplies. Maybe one in twenty found quantities of gold that bugged the eyes and minds of all the remaining fools.

"One ounce of gold per month for every worker," I'd tell those who asked.

"That's awful steep, José Jesús," they'd always answer. I got to know the words for "too much" in Chinese, American, and Iroquois.

"Take or leave it. There's plenty to pay the price."

So it was that the Miwok and Yokuts of the great valley earned food, a blanket, and either one shirt or one pair of pants for the same four weeks. "Hide what gold you can," I'd whisper to my workers. "I'll set you up with a musket and lead, or whatever you want, after you get a good poke."

It was early June when a white man named Weber tracked me down and waved a big "Hello!" in my direction.

"You want a crew? I charge two ounces of dust nowadays. One ounce of gold up front and the other after thirty days."

"I've got us a better idea, José Jesús."

I knew this white man from when he farmed over near the French Camp rancho. "What's on your mind, Weber?"

"You still tipne to the Miwok?"

"Sure, Miwok and Yokuts both."

"You want some Yankee tobacco?"

"I got all I need, Weber. Tobacco or whatever—I'm a rich man."

"This idea of mine will make you a whole lot richer, José Jesús, and it'll help out your people to boot."

"Don't give me a bunch of bullshit, Weber. Just say what's on your mind."

Weber worked on his chaw for a while, spit a few times, and stared hard at the dirt. "You and me will go halves," he finally said.

"Half of nothing is still nothing," I said.

"If you can get us some of those Miwok fellows from around the Stanislaus River, some good men that are both strong and smart, and then bring them on up to my diggings, I'll teach them everything I know about taking gold."

So here it went again. Another white man with a dream. Another opportunity for me to place my head in a noose.

"I know some good men from around the Stanislaus," I said.

"I got me a store now," Weber said.

"I heard you had both a store and a big crew working a bunch of dry gravel beds."

Weber kept his gaze down toward the dirt. "True enough."

"Looks like you won't go back to digging black dirt over at French Camp," I said.

He finally looked at me. "A body never can tell about life, José Jesús. Every time you got things figured, life comes along and kicks you flat between the eyes."

"Mostly it comes down to us Indios that gets kicked," I said.

"Well now, red and white alike, José—there's not much difference." Weber spit, but most of the brown goo drooled over his whiskers and down onto his pants. "It don't make no never-mind about color—we all get chewed up by the same worms in the end."

"So what's the deal?" I said.

"After I train these Miwok fellows of yours on what kind of gravel to look for and how to pan out the color, we send 'em home to look around their own Stanislaus River. Any gold they find I'll swap for goods in my store. I'll figure my expenses, and then you and me split any profit fifty-fifty."

Even back at French Camp, Weber had dribbled tobacco juice all over himself. He also treated his Chulamni wife with respect, so he had two points in his favor. In my experience, a good spitter never had much time for honest work, and a Chulamni woman could never tolerate a liar. There was also Ulati, my mother who was the best gambler in our Tachi village. She taught me to watch for patterns of response from my opponents, and to carefully study any change in the lines over my opponents' eyes. Not the eyes—it was the lines *over* the eyes that flashed one signal or another. As a youngster on my sojourn up the great valley, I put my mother's training to use and soon had my own reputation for winning more often than not. Sutter had ended as a lost opportunity, so what options were available for me?

"You got yourself a partner, Weber."

"We got to keep this real quiet, José Jesús. There's folks that are coming from all over the world to get some of this gold. Even Chinamen are swarming around looking for gold, like bees after honey."

"There's nobody on the Stanislaus that I know of—just the people who live there."

"Well now, that's what I'm talking about. From what I remember of the times I walked the Stanislaus, the rocks and the drop of the American River were much the same." Weber stopped chewing and stared at me to see if I knew what in hell he was talking about. "Look, Tipne Man, it just stands to reason that if one river shows gold from stem to stern, then the twin will be the same." He went back to chewing at a steady pace. "I'll pack up some tools so that you can get a few Miwok women to hump the lot up to your boys on the Stanislaus. We just have to keep everything quiet and see how it plays. Real, real quiet."

The July heat pushed my eyes far back into their sockets. Scrub jays complained from the deep shade of a willow clump, and even white men found an excuse to hide from the sun. It was noon when a half dozen of my men brought the first deerskin bags of gold into Weber's store. There were a few Americans picking up some bags of beans and flour, so I stayed out of sight behind a black stove made of old fifty-gallon barrels and Weber pretended he didn't know any Miwok fellows from a pack of wolves. When the store was empty of customers, he sent three of the Miwok boys to search around the place and make sure no one was spying on him. It was close to sunset before he spilled their gold. Mostly it was small flakes and chips, but there were some egg-sized nuggets that clumped down on the wood counter.

"Jeeesus and Mary both!" Weber stared at the pile for the longest while, and then reached under the counter for two whale oil lamps. He stared again at the pile for a long time before he got out some acid and tested the gold for purity. "Yup, she's the real McCoy." He took a hammer and knocked some quartz off a gold nugget that weighed a pound on the scale. Tobacco drooled down his chin. All the time he whispered, "Jeeesus and Mary both!"

"Looks good, hey?"

Weber sent three Miwok out for another run around the store to check for unwelcome visitors. He poured the gold back into the deerskin bags and wiped sweat from his eyes. "Never seen anything like it."

"How's that?" I asked.

"This gold here is real rough—there's edges to it, not like the smooth stuff we've been getting around the American River."

"So what?"

Weber moved closer and whispered into my ear. "Your boys are picking up gold fresh off the mother lode. You've got to know that flakes and nuggets with this kind of coarse texture haven't tumbled very far away from the source. There's hardly any sign of wear." He chewed and drooled, and both his hands had the shakes.

"That good or bad, partner?"

"We're onto the biggest strike ever, partner. Bigger than the one they had in Georgia. Bigger than anywhere in the world."

A pleasant memory of the New Helvetia Army flashed in my mind. There was that feeling of comfort that always oozes into your stomach when an opponent has picked the hand with no stone concealed. "What's next?" I said.

Weber looked around the store as if he were demented. "Tell your boys they can have anything they want."

"Anything?"

He rubbed both hands through his scraggly, sticky beard. "You decide what's best, José Jesús. You just tell 'em exactly what they should take."

I motioned for the crew to gather around and listen. "The gold is good." I nodded to each man in turn. "Your gold is different from the kind found here on the rivers of the Wintu, and it is more valuable."

The oldest Miwok miner said, "Tell us what to do, Tipne Man."

"Start off with taking one shirt and pair of pants for everyone. Make sure that they fit as well as if made by your wife."

"Sounds like a good start, José. What else?"

"Okay, add two blankets, a Boston hat, one steel knife, and a packet of needles to each pile."

"Tell us what will happen if the invaders discover the value of our gold."

"If the invaders discover our secret, they will fly to the land of the Miwok like a plague of grasshoppers. You will lose your Stanislaus River and all of your villages. The People will scatter and die."

"Give us also six muskets with sufficient powder and lead to defend our villages," the leader said.

"Yes," I said.

A young Miwok warrior stepped away from the circle and stood toe to my toe. He spoke to me in low tones, but with an even voice. "Tipne Man, just so you understand—we will kill any who invade our territory."

"Yes, you must kill the first trespassers as soon as they arrive." I waited until the other Miwok joined our little circle. "You have only one chance at success, my friends. You must gather a large amount of this gold in a very short period of time. In the natural course of events, your river and villages will see the inevitable invasion of greedy foreigners. We have this small moment of time to prepare for the onslaught of invaders. When all the villagers have enough gold to purchase food and weapons in sufficient quantity to survive for two consecutive winters, then the villagers must move away from the rivers to higher ground."

"Even with the gold we must lose our land?"

"The Miwok must act as the willow tree and bend to adversity in the effort to survive. Some will live, but more will perish if you do not follow my advice."

"No bending willows," the leader said. "We will stand and fight for our land."

❋❋❋

On the third trip to the store, and after they were paid with two muskets each and three steel knives each and all the metal pots their women could carry, the same young warrior spoke.

"We killed two Sonorans the other day."

Weber stopped chewing. "Did they see you working the rocker?"

"Yes."

"Were there others?" The pink under Weber's eyelids showed all around.

"One, maybe two, got away. We followed their trail down to the San Joaquin River, and then lost it."

Weber nodded a few times, gave a faint smile, and said. "We've got to work fast, boys."

"Maybe the other two Sonoran boys got drowned or killed by a bear," I said.

Weber just shook his head and said his piece. "José, you and me have got to leave for the Stanislaus today. It's probably too late, but we'll give it a try anyway."

"I'll get a bunch of women to carry what we need."

"Yes!" Weber bit off a fresh twist. "Get going, you Miwok boys, right now. Get going, partner—as soon as possible." He turned away to begin stuffing small packs of needles and knives into burlap bags. "Jeeesus and Mary! I'll bet we're too late already."

❋❋❋

By the time we made it to the Stanislaus River, there were at least two parties working the lower pools. One group of Califorñio boys, just arrived up from the San Joaquin River, was scrambling all over the place and pulling up gold by the hatful. One man held up a nugget as big as his fist and laughed at us with a long hysterical donkey's bray. There was another man with two fingers gone from his right hand—named Valdes—who toted gold around in a towel and mumbled to himself with words that I couldn't hear over the rushing water.

I knelt down and examined his hoard.

"In one day!" Valdes bent over to speak into my ear. "In one day there is too much gold for an old man to lift."

"Keep moving, Tipne Man," Weber yelled. "Keep moving. We're after the big strike. The mother lode!"

I walked up close to him. "What's your strategy?"

He waved an arm. "You go and hike upstream till dark. At daybreak you set up a small crew at the first likely spot." Weber turned to face me. "Have two of your men pan the gravel and two more pry around with their knives. Keep the rest moving upstream, and every mile set up another crew until we get a survey on a stretch of ten miles or so. Tell your boys to work fast. Give up on any place that doesn't give rough-edged nuggets of at least two ounces." He bent over and spit into the water. "You'll have to keep moving up and down the river to concentrate your boys in the best spots."

"What about you?"

"I'll take a half-dozen men and a dozen porters and move up into the hills. I'm looking for a stretch where there is no gold at all. Then I'll backtrack and spy out a quartz outcropping. That's the sign I'm after. All the smart engineers around hereabouts say that a bunch of quartz shining in your eye will cap a big goldfield. The vultures can have the river—we'll take the queen mother."

The next day I left a crew at the most productive bends in the river and leap-frogged ahead with the remaining twelve of my trained miners. When they were all busy with their pans and knives, I walked downstream to the Lacquisamne Miwok village.

When the steam was heavy in the sweat lodge, and after the village chief and the tipne had exchanged the requisite greetings with me, I spoke to the assembled men. "The damned white men will soon arrive in your territory."

"Do you think we're blind and stupid both?" The Miwok chief whipped sweat from his eyes and scowled at me through the steam. "Maybe the great Yokuts tipne doctor thinks that the Lacquisamne are blind old hags."

"Tipne to both the Yokuts and Miwok," I said.

A few of the young men near the rear of the sweat lodge mumbled together, then spit onto the hot rocks.

The village chief stared at me. "Yesterday the whites killed two of my men."

"What happened?"

"Four of my men were operating the ferry on our river when a mob of Sonorans attacked them. Two of our ferrymen were shot dead, but the other two ran back to the village and warned us of the violence."

"What did you do?"

A young warrior, as broad as a yellow pine, stood. He was angry but maintained his dignity. Each word was an arrow to my heart. "If we kill these white men who have killed our men, an army will quickly appear. The whites have guns without number, cannon that destroy our lodges, and huge cocks to penetrate our women." He turned his body slightly and joined with me to study the steam pit. "If, on the other hand, we ignore these whites, they'll see the Lacquisamne as helpless children. They will steal our river and orchards and souls." He coughed once and turned back to face me again. "What will you have us do, José Jesús?"

I pulled a leather bag from my shirt and emptied gold onto the floor. "This is what the white others seek. They will kill any who obstruct their quest."

"Tell us what we do not know," said the chief.

"I join with a white man whose name is Weber to take gold from your river. Every day we will give you a bagful of gold in exchange for your permission to invade your territory."

"Can we expect the same courtesy from the hairy invaders?" the chief said.

"No. They will kill you if you make any effort to restrict their attack."

"Tell us our options."

"Move your village farther up into the hills. Avoid the whites as much as possible because they will make you witless with their whiskey and they will steal your women and children."

The chief moved his hand as if to chase a very slow mosquito. "What is the difference, José Jesús? You tell us to die quickly or to die slowly—either way the Lacquisamne are dead."

I tapped the small pile of gold at my feet. "The gold may save some of the Lacquisamne."

"Tell us," the chief said.

"Those who join with me and the white man Weber will learn how to find the gold in your river. I will also teach you how to exchange the gold for items that you need to survive the white others."

"How will we eat? The white others will eat our fish and game. We must abandon our orchards of oak. Can we make soup of this gold?"

"Neither soup nor atole, but the gold will buy cattle and flour. The gold will also purchase salt and kettles and beans. The

Lacquisamne must accumulate large quantities of their gold and learn to live as the white others. They must use the gold to secure claim to some small part of their own land." I stopped for a moment to let my heart catch my tongue. "You must learn to grow the wheat and corn and to raise the cattle and horses as do the white others. The gold will give the Lacquisamne time to learn such strange habits."

I sat still and quiet.

The steam diminished into a chilly cloud before the chief spoke. "I am very tired, José Jesús. The spirits refuse to answer my questions." He moved his shoulders up and down to release the immense tension. "My powers are gone. I have no ability to advise my people. They may do what they will with no support or criticism from me."

When the lodge was completely clear of steam, a handful of the Lacquisamne followed after me, and I led them to my first crew. "Teach these wild Indians how to find the gold," I told my foreman.

"Sure." He motioned for them to move toward the rocker, and they stepped forward like antelope on a windless day.

✻✻✻

Weber was so excited he could barely hold the cup to his lips. "There's color everywhere!" He sipped hot soup and spilled half down his beard. "She lets up for a bit, but the next bend gives up a whole bucket of those big rough-edged nuggets."

"The Lacquisamne killed a couple more Sonorans last night."

"We're getting closer to the queen, José Jesús. Keep your men moving on up the stream."

I moved closer to Weber and made him listen to my words. "Do you know Doc Angel? A one-eyed fellow who carries a gun on each hip?"

Weber looked at me like I'd just arrived. "Sure, I know the bastard. He's a gambler fellow and a mean sonofabitch."

"He's on the river and moving upstream."

Weber squinted at me. "How about putting some of your Miwok hot bloods on him? Slow the bastard down a bit."

"Look, Weber, nobody cares about the Sonorans, but we'd have an army on the river if an Indio killed an American." I shook my head. "Even Doc Angel."

Weber went back to staring at the fire. "What can we do?"

"Nothing, not a damn thing. In a week or two this place will be like flies on dead meat."

He clawed his beard. "You're right, José Jesús. Dead right."

We stared at the fire until both evening planets were clear of the trees, then curled side by side on the bare dirt and fell asleep. Nothing either one of us could do. Another Cahuenga and no Sutter to blame.

✳✳✳

Two nights passed, and at dusk of the third, one of the Miwok women we had working around our camp gave Weber half of a nearly raw green-headed duck. I got the other half. We chewed and stared at the fire for a long time. "There's a couple spots that look real promising," he said.

"Up where that second creek joins by the big sugar pine stand?"

"That's one. Then there's another farther upstream under a quartz wall. It's where the river shoots out from a little canyon and flattens for a bit. There's some nice boulder traps and two rich racks of gravel."

"Can you hold both those claims, Weber?"

"A white man and twenty Indians could probably hold one, but not both."

"I heard that my old partner, Sutter, and a guy by the name of Knight landed a barge down at the mouth of the river today."

"How many were there in the barge, Tipne Man?"

"My messenger said that Sutter's got maybe fifteen white men with him and Knight's got about the same. My messenger also tells me that there's a regular ant trail of white men coming down the eastside of the San Joaquin, and they're all headed toward us."

Weber hunched his shoulders forward and ignored the mosquitoes. He started to say something, went quiet for a while, and finally he spoke. "I'll set up a crew at the sugar pine creek, and you do the same at the quartz canyon. We've got to figure which is the best claim before we get shut out of everything."

"You giving up on laying claim on the jackpot?"

"Maybe yes, maybe no. Let's go for what we know and take what we can." He hummed in tune with the mosquitoes and rocked himself back and forth.

Weber wouldn't look at me, and the lines over his eyes were thin and straight. "We still partners, Weber?" He kept looking at his shoe. "I hear Doc Angel was walking along the river with you—yesterday and today both."

Weber stayed in his hunched-over posture. "He was merely asking my advice, José Jesús. Nothing more."

"He's a black-hearted sonofabitch." I threw my duck carcass into the fire. "He's the worst of the Missouri fellows and almost as bad as Frémont."

Weber stayed silent while he sipped an empty cup and stared at the fire.

"Weber!" I raised my voice a notch. "If we're not partners, let me know, and I'll get my boys on outta here. I don't want any kind of trouble with that Doc Angel fellow."

He startled a little, like a doe when a crow flies overhead. "Sure, José Jesús. Don't worry the least about us. We're both going to come out of this partnership richer than any white man can imagine. There's no need for you or the Miwok fellows to worry. We'll work things out. Yes sir, indeed."

I didn't need Sedit or Brother Coyote to tell me the lies falling out of Weber's mouth. Which way to jump was one thought, and how to get my Miwok boys organized was the other.

※ ※ ※

Weber and Doc Angel came up on my men and me not long after sunrise. We were talking about where to go and how to get there. I had some women steaming a young doe under some river stones for us to share after we made our decisions. Damn fool that I was, there wasn't a single warrior looking out for trouble. Doc's single eye was glazed, and he couldn't seem to look at anything but the belt around my waist. Weber pulled and twisted at his beard with both hands.

"How do?" Doc Angel said to my belt.

"Well enough." I knew bad trouble was here. My stomach churned like I'd been eating green chokecherries. "Last I heard, Doc, you had a crew working down the river near Sutter."

"It was upstream from Sutter, somewhat." He squared his shoulders toward me. "I've got my crew near that first fork, but I'm fixing to move." Now he looked toward my chest. "Weber's been telling me about this part of the river. Seems real pleasant up in this neck of the woods. Yes, indeed."

My stomach felt loose and tight, both. "Well now," I said. "We're about done ourselves, and just about to mosey on to some other place to the south of here."

"Sure," Weber said. "That sounds real good, José, real damn good."

I signaled trouble to my men, and they eased out of the campsite and toward the shadows.

Doc Angel pulled two .44 caliber pistols from their holsters. Both barrels were pointed directly at my head.

Weber jumped up from a log like some red ants had settled in his pants. "Now, José Jesús, times they are a-changing." He did a quick jig. "Real fast, they are a-changing."

Doc Angel moved two steps closer to me. "Well now, José Jesús, I thought that you'd like to know that me'n Weber are legal partners on this here quartz claim. We got the legal papers all signed, and I want all you diggers to move on out, quick as scat!"

"Indeed, sir, I was just about to head downstream this very moment." I looked straight at the long barrels and kept real still.

"You'd better get on out of here double quick." Doc extended both guns toward me. "Get!" he hissed.

I slowly moved a few steps backward, and Doc jerked his head toward some brambles. "I got me six men with rifles over there. They're all real good shots, and they all hate diggers."

"What've you got in mind, Doc?"

"Me and my boys is all sports, so I'll count off to five, and we'll see how things work out. One . . . ," Doc Angel said.

Bullets swished through leaves and pinged off rocks near my feet. I zigzagged toward holes of silence, dove behind a fallen pine, and wiggled recklessly through a tangle of gooseberry and poison oak vines. I could hear my men crash through the woods. One called out in pain, and then it was quiet.

Later, when the campfire flared and shadows danced far into the woods, I yelled toward the Missouri sonsabitches. "Weber! You are a goddamned liar!"

"Am not!" Weber shouted back. "Indians ain't nothing, so a white man can't lie to a damn Indian."

A barrage of rifle and pistol shots exploded. Lead clunked into trees. Branches fell nearby.

I never moved, but made each word sound from a different spot. "I'll get you Weber. You too, Angel. Sonsabitches!"

Doc Angel laughed, and his men fired off another dozen rounds into the dark.

We used the tree frog signal to find one another. The only wounded man was shot in the arm, so we cleared the quartz canyon before the half-moon came up, and a week later I threw in with Sutter. Not partners this time, just neighbors on the Stanislaus River. We each listened to the other complain about Missouri sonsabitches and the perpetual cold water.

"They kicked me out of my own fort," Sutter said.

"You should've listened to your partner," I said.

"Maybe," Sutter said.

"Guess we'll never know," I said.

I filled a small sack with nuggets after three days of hard work, but then Sutter wandered away as if I were covered with black pus. The hard looks from the white boys got dangerous, so I moved back into the woods and put my crew to work on some dry gravel beds high above the river and with guards posted wherever needed. I also put Carlos to work stealing cattle to sell in this southern mining district. He charged an ounce of dust per pound, and Carlos told those white sonsabitches how much the cows weighed.

That half-breed Carlos had a way of getting on with folks that I found intriguing. He didn't smile a lot or tell stupid jokes—he just did what he had to do without any bullshit. There was a whisper of Sedit or maybe Podnow in his audacity. I gave Carlos a quarter of the profit from the cow business, and he paid his vaqueros from his share. My Miwok miners split half the gold we found with me, and I kept them away from the white man's whiskey and from their whores.

After the heat died down and the first big storm flew in over the great valley, I packed four donkeys with deerskin bags full of gold and walked southwest toward the Tachi people. I was exhausted. I could barely keep my eyes open to guide the loaded animals on any trail I could find. Visions of rabbit-skin blankets and a steam lodge filled with loquacious men blurred all but the largest rocks in my path. The old-time songs moved through my nose and tongue and overwhelmed the sound of rain falling through the trees and onto my shoulders. The warm cocoon of memories filled my waking dreams. The People smiled at me in my dreams.

The rain settled to a persistent drizzle. It sputtered out at the last stand of pine trees, then stopped altogether where oaks gathered in elegant groves. Finally, the clouds disappeared and the sun made luminous the first raft of tule-reeds. Geese and ducks flew in swarms. The smell of damp grass and wood smoke eased into my skin and bones.

The People smiled at me. The People. The People. I was home in the south end of the great valley, the land of the Tachi.

CHAPTER FOURTEEN

Fall, 1848

M Y FEET TOOK ME HOME. There was no thought as to direction, only an inner tug that culminated on the shore of our beautiful lake. My Tachi village was gone, but I examined the steam lodge, a hulking mound of debris now, and paid a visit to each empty dwelling. The dense clouds of waterfowl still swirled like mosquitoes on a calm night, but there were no people. Herds of elk still hid among the tule reeds, but as I coursed back and forth through the southern portion of the great valley, I found only a few scattered Yokuts. They were tucked into dense thickets of willow or in uplands caves. The huge villages of the People had vanished; now there were but a few hundred frightened souls.

I stopped two white men riding toward the goldfields. There was no caution in this act—my head was empty of thought, my stomach full of bile. "Where are they?" I asked.

"What you yelling about, digger?" the older man answered.

"The People! Where are the People?"

Both white men pulled rifles from their saddle holsters. "There's no people around here, digger. It's too damn swampy for any good farms." They jacked shells into position and pulled back the safety catches. "Get on back, digger. I'd hate to waste a good shell on the likes of you. Back off now."

The souls of my father and uncles and all those ancestors who lived and died along the shores of our beautiful lake remained hidden from my dreams. There were fish and fowl and game to eat, but no spirits of the People to tell jokes or listen to tales of my journey through life. Our oak orchards had survived, but not my wife or only son. Sedit was dead, that lovely brown crane of mine.

❋ ❋ ❋

I guided my string of four mules along deer trails in the foothills and high country. In a few places I found villages that were mixed with Paleuymani, Yauelmani, Chukhansi, and Tachi of the Yokuts people. There were usually some Miwok and always a few half-breeds added to the lot, together with a garnish of Paiute and Chumash. I saw remnants of families achieve some small degree of comfort and power within each collection of strangers. Mission Indios were village chiefs and half-breeds served as tipne doctors. My disturbed mind found a peculiar comfort in these communities of recent invention. Almost everyone knew my name, and many had some bit of distorted knowledge of my past. All tolerated my odd behavior, and I in turn was tolerant of each odd collection of people, brought together for reasons no one could explain.

During the pleasant days of late fall and early winter, I moved from one small village to the next without the slightest plan. The older residents welcomed my advice about the spirits, and we old folks exchanged information of who was dead and who remained in this world. At the end of each conversation I always asked, "Sedit— have you heard what happened to my wife?" Old men always looked at the dirt and said, "No, José Jesús, I cannot answer your question. Some say she died among the hill-country Miwok, but only the spirits can say for certain." Old women paused to send their memory back through the hateful past. "I celebrated the death of your son at a Lonewis several years prior to the invasion of gold seekers, but of Sedit I know very little. Some say she died among the Paiute."

During the wet weather season I stayed as a guest in the chief's lodge in a small village near Kings River. Time moved to the slow pace required by the cold and mud. There were the same rabbit-skin blankets of my youth: the clapping, shouting games of chance, and the same nimble humor from my memories. But I missed the night wind whispering through tule reed walls, the night herons disputing territory, and the special subtlety of Tachi jokes whispered from husband to wife while playing under the blankets. I missed the whispers from my Tachi ancestors, and I missed by brown crane, my Sedit.

There was another problem with the new villages. The familiar smells of smoke and sweat failed to evoke a single whisper of welcome from Brother Coyote. Even with the soft taps of rain about the roof, the many pipes of jimson weed, the singing—nothing helped. Pain exploded in my head. Dreams roared with the constant din of shovels in wet muck, but Brother Coyote remained aloof. He strutted about on the hazy horizon and howled. He lifted his leg to every waist-high stump, but he never smiled, and he never moved down the dream trail to sit at my side.

Each chief of every village accepted my gift of gold. I explained how the abalone shells and small white shells of the old days were not acceptable to the Americans. I explained that now only gold served to store the value of elk-skin moccasins or acorn flour through the wet winter, that only gold would purchase sharp metal knives and needles and muskets. The Americans gave value to gold, not to the beautiful iridescent abalone shells. I answered their carefully crafted questions with stories of Coyote and Eagle besieged by problems caused by the white man. I taught the young men some words of the Americans and cautioned them to behave as the coyote and not the grizzly bear when confronted by the sonsabitches. I recruited a few in each village to spend time during the subsequent summers searching for gold and told them of likely places to look.

"If we bring our gold to the white men, how will they treat us?" the young men always asked.

"They will call you digger or damn digger and steal your gold," I said.

"If there are no advantages in finding the gold, why should we bother?"

"During each winter I will return to this village," I told them. "I will trade your gold for the white man's cloth and metal pots."

"What about muskets?"

"One musket will cost a deerskin full of gold. You will find more advantages in trading gold for food and cloth and seed than guns."

"We can kill elk and bear with the musket."

"The white man will kill all Indios who carry muskets. The invaders have laws and armies to enforce those laws that deny guns to Indios."

"We are smarter than the white man. He will never know that we have muskets in our possession."

I shrugged my shoulders. "When I was a young man, the white man always seemed exceedingly stupid."

"Now you are an old man, José Jesús, and not long for this world, I would guess," said a voice from the sweat lodge.

"I welcome death over every desire," I answered.

✳✳✳

I followed the King River up into the hills until it became a small stream. On a secluded meadow, surrounded by groves of white oak and sugar pine, a small village detained me for three cycles of the full moon. It was here, in this distant place that my mind and stomach settled into a comfortable routine. I smiled when jokes were told at my expense. Brother Coyote finally joined me on long walks, and we held the peace without a single noxious dispute. The sight and sound and smell of women titillated both my evening dreams and those of the day. I married again. Twice, in fact, because I married twin daughters of the chief. They were both widows of brothers from a village on the San Joaquin River. It happened that one husband had been gored by a bull elk, and soon after, the husband of the other twin died of a persistent cough that continued for weeks until he expired. The children of these two dead men went to live with their father's relatives, while my wives returned to live on the land of their birth.

My wives told me that they had cried when they left their children, but there was nothing to do except follow the wisdom of their ancestors.

"Everything was already in turmoil," I noted. "Why didn't you both just bring your children up the river to the home of your own father?"

"The tipne doctor of our husbands' village threatened to kill our children if we didn't follow his directions. He said that he would poison our babies and poison us too if we weren't careful."

"What name did this audacious tipne doctor use?"

"Hineh," said the twins in tandem."

"Ahh," I said. "Hineh, a vicious doctor indeed."

"Anyway," said the taller twin. "It still holds that when the nenas—the families with the same male lineage—travel up into the mountains for summer hunting or again during the ceremonial gatherings of both spring and fall, we can see our children."

"We can laugh and roll on the ground with our children," said the shorter twin. We can tell each other of the tiny adventure since the last meeting."

They were good mothers, my wives.

I loved my wives for their affection to me and to their children. My wives smiled at everyone, even to the mothers of their dead husbands. They smiled at me in the firelight, and they giggled constantly when we played ingenious games under the blankets. They listened when I told them of Sedit and of my son, and they cried when I cried with her memory.

Kalu was short and chubby with a long tongue that she used in truly miraculous ways. In the spring she wore the coiled orange flowers of her name around both ears. She listened carefully when I spoke, and during the cold, damp nights of winter, she told stories about the old days.

Haienen was taller than her sister, with widely spaced eyes and full lips and the complexion of the gray-brown alder tree. She listened with the same diligent attention of a small bird to her sister and me and to all who would speak. Haienen smiled with her eyes and danced like the moonbeams on a large lake. When she sang, my throat became very small. I could barely breathe.

Kalu and Haienen liked each other, and they grew to like me. They massaged my shoulders and tickled my ribs and whispered hot breath into my ears. The pain eased from my stomach. The headaches disappeared like bubbles from deep water. Coyote peeked under our blankets and laughed at the tangle of bodies. "Wait!" he called. "One more penis will help your pathetic daisy chain!"

"Quiet, mutt," Kalu yelled.

"Another tongue could serve you well, my sweet girl." Coyote slobbered his genitals in demonstration. "See the length, my girl, and the ferocious vigor that I am willing to extend."

"Maybe he's right," whispered Haienen. "Try as we might, there always seems to be an unfilled void."

"Quiet!" I yelled.

"Quiet, yourself!" yelled my wives and my spirit brother.

Each morning Kalu and Haienen greeted me with satisfied smiles and a breakfast of grasshopper atole. During the day, Brother Coyote took long walks with us through the yellow pine forests. And so it was that through the long, cold nights of winter and into the soft, warm spring, we four talked and laughed and joked. When the rocks began to show in the river, we sat in a quiet glen, and my twins listened.

"I must leave for the summer." When they remained quiet, I continued. "I must observe what the white men are doing up and down the rivers, and discover what dangers they present for our villages."

Kalu waved a hand to dismiss such an absurd thought. "The chief will send his spies to observe the white men. Let the chief manage his job as he should."

"There are white men who know me, and they will provide information unavailable to the chief of any village. I will return to our shared bed with the acorn harvest, at the very latest."

"Stay, Husband," said Haienen. "You have served the People for many years, and now they can serve you."

Kalu smiled at me "How old are you, Husband? Isn't it the time for you to sit with the elders and let the young men act as fools?"

"The Mission San Juan Bautista records proclaim that I am near sixty of their years— but the invaders lie for little or no reason."

"My," said Haienen, "I assumed you seventy summers or so."

Both Kalu and Coyote giggled with malicious glee.

"A Tachi warrior in his mid-fifties can easily handle the sensual needs of two women." I gave the three skeptics my best tipne doctor glare. "What! Who is the first to complain of my virility? Who?"

"You must admit your true age, Husband, and then you must allow us the pleasure of our ministrations to your aches and pains and carnal aspirations," said Kalu.

"Go on any foolish mission that you desire, brother mine," said Brother Coyote. "Don't you worry about your wives in the very least." He flashed his eyes first red then yellow. "Go to the white man, José Jesús, and I'll stay to help minister to these two beautiful women."

"Ha!" said Kalu.

"Come, come, Brother, fly from this mountain retreat and make your survey of the rapacious white men." Coyote licked his forepaw and smiled at my wives. "Go," he said. "Hurry to save the People. Hurry, hurry."

❈ ❈ ❈

I traveled west down from where the Kings River was a small stream wandering among tall mountains, to the last fork bearing north and into the San Joaquin River. The changes from my last year became quickly apparent. Every single river, and every stream of any consequence, was filled with gold seekers. Even the lower reaches of the remote Kings River was choked with temporary dams and rockers of every size. Hordes of miners moved dirt and rocks through every day, and at night they gambled and whored and shit and killed those who might interfere with their pleasure.

Almost all the miners were the white invaders—Americans in the vast majority—but there was also a large contingent of vile and brutal Australians and Europeans of every language. Those from Chile and Mexico were scattered here and there, but they were now forced to work the remote edges of sites showing significant gold. As I traveled further north, Chinese people were also evident. Some of the yellow people were making an effort to find gold without interference by the white miners.

"You foreigners got to pay twenty dollars a day to work this river," the white sheriff yelled at the Chinese and Mexicans. "You damn foreigners have got to get a license to work this river," he yelled at the Californios and black niggers. "No tickee, no workee," he chortled. "You must buy a tickee from me, and then you maybe get some workee."

Most of the Chinese people were slaves available to the white miners for a daily wage. The Indio slaves worked for the cost of pants and a blanket. The Indio miners yearned for the possibility of some food or maybe a shirt or a stray chip of gold, but both Chinese people and Indio people died in large numbers. Both were expendable, of course, and easily replaced as slaves to the white miners.

At night, when I whispered to the Yokuts or Miwok people huddled around small campfires, they looked all around for evidence of their white masters listening before answering any of my questions.

"Run, Tipne Man," they warned. "There is nothing here but cold, wet death. Tell the People to run and hide."

"Have you seen any of my vaqueros? Any of my family?" I queried.

"No," they all answered.

So I traveled further north up the San Joaquin past the mouth of the Merced River and then the Tuolumne River. "Have you. . . ?" I asked.

"No," they all answered.

It wasn't until I explored the diggings on the Mokelumne River that one old man answered. "Only that Sonoran," he said. "The smart Sonoran from your army of bandits. The one with the big smile. He is north of here, on the Yuba River."

I watched and waited for two full days and nights before making contact. From past experience, he probably knew that I was spying about and full of questions—but Joaquin let me set the pace and allowed me the time to observe until I joined him for coffee on the third morning. He looked up from contemplating a small campfire, suitable only for sustaining a single pot at a slow boil.

"How are you on this fine day?"

My old friend from the vaquero days, Joaquin Murrieta, smiled at me through his beautiful new mustaches. He handed over a tin cup with hot coffee full to the rim.

"One foot still follows the other," I said. "And how are you?"

"I'm worried," El Famoso, as he was known, said. "The Americans are countless maggots this summer. They claim every bend in every river for themselves. They claim you and me as foreigners and all the land as theirs. 'No niggers or diggers allowed,' they warn."

"Which are you, my friend—nigger or digger?"

"No jokes, José Jesús. These Americans will kill you for making light of their pretensions. They have no humor and no honor. Beware!"

"I need many sacks of gold, Joaquin. Last year I charged an ounce of gold for workers and the same for a pound of beef. What can I charge this year?"

"Nothing. Even if you could give these invaders all the free workers and free beef that they desire, they would still kill you for your arrogance."

"Last year white men welcomed my services."

"This year they are wild with greed."

"I need to help the villages, and it appears that nothing except gold will help the People survive their fate."

"I fear you are too late, my friend."

"Again, I'm too late." I moved to embrace this Sonoran, this wonderful trickster. "Help me, Joaquin. What can I do to help the People?"

Joaquin pushed me away to an arm's length and smiled. "Can you still pull a scorpion from my ear?"

I opened my hand to reveal a lively resident from his ear.

"Good," he said. "You're hired."

✳✳✳

Joaquin Murrieta's tent was a big sun-bleached brown edifice, with two center poles and outside walls nearly tall as a horse. His wife and some of the whores that he employed served dinner to the miners for an ounce of dust. Two more ounces and a whore served dessert in one of the cribs in back of the tent. While the white men waited for dinner or a woman, I worked outside the tent with three walnut shells on an oak tree stump. After the tables were cleared, I ran a three-card monte game under the light of whale oil lamps. Both games were profitable, and even after I split fifty-fifty with Joaquin, many deer sacks were quickly filled with gold.

For the shell game, a bean was placed under one of the walnut shells, and then the shells were all moved in a rapid and confusing pattern. The player, of course, always tried to follow the movement of the shell containing the bean, and when I stood back from the stump, he placed a bet to prove the accuracy of his judgment. I always enlisted two or three of Joaquin's blond-haired cousins to build the suckers up with successful bets and loud cries of pleasure. "Lady Luck! Thank you! Thank you! A month's worth of work for one bean. Thank you! Thank you!"

Some of the cousins were less exaggerated in their ability to vanquish a no-account digger, but all were successful in their tasks. When a sucker placed his bet, the bean was never under any of the shells. Never. In the process of moving the three shells about, the rear of the shell covering the bean was lifted and the bean pinched between my thumb and first finger and retained until after the mark had made his guess. The empty shell was overturned, the wager collected, and one of the two remaining shells was lifted to reveal the bean.

"If you had picked this one," I always remarked, "you'd have won your bet."

Here was my monte spiel: "Look here, men, I have three little cards—two black aces and one red queen. You must find the queen. If you find the queen, you win your bet. If you turn up an ace, you lose. The queen wins and the aces lose. Remember now, I take no bets from paupers or pregnant women. I'll show you all three cards and throw them on the table. If your eye is faster than my hand, then you win the amount of your bet. Gold on the table or no bet. Okay, let's go!"

Every night six or eight men crowded around my table, and two or three were always my confederates. "Step right up," I'd yell. "If you don't speculate, you can't accumulate." Of course both aces had burred edges, so the cousins got the queen and the damn white miners got the shaft. I'd guess that except for those miners who made exceptional strikes in one river or another, Joaquin and I were probably the wealthiest men in California during the year of 1850.

✳✳✳

Joaquin kept his gang of Sonorans moving up and down the great valley with long strings of mules to haul food and clothes and mining supplies that he imported from Guaymas and Hermosillo. My vaqueros, with Carlos still serving as straw boss, stole cattle and horses from the coastal ranchos, and we sold them to the hungry miners.

"Dammit, Carlos, how in hell do you survive those damn Missouri devils?" I asked. "Why don't they just kill your ugly hide and walk off with your cows?"

"I don't go anywhere near them—that's how I stay alive." Carlos gave me a hint of a smile. "My boss does the selling, he collects the gold, and I get an eighth of every cow."

"Joaquin does all your front work?"

"No, it is a man named Miller. My boss calls himself Miller but he talks like Sutter."

"A Swiss man?"

"German, I'd say. A butcher by trade, but smart and tough enough to face down even the meanest of those Missouri bastards."

"He pays what he promises?"

"Dust or coin, whatever I want." Carlos gave me that same little secret smile of his again. "Miller says that it was you that trained me as a shrewd businessman."

The woods were full of Millers and Smiths because they were both common white-man names. I shrugged my shoulders at Carlos. "Miller? Where did I meet this particular Miller? At Sutter's fort?"

"Just hearsay, I guess. He never told me that you two ever met face-to-face, but my boss with the name Miller keeps telling me that the two of you are peas in a pod, and that he'd welcome you as a partner any day of the week."

"I've got Joaquin here on the river and two beautiful partners waiting for me up in the hills. I'm done with white-man partners, and you damn well better believe, my half-breed friend, that this Miller of yours will inevitably turn into more trouble than not."

"Hey, Tipne Man, 'breeds like me have got to learn how to swim through trouble and just keep smiling."

I gave the boy my coyote look, the one that said you ain't nearly as smart as you think. But just standing around Carlos settled my stomach. There was no way to tell the 'breed he was a good person, almost up to the level of some thoughtful Tachi warrior, but there it was—the smiling stomach, that is.

✳✳✳

Just after the first frost but before the first heavy rain, I was setting up for my first monte game of the day, and a big smelly Missouri fellow, complete with a scraggly beard and bad teeth, stopped to confront me.

"Hey, digger—wha'cha think you're do'n, hanging around here?" The man spit on my feet and slowly pulled a pistol from his belt. "Git," he said. "Damn sneak thieves. Damn diggers. Git on outta here before I waste good lead on yor flea-bitten hide. Git!"

Later that night Joaquin poured some coffee for his cousins and me. "There's too many, José Jesús. Every creek is crowded with Americans, and damn few of the idiots can manage their expenses. Fewer yet can find enough gold to pay expenses."

I held the hot metal cup in my hands but remained silent.

"You'll have to stay out of sight from now on. No more shells or cards—just keep track of Carlos and the cows I need."

"Okay," I said.

"You can help my wife manage the whores when she asks, but keep out of sight. This place is filled with those damned Missouri men."

"Sonsabitches," I said.

"It'll get worse," Joaquin said. "You can bet all the gold you've got hidden out back in the woods that us blond-haired niggers are next on their list."

"Well then, maybe we'd better get some mules together and get the hell out of here." I swallowed half the cup of coffee. "Sooner is better than later, because I've got a bad habit of outstaying my welcome around these damn sonsabitches."

"There's still time, Tipne Man. We'll get on with the gold right after the first big rain." Joaquin gave me a smile that matched Carlos's for mood and texture. "I think that we'll load up the mules and head for old Mexico pretty damn soon. We've got enough gold right now to where we'll never have to work another day in our lives."

"My twins will be real happy to see me, Joaquin. Maybe they'd even like a visit to your Old Mexico."

"Sure enough, Tipne Man, you can bring them to my village of San Felipe. We'll all sing and dance and eat, all of us together."

"No Missouri men down there?"

"None! Never will be, either."

"Well now, maybe a visit, for a few seasons anyway, is a good idea. I'll divvy up some gold to a few villages and then disappear from the land of the People for a short while."

"Okay, then, we'll all tail out of here right after the first rain."

"I'll make a short detour up the King River to collect my wives, and then follow along after that long line of mules of ours," I said.

✹✹✹

I wore an old brown wool blanket and let my hair get long and greasy. I tried to disappear from the Missouri men, just like a pea from a shell or a queen on a stump.

"Git outta my way, digger!" yelled one of the bastards, just as I was trying to take a leak.

"Wha'cha doing around here, anyway?" yelled another, just as I was dumping soapy dishwater out away from the tent.

"Git!" In the morning. "Git!" All afternoon and into the night. "Git!"

Not five nights after Joaquin poured my coffee and explained his dream of life in old Mexico, a bunch of Americans from San Francisco set up two stores and a gambling tent just downstream from where we'd been from early summer. The cousins of Joaquin told us that these newcomers charged twice our rates, and their whores were all poxed and skinny.

It wasn't but two nights after the Americans went into business that they burned Joaquin's tent. Then, on that very same night, the bastards stole his mining equipment, and while they were at it, they shot two of the cousins.

We were standing around looking at the hot ashes of the tent and the whore cribs, when an exhausted man came up to us. "Joaquin!" he said. "They burned all our rockers and shot three of your cousins."

Joaquin didn't start breathing hard or grinding his teeth, but turned to me and spoke with patient grace. "I'm needed, Tipne Man."

"It's ten miles in the dark," I said. "Send Three-Finger or somebody else."

"I need to see exactly what has happened," he said. "It is likely that I must bring all the survivors back here, and then decide our next step." Joaquin spoke over his shoulder as he moved toward his horse. "Be careful, Tipne Man—but help where you can."

So it was that Joaquin was tending to his injured relatives when the Americans raped his wife.

Rosita Feliz was a generous woman, with eyes that always smiled even as she stirred iron pots full of beans. She treated her servants and the whores with stern respect. When the Americans grabbed her to drag her into the woods, she did not scream. They beat her with logs and mounted her, one after the other. I sent two of Joaquin's cousins to intervene, and they were shot. One died immediately, and one stayed until the final penetration of Rosita, and then that brave man crawled over to where I was hiding and very slowly he identified each assailant while I listened.

Ten Sonorans traveled ten miles downriver to tell Joaquin Murrieta that his wife, Rosita Feliz, was dead. They gave him every detail of the rape, including the name of each white man who committed the monstrous act, and without a word of response to the messengers, he mounted his horse and rode slowly back toward his Rosita. All the messengers and all of the survivors followed after their chief.

✳✳✳

The first on our list we caught sitting with his bare butt hanging over a small oak branch propped between two stumps. "Hey, you greasers. I'm trying to take a shit. Git on outta here."

Joaquin clubbed the man to the ground with his fists and tied the whimpering man's hands together with rawhide rope. The cousins and I laughed at the sight of El Famoso leading the American around a clearing in the woods from a long rope secured to the pommel of his saddle. At first the horse walked at a slow amble, but soon the man tripped over his loose trousers. He screamed as he skidded through scattered patches of nettle, but soon went quiet. When Joaquin spurred his horse to a trot, we stopped our laughter and watched as the man bounced against trees and rocks. At the gallop, the rope stretched in a taut line and shuddered with each collision until only a pair of arms, tied at the wrist, flopped in a bloody dance through the dust.

We retrieved the scattered parts and piled them under a small tree. Joaquin carved his name in the bark, then plunged his knife between the eyes of the rock-scarred head. "That is the first, Rosita Feliz," he said. "Only the first."

The next three we caught panning the dried loop of an ancient stream. We roped and tied them in vaquero fashion, and then Joaquin pulled all three in a race among a field of rocks. In the end, each received a dagger between the eyes and the epigraph "Joaquin" on a wooden board.

Mounted militia searched the hills for the murderers of honest Americans. Innocent Sonorans and Indians were killed. "A lesson to the damn greasers," they yelled.

Very quickly, however, the gold and whores and cards called the militiamen, and one early morning Carlos whispered into my ear: "Six of them are coming. Six of the marked men are riding toward us."

The ambush was a complete success.

"Don't shoot!" they pleaded.

"As you wish," and Joaquin ordered us to tie the men in pairs, with wrist secured to wrist. Nothing changed after that—the race, the daggers, and the epigraph.

One additional rapist fell into our net, and the remaining two fled east up into the hills and over the far mountains.

"What will you do now?" I asked Joaquin.

"I am not finished punishing the Americans."

"Give it up, my friend. Take your buried gold back to San Felipe and grow old."

My wife is dead, and the gold is gone. Every last nugget, stolen by the same tribe that killed my Rosita." He put his hand on my shoulder. "I'm sorry, José Jesús. Your gold is also robbed. We are both beggars again."

I felt no loss for my gold, only the look on the face of Joaquin distressed my mind. Another friend was drifting toward a useless death. Another good man doomed to dying for a vanished mission.

"Come with me, Joaquin," I said. "Spend a quiet winter in my lodge. Learn to laugh again. My twins and spirit brother will teach you to sing and dance in the proper manner."

"I must stay and kill my enemy."

"They will kill you."

"If they do, Rosita Feliz will welcome me with her lovely smile. If they don't kill me, the angels will join her in rejoicing my success." He gave an awkward shrug. "How can I lose, José Jesús?"

"Come with me, Joaquin. Smell the juniper berry with me. Listen to water whisper over smooth rocks with my twins and me. We'll tell old stories to the youngsters of my village, and we'll both learn how to laugh again."

Joaquin waggled his head a few times and then turned to walk away. Joaquin Murrieta. El Famoso!

CHAPTER FIFTEEN

Winter, 1851

IT WAS NEAR DUSK WHEN I approached the village. The lower Kings River was still filled with white miners and yellow servants, but once the stream narrowed among high mountains, there were only a few of the sonsabitches, scattered here and there. I stood outside the lodge of the village chief and asked permission to return to his village and my wives.

"Stop, José Jesús. Stay where you are, my son, and I will come to stand at your side." His voice was gentle and ominous at the same moment.

"Certainly," I said.

Both the chief and his wife emerged from the lodge. The chief kept his eyes on the ground while his wife stood in front of me to show eyes clogged with tears. "Our daughters are dead." She moved a step closer. "They were murdered, my lovely daughters, murdered."

We closed to hold the other and let tears flow until the first owl called into the night.

"Hold me," she kept repeating.

"Hold tight to my wife, José Jesús," said the chief. "Take no action until you and I can discuss what happened to my daughters and what we must do."

I thought of Joaquin and his dead wife. My tears stopped, and my ears buzzed in the silence.

"Come into my lodge," said the chief. "We will cut your hair and plead with the spirits to honor my daughters."

"Yes," I said. "Lead the way, my chief."

✳✳✳

My wives had been cremated two days before I arrived home. When the ashes cooled, two older women had filtered out the bones of Kalu and Haienen and carried the remains far into the woods where they could rest in quiet retreat. The old women told me that maybe the little owl Pokook would guide my wives to Tipiknits Pahn.

"Yes," I said, "In Tipiknits Pahn they can giggle and play with their dead husbands and they can make everybody happy. Merely watching those two wonderful women will bring smiles to every face."

I thought that maybe they could eat lots of greasy horse meat and grasshopper atole and dance and sing and sleep the dreamless sleep of good souls. My sweet and modest and faithful wives.

I thought that maybe the God of all Spirits was not dead. Maybe he would welcome these good wives and mothers and sit with them and laugh at their jokes. He would certainly smile with the joy of observing the singing and dancing of such humble women. He would cry and burn his hair short with the knowledge of their unseemly deaths.

Maybe the burning of my eyes would diminish, and maybe someday I would understand why I delayed fording the rivers and climbing the mountains to lay beside them in our lodge. Maybe someday I would forgive myself for the time spent hunting the killers of Joaquin's wife and the time spent shoveling gravel into wooden hoppers instead of watching the sun and moon drift one after the other with my wives. Maybe, but probably not.

On the second day of my return to my village, the chief called all the men and big boys into the sweat lodge. After a suitable interval he spoke to us in his low, gravelly voice. "Listen, young men of my village and husband of my daughters, listen to me." A youngster spilled water on the hot rocks. Steam obscured the old chief. "You all must diminish the strength of your anger," said Chief Kodja.

Two elders began clapping.

"You must avoid haste in making decisions." All the elders joined with the slow beat of hands. "You must be kind to everyone, even to those who are evil."

Water splashed again, and the steam obscured my tears.

"No revenge!" said the father of my wives.

"No revenge!" echoed the elders.

I remained silent through the time in the sweat lodge and into the time of bright stars.

When I could restrain my legs and feet no longer, I departed from the village of my wives.

It took two days of searching each pool and falls, and slowly walking with the current down the Kings River. There were only a few miners this far up the river. I would guess that it was only a half-day's hard walk from my village to where I found the first white sonofabitch. The first fellow and also the next two didn't know anything about two Indio ladies.

But late in the same day, I sat in the deep shade of alder trees and watched two men shovel wet mud onto the wire mesh. The taller and older of the two talked through each pause between striking the shovel into muck and heaving it toward the rocker. A cold gray mist settled through the pines and trickled over the top of water-bound scrub willow. I walked the arc between river and their lean-to for the third time and made short diversions to search through the scattered groves of oak and manzanita and pine. There was no one else around.

Brother Coyote told me that only a yew bow with obsidian-tipped arrows would serve my purpose. "The ten-gauge shotgun is all right," Coyote admitted, "and the bang and stink of it would probably ease some of the pain." His yellow eyes looked into mine. "But listen, brother, the *thonk* of an arrow into white meat will best please the spirits. Use the yew bow with obsidian-tipped arrows, and the God of all Spirits will smile upon you."

"Hey! Now lookee here! We got us a digger chief right here on our own claim." The talker put his right foot on the embedded shovel. "And just in time, I do believe." He waved an arm to gesture his welcome. "Git yourself on down here, you old varmint."

I took a few steps toward the men. It was only fifteen paces now—an easy shot if they proved to be the murderers. Even with the little practice I'd had in the past years, there was no thought of missing my intended targets.

"You got a name, digger?"

"José Jesús."

"Haysoos, huh. Joe Jesus." The talker elbowed his companion. "What do you make of that, Mac? This here digger says he's got the Lord's name. Doesn't sound right to me—how 'bout with you?"

"Nope, not right t'all." Mac shoveled two more loads, then stopped. He looked up and down the stream with the flighty twist of a scrub jay.

"Can't have no part of it, no sirree." The older man gave me a hard stare. "Get on down here, digger. It's not right for a white man to shovel shit when a damn digger's standin' around calling hisself the Lord. Damn, boy! Don't you hear me? Git on down here."

I took a few more steps, as if in a dream.

Brother Coyote whispered. "Slowly, now. Ever so slowly."

I unlimbered the bow and placed one end on my moccasin. The two Americans were only five paces removed. "Tell me now, did you boys have some fun with a couple of Indio ladies a week or so ago? Twin sister ladies?"

"Ladies!" The talker bugged his eyes. "You cain't be talkin' about them pox bags who kept crying for more of our good white cock, can you?"

"Dammit, shut up." Mac twitched his eyes first at the talker, then at me. "They shouldn't oughta run." Mac swallowed his spit. "We was only funnin' with 'em, and they up and ran. We called for them to stop, but they's ran from us."

The talker slapped both hands together and smiled. "We showed them ugly bitches a thing or two, didn't we, Mac?" He gave me a big gap-toothed smile. "Faster 'n bush rabbits, they was, but we catched 'em, and that's a fact."

Mac dropped his shovel and began backing away from the talker. He never took his eyes off me, so he was able to watch the first arrow flutter with a twisting leisurely flight into his shoulder. He grabbed the shaft, tripped, and fell backward into the water.

Over the next sixty heartbeats I released twelve arrows—six into Mac and six into the talker. Brother Coyote sat on his haunches and watched my every move and smiled that foolish lopsided grin of his. I walked over small rocks to the talker, pulled his knife from the scabbard, and plunged it between his eyes. Mac received the same present with his own knife. A man's knife between the eyes was El Famoso's prank, so the whites would probably blame him for the murders. Two more was no matter for Murrieta. A hundred dead whites was no matter to him.

Brother Coyote advised me on the proper etiquette for the last trick. "Pee on them," he said. "Leave your mark on the bastards."

I peed on the bloody faces, a full stream into their mouths and eyes. As my yellow pee mixed with their red blood, I felt a feathery weight on my shoulder. A caress followed by a gentle whisper.

"Thank you," the whisper said. "Thank you."

They were good wives, my twins.

The first three ravens slid out of the sky and plopped onto the gravel. One shiny black bird bounced four hops over to the talker and sat on the dead man's chest. The bird turned his head aslant, muttered a few husky croaks, and then pecked both eyes from the man's face.

Maybe the twins could ride to Tipiknits Pahn on raven's wings. Maybe the twins were smiling now. They always smiled, my wives— they smiled and sang and waited for me to return to our lodge. They were good wives and deserved the cleansing blood of revenge and the warm yellow insult on a defiler's face. I felt good about every moment of killing the two, pissing on them especially. Maybe I should have gone and found Joaquin and advised him on this proper gift for the eyes of murderers and rapists and probably for most of the white sonsabitches.

There was a twitch of leaves from a downstream alder, but I ignored the intruder and watched the growing mass of ravens. Fifteen now. They pecked and ripped and pulled bloody skin. Black devil birds feeding on the Black Angel of death. They croaked and squirted white shit over the white men. Red blood. White shit.

"Thank you," came the whisper from my wives.

The first redheaded vulture spilled from the sky and chased a mass of ravens from a body.

"Savage!" I called. "If that is your sorry ass over there, bring me some of that Yankee tobacco."

I heard the *click-click* of iron hitting iron, followed by the acrid smell of tobacco smoke. White man's tobacco. Footsteps crunched over gravel, and Savage squatted next to me. We shared the stubby pipe and watched the birds squabble. It was full dark before the last vulture flew away to a nearby roost.

"That's a mighty fine job you did there, Tipne Man."

I didn't respond.

Savage coughed a few times, filled the pipe, and sparked it back to life, then edged around to face me. "Some people might get real upset with such carrying on, you know. Those militia boys always carry a big rope they can sling over a tall tree in a case like this."

"So you think I shouldn't kill two toadstools that raped and killed my wives?" I looked hard at the white man for a long time. "You can tell anybody you want that I think it is damn well okay for me to shoot the sonsabitches full of holes."

"You are right as rain about your thoughts, but the law's coming to California, and real soon, I think."

I could barely make out his face in the dark and kept my mouth shut.

"You've got to learn how to use the law to get your revenge, José Jesús. You got to stop listening to that damn coyote friend of yours."

"White man's law doesn't mean a damn thing to a digger."

Savage spewed some smoke at me. "Tell me this, Tipne Man. If some stranger came walking into your country—your village—what laws would you use?" Savage held quiet for a stretch until it was obvious that I wasn't going to answer his stupid question. He nudged me on the shoulder. "The laws of your ancestors, right? The laws of your village."

"Our land, our people, our laws," I said.

He handed over the pipe. "You are still right as rain, Tipne Man. Just what I'm saying is that you call yourself the People as if everyone else in this world is less than you. Am I right with this supposition, or not?"

"Right as rain," I said.

"I'll tell you something else that you probably already know, my friend. Laws are nothing but rules to give the powerful folks more of what they want. You've got your chiefs and tipne doctors, and you've got your low-down folks who have to follow their rules. That's why a stranger in your village always does what the powerful men want him to do, or something bad happens to the stranger. Am I right in this matter also?"

"Talk," I said. "You white boys are always full of cheap talk."

"That may well be a fact—and we've still got the white man's rules now, Tipne Man. Soon enough the white men will spread throughout the great valley and all over California. There's nothing you can do about this fact of life except to follow along or curl up and die."

He put his hand out for the pipe, and I gave it over. "You red men have got to figure out what the powerful white men will tolerate from you boys, or you're all dead as any doornail."

"I'm ready to die—any day is okay with me. Sixty or so years is enough for any man."

"The People need you, José Jesús. Most whites don't know it, but they need you too."

"Savage, you just listen for a change. My wives are dead, white man, and I'm ready to join them any time at all—so cut out with the bullshit."

"I believe that I can help you, José Jesús. A little bit, anyway. For that matter, we can help each other, and maybe we both can help the People."

"You been talking with Sutter? This line of yours sounds real familiar."

"Listen to me—I'm telling you the truth. I don't care what anybody else said to you."

"Anytime some white man says he can help some red man, that very same red man better run like hell. I'd rather go walking hand in hand with a grizzly bear than take up with another white man."

Savage stood. He was trying his best to keep his mouth shut, but he had to say something. "You want any help with those two dead men?"

"Ravens and vultures—that's all the help I need for them bastards,"

"I'll be around hereabouts, Tipne Man. Come look me up if you see any way of our getting together."

"Sure, white man. I'll remember your little story."

"Adios, then. See you when I see you."

"True enough, white man."

Chapter Sixteen

Spring, 1852

"TELL ME AGAIN, WHITE MAN—how does running a whorehouse serve the People? Especially a damn whorehouse on the south fork of Tuolumne River, the hell and gone from enough customers to pay expenses." I was drinking whiskey again, but not enough to drive me over the edge. "C'mon, Savage. Twist some words around that slippery tongue of yours, and let me know the real truth of the matter."

The actual real truth of the matter was that Savage pulled me out of a gutter someplace—Oakland? Fresno? I've got little or no memory from after my wives died. Downhill I went, and that is a certain fact. Downhill from the place where ravens plucked eyes from the two white sonsabitches that killed my wives. Downhill in the eyes of the People because a drunk is no good to anybody, including himself. And still no word at all from Brother Coyote, even with me sober most of the time.

I also believed that Carlos was somehow involved with Savage getting me back from wherever I'd been. The damn half-breed. Those two made a pair the time I tried to kill Frémont. Carlos and Savage—both could talk their way past ten ornery rattlesnakes.

I do recall that it was Savage that forced me to take a long walk. "We've got to get rid of the whiskey in your system," he told me time and time again. I can't remember the first few days of wandering around the rocks and caves near Mission San Juan Bautista, but I do remember Savage tying me to a tree at night so's he could get a little sleep. The sonofabitch. It was probably Fresno where he found me, with Fresno closer to the caves south of Bautista than Oakland. Anyway, I got mostly dry with his walking cure, and now here I was sitting in the mess hall of his damn whorehouse. Savage was encouraging me to go in his direction of thought with a little whiskey mixed in with my cup of coffee. The sneaky sonofabitch.

"Those women have got no choice, and that's God's own truth." Savage spilled another splash into our tin mugs. "I know for a fact that to you and me it's a real sorry affair, seeing these ladies on their backs every day, but what else can they do?" Savage moved his nose across the table to nearly touch mine. "They got no villages to call home and no family to provide for them. If we didn't take 'em in, you know damn good and well somebody else would do worse by the poor, sad creatures." He let a small tear drift down the cracks on his face. When Savage was in the hunt, he could make tears with one blink and a big laugh with the next. "Now you and me, we can treat every single one of those gals like family, José Jesús, and you damn well know that I'm speaking the honest truth." Savage took a long drink and plopped the mug back on the table. "So help me God if that's not the honest truth."

I let the man wipe the tear away and compose his delicate disposition. "Savage," I said. "You could sell horseshit and call it strawberries. The trouble is, some famous French chef would call your shit the best strawberries he'd ever tasted."

"Well, thank you, José Jesús. I take those words of yours as the best compliment a man could ever get."

I matched his long drink with one of my own. "The girls all want me to tell you that they also think that you are the best horseshit salesman they have ever encountered."

"I try my best, partner. My honest best."

"We know you do, Savage."

"Are we partners or not, Tipne Man?"

"Hell no," I said. "I'll just hang around here with you and the girls and keep out of your way. I got nothing better to do with my time. Just keep any talk of partnership out of our conversation."

"Whatever you say, José. Whatever you say."

✹✹✹

The girls were mostly valley mixed-bloods, but we also had one Karok and one white woman. The Karok whore we bought from a Mexican fellow, who bought her from a white man who came from up near Eureka and needed money more than he needed the Karok because he sure as hell couldn't find any gold on the Stanislaus River, or the Tuolumne River either. There were two Mohave traders that sold us the white whore.

There was no brawling among the whores of Savage like there was in so many other places. I think this fact was all because from the very beginning he established two very good rules. First, there were no tricks during the day, and second, every one of the women had a day job in the store, kitchen, or laundry—no exceptions. Together—by total accident, I admit—we also created another rule that defined the border between one job and the other, and that was mandatory choir practice directly after the last miner had been served his dinner.

Savage had a nice tenor voice, and I played the guitar or violin, depending on the song. Mostly we did hymns that I remembered from the mission days, but it wasn't long before the girls and customers got to singing a bunch of raucous chants or dirges about ships at sea.

When we had a mob of Frenchies or Chileños around, they always insisted on teaching a song or two in their own language. They weren't all hymns either.

The choir started when Savage and a few girls started singing a Yokuts song while they were cleaning up after the evening meal.

"Cut out with that blamed singing," one of the miners yelled. He was an American fellow who came around the whorehouse every night. He never ate anything we prepared or bought supplies at the store—he just came to service the whores. "All that singing makes me hornier than ever," he yelled. "Let's get down to business and leave off with the damn singing."

Savage gave the man a big wink and a bigger smile and then turned to me. "José Jesús. Tell me if you don't think these girls sound like angels from heaven."

"To my taste they are sweet as maple syrup," I said.

"Well, now." He gathered the girls in close. "José Jesús, would you please get down that guitar of yours and play along with me and the lovelies?"

"Whoa now!" the American yelled. "Here's a five-dollar gold piece with not a nick. Gimmie that Karok bitch and go right on singing all night, for all I care."

Savage ignored the man. "Girls, gather around and listen." The entire batch of ten whores stood in a semicircle around Savage. "When you've got a smelly goat of a man puffing away on top of you, here's a song to sing in his filthy ear."

Savage sang two verses of "Rock of Ages" a cappella, and even the American shut up and listened to him sing. "Now, this is what we'll do," he told the girls. "I'll sing a line, and then you and José Jesús follow. First me, then you."

"Ten dollars!" the American shouted.

Savage turned to face the crowd of forty men. "You all are about to get a little culture from the Mariposa Ladies' Choir. We'll learn one song tonight and add another each night until we've got a grand repertoire." He gave them a stiff little smile. "Mark my words, boys—pretty soon we'll be so good that you'll be forgetting that hard-on down at the end of your pocket."

"Fifteen dollars!" the American shouted. "I'm taking that Karok squaw right now, or I'm leaving right now. One or the other."

Savage pulled the Karok woman forward and twirled her around like a fandango dancer. "Twenty," he said. "Do I hear twenty dollars?"

I've got to admit, Savage was a damn genius in getting what he wanted. Never a bluster or threat to anyone, just his big smile and soft words and moving his victims to absolute and total surrender. In the days before the choir started, Savage let the men stand in line in front of the crib of the whore of his choice. There was no special order in the procedure—as soon as the supper meal was over and Savage said, "The cribs are open," the stampede commenced. If the line exceeded three men, he charged five dollars for that particular whore. The shorter lines paid three dollars each.

After that night, when the Karok lady garnered a hundred dollars in gold coins for her initial service, Savage took bids for each girl, and the victorious bidder followed his girl immediately to her crib. One half-hour later we rang a bell that Savage had stolen from San José Mission, and the next highest bidder for each girl got his turn. Naturally, he got half the time also. Every man after the second paid the fee of the second man and got the same time allotment. It was a good system because the first-round winner got to spend a good long time with our genuine, officially certified by Savage, virgin.

Savage made buckets of real gold coin and buckets of gold dust, and he filled deerskins full of both and let them molder under our beds. He had two Yokuts warriors outside the door of our bedroom with ten-gauge shotguns, day and night.

"This gold will buy a lot of good things for the People," Savage said.

"Sure enough," I said. "Sugar to rot their teeth and whiskey to rot their guts." I wasn't about to let Savage take the high road here. He was still trying his sneaky best for me to fall in line as his partner. I guess he figured my name combined with his would bring more regular customers into his store. The whores were good for any miners trying their luck in the area, but the new villages in the valley and foothills were starting to spend money in his store, and Savage had his eye on milking that cow.

"Listen to me, José. The gold I give to the local villages will be for plows and seed and land and respect—that's what this money will buy the People." Savage put a splash of good whiskey in each of our cups. "It's only a matter of time, José Jesús. The People will catch on to the proper way of life, and then they'll be as good as any white man. If you'd just stop with that stubborn streak of yours and sign on as my partner, we could move the People along even faster than with just me flapping my mouth at them."

"Hit me again with that whiskey of yours and shut the hell up," I said.

Savage trained a couple of young Americans to assist us in the store, and he kept a barge going back and forth to Stockton for supplies. He carried most everything a reasonable person could desire, and there was never any special hurry in making one purchase or a dozen. He had seed and hoes and even one steel-plated plow, but mostly he sold dried beans, flour, maple syrup, pepper, and salt. Whiskey too, of course—local rotgut or American rye, whatever a customer could afford. I did maintain a crew of Sonorans, plus a few of my old vaqueros from Sutter's army, for stealing cattle and sheep and horses from the nearly deserted ranches south of San José Village. Carlos told me that he was too busy working for that Miller fellow to help me very much, but he did arrange that my stolen critters went to Miller to get butchered and packaged. My vaqueros did all the work while Carlos and that damn Miller fellow gouged an easy profit for themselves.

"Just have your boys get the beasts you want butchered up to our place near Fresno, and we'll wrap up the best parts for your customers," Carlos said.

"What about the guts and skin and moo?" I was teasing the damn half-breed a little.

"We'll take even the moo and make a little profit," he said

The Miller fellow stopped by our place early one morning, just at the time when all the women were carrying loads of scrambled eggs and flapjacks to the voracious miners. There was also a line out the door of our store with folks waiting to buy a shovel or a bag of beans or a tin of maple syrup. It was a typical day for our place. He walked up to me with an outstretched hand and said, "José Jesús, I'm very pleased to finally make your acquaintance. Yes, indeed."

"Do I know you, sir?"

"Not to my face—not until today, anyway." He had a funny curl of hair that circled his right ear, and his eyes were stone gray. "My name is Miller, and I run the biggest butcher shop in California."

"Is that so?" I'd trust Savage way before this Miller fellow, and I'd trust ten rattlesnakes before Savage. Both men were easy with words and smiles, and a both had a way of looking at you that might make you think they posed no threat—that they were just passing through your space and wanted to say "Howdy." Podnow would warn me against this pair. Brother Coyote would pee on their shoes.

"Carlos is one of my best foremen, and he has many fine words for José Jesús."

"Carlos is a good man—for a 'breed, anyway."

"He works hard and always keeps his word," Miller said.

"Well, I like Carlos good enough. We may even be related in some way."

Miller stood there, not two paces away, nodding his head, not at all anxious to move along.

"The boy's got a real good smile," I said.

"That he does, and I want to tell you, sir, that from this day forward, Carlos will stop by wherever you say to pick up all your critters. Once a week or so, that is. My drovers will move your stock up to Fresno at no cost to you whatsoever, and I'll send a wagon with your butchered beef, posthaste."

"Same deal with you keeping the skin and guts and moo?"

"Yes sir, the same excellent deal for both of us."

"Well, thank you. I appreciate your excellent service."

"My pleasure, José Jesús." He nodded one more time, turned sharp on his heel, and walked away.

He was correct, of course. The butcher had a good deal, and I was satisfied keeping my vaqueros close at hand and still making a good profit. I never signed a paper or even nodded my head—yet here I was with a partner. Same with Savage. I never agreed, but our partnership put gold in both our pockets. Those sweet-talking sonsabitches were something else.

I hardly ever thought of my twins any more. My lovely, warm, sweet, affectionate twins. Hardly ever. Only when the rain drizzled down the eaves of our shack and made little shushing noises in the mud. Or when I smelled the juniper berry. Or when the hoot owls called one to the other in the early evening, back and forth: "*Hoot, hoo. Hoot, hoot, hoo.*"

Getting through one day after the next was the best I could do. I found that a little whiskey could help to forget my twins, and a little work with the boys in the store was good for a joke or two, and a little help with the whores to slow down the cleanup after supper was always good for a smile or two or three.

❉ ❉ ❉

Savage was speaking. "Listen, partner. A strange thing happened yesterday when I was up in Stockton."

"Did you get the sugar and maple syrup that the boys added to your list?" I found that it was always a good strategy to put a question after a question if you wanted to slow a conversation down.

"Sure. I got the eight bags of rice and ten bags of wheat flour too."

"I'm not your partner, Savage, but go ahead and tell me what the strange event was that you observed up in Stockton."

"Some guy by the name of Miller came right up to me out of the blue and told me that three federal government judges were nosing around and that you and me should pay attention."

"Miller is a friend of Carlos, and as you know full well, the 'breed is a friend of mine. The Miller fellow is a butcher."

"Do tell."

"Well, go ahead, dammit. What troubles are the Great White Father and his boys up to now?"

Savage winked both eyes at me, just like Brother Coyote always did, except Coyote had red and yellow eyes and Savage was stuck with blue eyes—the blue that witches possessed. "I think maybe we can work us a little deal," he said.

I looked up at the corner of our bedroom as if making a study of spider webs was more important than anything he had to say.

"Listen, partner," Savage said. "This is damn serious business." He tossed a twist of tobacco on the table to get my attention. "These government folks are looking to give some land to all the tribes in the great valley."

"Savage, how many times must I tell you—tribes are from back where the Great White Father resides." I put the entire twist in my mouth. "There are no tribes around here in California and no big-time chiefs. There are just villages, each with an old man who might listen to complaints once in a while."

"Sure, sure, I know all that stuff, but these federal boys are going to give land according to the number of people in each tribe," Savage said. "They've got land and farm equipment and seed to give away, all according to the size of a tribe."

"No tribes and no people," I said. "Most of the people in the great valley are dead or scattered up in the hills. Nothing much around here anymore but you white folks."

Savage hit me a blow on the shoulder. "Partner, you are exactly right, and that is exactly why you and me are going to conjure up some tribes so they can get their rightful share of land here in old Cali-for-nye-ay. Yes sirree, Bob."

❋ ❋ ❋

The very next day Savage and me found our first chief and our first tribe. The old man shook his head. "I'm not a chief, and the Paleuyami aren't a bunch of Sioux or Mohawk people." He scratched his bald head. "What's the matter with you, José Jesús? You a white man now?"

Savage handed the Paleuyami elder a twist of Yankee tobacco. "You folks have to behave like the coyote. You've got to be tricky and smart with these treaty folks that are coming your way."

"Tell you what, Savage—if any more damn white people come onto our land, I'll just move up into the hills with my daughter." The elder bit off a small plug from the tobacco. "All the young men are dead or off looking for gold. We can't protect the land of our ancestors, so those of us still around might just as well pack up and leave."

"Stop your whining," I said. "Think like a coyote, not a camp dog."

He swallowed his cud. "José, take this devil away, will you? I'm not a chief. I'm a tired old man ready to die."

I spit a brown stream at his foot. "Dammit, I'm a tired old man too, and you are now Chief Bumuk."

A smile cracked his lips. "Bumuk? I'm chief of the cattails?"

"Do you see the joke, old man?"

"We're fooling around with white hairy children." Chief Bumuk pawed his left ear. "Well now, you boys, go ahead and tell me what I need to know."

Savage poured hot water from a tin kettle into a clay cup. He plunked a small twist of tobacco into the cup and gave it over to the new chief. "You got to keep telling these white men that you're the supreme chief of an ancient tribe. Tell them that a long time ago, the God of all Spirits gave the Paleuyami people all the land that drains into Poso Creek."

"Poso Creek?"

"The white people call your river by the name Poso Creek."

Chief Bumuk sipped his tea. "Maybe I like this chief business."

Savage filled the cup with more hot water. "You've got to act dumb with these treaty folks. Don't ask any questions—just repeat the Great Spirit stuff and Poso Creek whenever they stop talking."

"A good joke," Chief Bumuk said. "Tell me what the white men will say to me so that I can keep the smile from my face."

"It's all real simple," Savage said. "The treaty folks will arrive the day after tomorrow. They'll count all the Paleuyami, then they'll powwow with the illustrious Chief Bumuk and award a settlement of land based on their findings."

"There's no more than a dozen Paleuyami scattered up and down their Poso Creek."

"A big chief doesn't worry about tiny details of fact," Savage said. "Just remember about the Great Spirit, and we'll take care of the rest."

"A chief requires lots of tobacco." Chief Bumuk rubbed his chin and looked around his tiny lodge. "I'll need lots of tobacco and lots of red feathers for my hair." He smiled at me and then at Savage. "Maybe you boys could find me a few of those nice blue heron feathers." After a decent pause he started up again. "Some of those white heron feathers would go nice with the blue, I'll bet."

"Why's that?

"Well I once saw a picture of Indian chiefs from back east where they have tribes, and they all had feathers hanging from their heads."

"Of course," Savage said. "Your every wish is our command, so I'll send a couple fellows out to the swamp with a .12-gauge shotgun—that should do the trick."

"Good," said Chief Bumuk. "Quickly now, for I must put my wife to work on the headdress."

❋ ❋ ❋

All the whores got ready to put feathers in their own hair and to put paint on their faces. Even the white whore and the stuck-up Karok whore went along with the joke. I had children running around to nearby farms and swamps to find turkey, duck, and woodpecker feathers. Carlos volunteered all his muleteers for our expedition, and he promised to turn them into Paleuyami warriors. Then there was a dozen Chileños who signed up as Paleuyami elders if they could also wear proper Mohawk paraphernalia.

Feathers, lots and lots of feathers! The Great White Father liked lots of feathers on his Indians.

"Ugh!" I said. "Ugh! Great White Father. Ugh!"

"Very witty," Savage said. "Maybe I'll just make you the chief of all the villages. It'll save us having to find a thespian as capable as Bumuk in each village."

The river was still high from the late spring flood, so for the first day and more we were able to pole the barge south past the Tuolumne River. The women laughed and ate and trailed fishing lines until a little past the Merced River, and then for the next day and a half we walked along the riverbank. Savage and the Mariposa Choir led the way, singing "Rock of Ages" two hundred times or so, until even Savage was willing to shut up and listen to the ducks and geese make their kind of music.

Just north of where the north fork of the Kings River came into the San Joaquin River, we met the commissioners from Washington DC. Savage waved his arms all about until he had it arranged so that the commissioner had to face into the sun, and then I started Carlos and his vaqueros riding circles around the damned white men. They stirred up dust and shouted like a bunch of Kiowa or Apache. Three massive clouds of mosquitoes gathered to welcome the banquet offered by three tender white men.

"I am Chief Bumuk, supreme chief and sole spokesman for the ancient Paleuyami tribe." The old man rolled his eyes to remember his lines. "The God of all—"

"Yes, yes. Quite so," said the fattest of the commissioners. "How many in your tribe, Chief Bumuk?"

"More than acorns on a tree. More than the green-headed duck in the fall."

Savage stepped forward. "I'd say about a thousand, sir." He shrugged. "I know for a fact they had near two thousand a few years back, but they'd probably settle for something less."

The fattest commissioner mashed a thousand mosquitoes with his hand. Blood oozed down his jowls. "Quite so," he said.

"Who in hell are you?" asked the skinniest commissioner.

"Jim Savage. I've got a store nearby, and I've been working with these Indios around here for over two years." Savage took another step closer to the three-member panel. "These are good diggers around here. No trouble at all, and I can give you my word on that fact."

"Quite so." The fattest commissioner waved to his clerk. "We'll credit the Paleuyami Tribe with a thousand people and award them exactly two hundred acres along the southeastern shore of Tulare Lake."

The clerk put parchment paper, quill, and ink pot on a stand in front of Chief Bumuk. "Go ahead, Chief. Make your mark," he said.

The old man stuck his finger in the inkpot and put one smudge on the paper and another on his forehead. "The God of all Spirits—"

"Yes, quite so," said the commissioner seated in the middle, silent thus far. He had a heavy black beard that hung nearly to his belt buckle. Up he stood, like a prairie dog from his hole, and waved his arm toward Savage. "I want the next tribe standing here in two days," he shouted. "Every other day we will review and examine those tribes eligible for our consideration. Do you understand what I am saying, Mr. Savage?"

"Yes sir, I most certainly do understand what you want me to do."

The whores clapped and cheered, the Sonorans fired pistols into the air, and my vaqueros made their Kiowa screams.

Savage and I continued our farce for the three men from Washington DC. We managed to get most of the villages in the southern reach of the San Joaquin River signed up for a few miserable acres of their own land. Savage did most of the talking, and I sat in for Chief Bumuk. Savage explained that the Yokuts were a confederation of independent communities, just like the Iroquois nations, and that I was their elected spokesman. He told them that the Yokuts had a common language, and that they did a lot of trading with other tribes from New Mexico all the way up to Oregon. His best talking, however, he reserved for the day the commissioners finished their job.

"We've done the best job we can with these diggers," said the fattest commissioner. "Now we've got to go back and convince the US Congress to fund our treaty commitment."

Savage walked up to the three of them and stood quietly before the august group until he had their attention. "I've got a proposition for you folks," he said. "Actually, this is a deal from both me and my partner, José Jesús."

"We're finished with this damn place. Go away," said the fattest commissioner.

Savage put both hands on the table. "What I've got to say could make you folks real heroes back in DC. The Great White Father and all those folks in Congress might even break out with lots of smiles if you listen to what I have to say."

"Be quick about it," the least fat commissioner said.

I stood next to Savage, dressed in my finest regalia. This was my first stand-up performance, because in all my previous appearances as spokesman for the villages of the Yokuts Confederation I had sat in quiet contemplation while Savage made all the noise. I nodded my agreement at appropriate moments, of course, but all the commissioners ever saw of me was a body covered by an old army blanket and a head with some feathers sticking out, here and there.

"Bad Injuns on warpath," I said. "Chauchila warriors and Waksachi warriors. Big trouble."

The three commissioners looked at me as if they were emerging from a horrible dream. I was buck naked except for the black-and-white stripes all over my body, even including my cock. But it was the headdress that bugged their eyes. The train of the bonnet dragged in the dirt, and I had an old potato bag wrapped around my head and a bunch of goose feathers stuck through the weave at every possible angle. At the very top of everything was the pincushion of porcupine quills. The whole mess itched my back like a tangle of poison oak vines.

I raised my right arm in a stiff salute. "Big trouble for Great White Father."

Savage leaned forward and looked each man in the eye. "We can stop those hot bloods for you."

The fattest man studied Savage, then me, and back to Savage. "You boys aren't nearly as clever as you may think," he said.

"Not clever at all," Savage said. "If you want to go back to Washington DC as heroes, you've got to listen to my proposition. Otherwise. . ." Savage shrugged his shoulders.

"Big trouble for Great White Father," I said. "Ugh!"

"Knock off the bullshit," the bearded man said. "Two con artists is what we've got—two bullshitters that're interrupting our mission. Dammit to hell!"

"Quickly," said the nearly slender man. "Quickly, give us your proposal!"

"It's simple as pie. If you give me the exclusive license to trade here in the southern San Joaquin Valley, then we'll make the valley safe for white farmers and ranchers," Savage said.

"No soldiers? No money?"

"Neither. Just a sheriff once in a while to help keep out any other white traders around this end of the valley."

The bearded man didn't hesitate. "Clerk! Get the name of this fool. Write up a contract for exclusive trade rights to this wasteland, and we'll sign it right after I finish my coffee."

"Yes sir," said the clerk.

"You won't be sorry," said Savage.

"Ugh!" I said.

✳ ✳ ✳

We tacked copies of the deal Savage made with the federal negotiators up and down the valley. The sheriff in Fresno came by every few weeks or so to see how we were doing, and we gave him a free sample of the Karok whore, even if it was broad daylight and she was supposed to be working in the laundry. A small bag of gold coins also always got stuck in one of the large saddlebags hanging on the sheriff's big black horse. Business was good. In fact, it wasn't but a few months after we posted the facts of who could and who couldn't operate a store in Yokuts territory that we were digging a hole to bury some gold. Savage held the lantern while I dug.

"There's a bunch of ignorant people around here," Savage said.

"Me, for one," I said. "Just another digger for the damn white man."

"We need to civilize the people around here," he said.

"Sounds like more trouble for the People. I don't even like the smell of that word. *Civilize*. Gives me the willies."

"We need to set up a bank to work for us." Savage sat on his heels and stared into the hole. "You people need to learn about banks because there's a lot of gold going to waste. I'll bet every village has a bunch of gold buried someplace in the woods."

"Not like us smart and civilized folks," I said.

We both laughed, and Savage held out a short plug of tobacco for me. "We're pretty rich right now," he said.

"I have no idea where we've buried all of our gold. Do you?"

We laughed again and chewed and spit and watched a few moths die in the lantern flame. "The bank idea is my best ever," Savage said. "Better than singing whores or cheating the Great White Father."

"That was my idea," I said. "The mosquitoes and feathers and Kiowa—they were all my ideas."

We filled the damn hole and settled our bones on a couple of nail kegs. Even Savage shut up for a comfortable period of time before spitting out what he'd been thinking about.

"How about if this coming spring, after the water drops from the rivers to an easy flow, we take a mule train full of gold to San Francisco." Savage gave me his pipe for a stretch. "We'll give the gold to one of those big banks that came from New York or Boston or even London. Come every fall that big old bank will pay us enough so's we can buy some land for the People, and we'll still be so rich that we won't have to take any shit at all from any man—not white, red, or yellow—nobody!"

"What's the trick?"

"Interest is the trick." He took back his pipe but made no effort to make use of it. "Do you remember when Sutter agreed on a price for Fort Ross, and he didn't have the gold or furs or wheat to pay the Russians?"

"Sure, they gave him some time to pay the debt."

"Correct. They let him pay for the land over a six-year period, and those Russian fellows charged Sutter extra gold for the inconvenience of waiting all that time. The extra amount over the original price is called interest."

"It was the same with Murrieta," I said. "He was always lending some busted miner a little poker money. Usually a ten-dollar loan and twenty dollars back."

"Banks don't pay like that. They'll give three dollars for every hundred we leave with them for a year."

"What's the profit for the banks?"

"Well now, they take our money and lend it out to some poor sucker for ten dollars per hundred over a year. Even more if some muleskinner had all his mules drop dead and he wanted some quick money to get back in business. They might charge that fool fifteen or even twenty dollars per hundred for renting our money. Do you understand now? We get paid for letting the bankers use our gold to rent out to somebody else. There's interest paid both ways, with the banks way out front on the profit."

The hairs on the back of my neck got itchy. "What happens to our gold if your banker takes it all back to Boston?"

"The banks always honor their commitments, just like the chief in any village always makes good on his promises."

"Sometimes a chief makes a mistake. Sometimes he dies of malaria or the pox or old age."

"It happens. Not often, but sometimes banks get sick too."

"Or die," I said.

"Or die," Savage said. "But what the hell, at least there's a fair-to-middling chance that the bank will remember who we are, won't catch the pox, or get robbed of all our gold. Think on the good side of things for a change, José."

CHAPTER SEVENTEEN

Spring, 1854

SAVAGE KEPT NAGGING ME WITH the bank idea most every day, and he even spoiled a night or two with his talk about interest and ignorant Indios. So finally, five full moons from that first night of his babbling bank bullshit, I broke into his monologue to say, "Tell you what, Jim—I just made up my ignorant mind."

Savage stopped smiling and babbling and nodded his head toward me. "What?"

"You just go on ahead with your gold up to Frisco, have all the fun you want, but I'm going for a little sojourn and find me a nice warm, comfortable spot with nobody around to cause any bother." I signaled to Savage to listen for a bit longer to what I wanted to say. "I'll help myself to any gold that you left for me; plus, I've got my eye on two wood boxes full of Boston rum that will ride comfortable on either side of a big mule." It was my turn to give out with a smile and stop talking. "No hard feelings, I hope."

"Not a one, partner. I do hope we can get together again, somewhere down the road, because I always enjoy your company, good times or bad."

"Watch out for the white men, partner—there's not many of the sonsabitches you can trust."

✳ ✳ ✳

Coyote and I took a nice slow walk up to a little lake in the eastern mountains, not far at all from where my twins had sung to me and rubbed my back and toes until, for no reason I can recollect, we started laughing and crying and holding one another. The truth is, making love with my twins was always very nice, but the main reason we hugged was to feel warm skin against warm skin and to kiss the other behind the ear or just to stay close and listen to the good sounds of slow breathing and to smell our shared perfume. The boxes of Boston rum stayed on the big mule or parked beside the lovely beast, but I divvied up the gold Savage left for me just crossing the great valley a couple times and then walking up and down a few hills. One big mule with two bitty boxes and an occasional coyote spirit was all I needed through the hot summer and warm autumn. For no reason I can fathom, the first snow drove me down from the little lake, and down past the lovely oak orchards, and finally down to the town of Fresno.

I shared my rum with any who asked, and then I shared whatever was offered back. Whiskey bottles multiplied like ground squirrels after a dry winter. Paper labels and moldy corks welcomed me as much as the mason jars full of clear liquor. I went down into the quiet black holes after the ground squirrels, but they were too fast for me. I heard little scratching noises from deep inside the den but nothing else. Once in a while I managed to gaze up toward the sunlight, and Brother Coyote called down to me. My mouth moved to answer him, but nothing came out. Vague mumbles up toward the light—hisses and such—but no words.

My spirit brother drifted further and further away, until finally I couldn't hear him and he certainly couldn't hear me. He disappeared, just like Savage. They both drifted into the speck of light way over my head, and they left me in the pitch-black hole of whiskey. I roiled about in the black clouds. Not the red clouds of Tipiknits Pahn but the black clouds of the white man's hell. Padre Carlos Maria stomped about the barren landscape and mocked me with his laughter.

Cousin Hineh joined in with his rough words. "Teat sucker," he chortled.

"Murderer," Padre Carlos Maria screeched.

Two or three years disappeared down my black hole. Maybe more.

A scratchy whisper demanded that I open my mouth. I forced the crust on my eyes to part, and an old lady moved her lips. "Open your mouth." She pushed a ladle of soup down my throat.

I coughed and spit the mouthful over my chest.

"Try again," she said.

I put my hand on hers to stop the ladle. "Am I dead?"

"You should be way past dead, old man. Shut up and drink the soup."

"Let me die," I said.

"Time enough for dying," she said.

I felt the warm fluid ease down my throat. A bitter flavor partially masked the sweet duck grease. A bubble of gorge rumbled from my gut. "Stop! Let it rest for a bit."

"We have time," the old lady said.

I shut my eyes. "The bitter taste. Is it alder bark?"

"Yes, the white alder bark. You have the stomach of a sick child, and the duck grease and the bark will make you strong again."

I felt the medicine course down my throat and spread to my very toes. "What's your name, old woman?"

"Palu."

"You are of the Yaelmani people?"

"Yes."

"Where am I, Palu? How did I get here?"

"Poso Flat, near Bekiu Village. You've been here a week now." She coughed into her hand. "You are José Jesús, tipne to the People."

"My name is Damned Digger," I said.

"The People need you, José Jesús." She waited until my eyes were open. "A 'breed from over Fresno way found you and brought you back so you could give us a hand."

I tried for a deep breath, but my stomach wasn't ready for such demands. "I'm ready for more soup, Palu."

"Here, one spoonful, then rest," she said.

I listened to the tule thatch rustle in the light breeze and to the blackbirds with their gurgling *o-ka-lee-onk*. "Tell me the 'breed's name."

"Carlos."

❋ ❋ ❋

I pulled a ragged red blanket over my shoulders and settled with my back against a Box Elder tree. My blood was still clogged at every bend, and the black whiskey cloud still obscured my eyes. That damn Carlos was still messing with me—the fool still had ideas that I wanted to stay alive and help somebody or other. Maybe he thought that going through each day with no hope of pleasure or even hope for a nice easy shit was okay. Damn nosey 'breed.

"José Jesús," called Palu. "Go for a walk with this child of my daughter. Show him where it is best to snare the green-headed duck."

"My knees will not bend," I said. "My stomach hurts."

"Take this stick from him and go—the boy is young but sturdy." She pulled me up from the shady spot. "Go. He will help you up if you fall. Go!"

We laughed, the child and I, when the white heron flew—croaking and straining—from under our feet. I felt the wrinkles above my eye curve when Brother Coyote raised his leg on a willow bush.

The eyes curved yet again when Sedit waved to me from atop a red cloud, and curved even higher when Kalu and Hainan peeked from behind a lightning-struck pine tree. They grinned and laughed with the same laugh as the red-winged blackbirds, "*O-ka-lee-onk,*" they giggled.

"Today you will walk to the first line of pine trees and back," Palu said.

"Today I will sit in the shade and dream," I said.

"When you return from the walk I will feed you salmon and atole. If there is no walk, then there is no food."

"Damn Scrub jay," I muttered.

"Get moving, old man. Tonight some visitors will share your food. A couple vaqueros want your advice."

"I'm a stupid old man, Palu—send them away," I said.

"The guests will arrive near sunset. You will have time to bathe in the creek after your walk."

The two elders from Shikadapaw leaned forward—both had skin the color of Yankee tobacco. "We can't gather acorns in our orchards because the white folks shoot us. We can't hunt deer or elk on our land because the white folks claim our land is, in fact, their land."

"What about those treaties that Savage and I negotiated? Ask the army to protect you, or the sheriff. That is the American law."

"There is no treaty," the oldest elder said.

I peered through the smoke of Palu's cook fire. "Now listen to me, my friends. I was there, and I saw the commissioners sign treaties for most every village. That damn Great White Father sonofabitch gave hundreds of acres to every village in the great valley."

The younger of the two elders shrugged. "The white sheriff says that the Great White Father never signed your damned treaties. He told us that there's no land for the People, only the damned reservation."

My hand started shaking for the first time in a month. "You mean all our tricks came to nothing?"

"That's right. The People have nothing, just the dammed reservation."

I sipped my bowl of elderberry cider. "Tell me about the reservation," I said.

"If you take your family to the reservation, the white boss will make slaves of the children and young women." Both elders leaned closer to the ground, but only the younger man spoke. "We cannot protect ourselves from the whiskey sellers or ruffians who invade the reservation. When we try to farm like the white farmers, the ruffians come to the reservation and steal our oxen and plows and seed. They even steal the fence posts and run their cattle through our gardens. The reservation is a place for death and sadness, nothing more."

"Where do you hide?"

"With the whiskey," said the younger of the elders.

"Of course," I said.

I sat with my eyes closed and felt the tremors of my hands. My knees knocked. The foot-drum in my chest boomed in rapid beat. "What do you want from me?"

"You understand the white devils, José Jesús. Find us jobs with a white man that will not kill us. Find us white men who will not sell our wives and children into slavery."

I lowered my eyes to Palu's food and started to eat. Soon the others joined, but neither joked or complained any further. The frogs erupted with their chorus when Venus finally jumped above the eastern horizon. The men departed, and I crawled to my bed and pulled the blanket over my head.

"Go to bed, Palu," I called. "No more with your wild stories—no more with the constant complaints of old drunks. Go to bed."

Palu sobbed once and then went quiet.

I rolled to face the thatch wall. Foolish old woman. Foolish old men.

One morning a week or so after my two visitors came and went, Palu brought me a nice gentle mare. "Ride up onto the hill," she said. "Stay away from any villages and stay away from the whiskey."

I walked the mare over to a stump and hauled myself up into the wooden saddle. "I'll return at dusk."

"Salmon and atole for the evening meal," she said.

"Horse is what I prefer. A nice young mare steamed under rocks for a full day and night."

CHAPTER EIGHTEEN

Summer, 1859

"**H**EY! TIPNE MAN!"
It was that damn half-breed Carlos.

"I hear you've been out riding most every day." He moved his sorry-looking castrated beast next to my little mare. "Mind if I come along?"

There was no sense in encouraging him, so I just kept the mare at an easy jog toward the pine trees and a little stream that reminded me of the time when the twins dragged me off a little beach into the cold water—how, after they let me up to breathe, we had hugged and kissed and flopped around like bears after a feast on salmon. Carlos knew enough not to talk, and he kept his ugly gelding far enough back so it wasn't the least bothered by my sweet-smelling mare.

On the very next day, Carlos brought along two old-timers, and the three of them joined up with me and we jogged along for most of the morning without a single word. Palu had packed a sizeable lunch of cold tortillas filled with pork, which we ate next to a little stream and then digested under the shade of a big white oak tree. Finally one old man told me that he had worked with me at Mission San Juan Bautista as a vaquero, and then the other explained that he had learned his trade at a rancho south of San José Village. They were good men, and quiet.

Before the end of the moon phase, there were six to eight men trailing after me every morning. Most of them were old men like me, but a few were the age of Carlos. All were vaqueros who could ride and rope and move cows from one spot to another. There were two half-breeds, counting Carlos, but the rest were of the Yokuts or Miwok people.

At first we just explored the creeks and gullies and spied on some of the white farmers. Carlos brought some clay pots full of cooked beans one day, and we found a nice cool cave to have a pleasant meal. There were some bits of pork for flavor, and fresh tortillas for getting the beans up to our mouths.

The boys did what I told them without any discussion, so we practiced moving cows here and there, and lassoing a heifer or two, but we never stole more than two or three cows from any of the white ranchers. The damn ranchers probably never even missed a single one, and Palu was happy with laying the livers over some hot coals. She made a real nice tongue atole that had all the boys full of smiles and good farts.

One day a white rancher came along, riding across a field to intercept my little band. Since he was alone and kept his rifle shoved into a leather scabbard, we sat and waited for what he had to say.

"Howdy, boys," he said.

"Howdy," I answered.

"My name's Parnay, and I've just got me a place over near Dudley."

"That so," I said.

"I'm looking for a foreman to run a herd of shorthorn cattle that I just bought."

"Do tell," I said.

"I've been talking with some folks around here who say that you could handle the job." Parnay leaned toward me. "They say that José Jesús has got a crew of vaqueros all set to go."

"Folks sure have been flapping their jaws," I said.

Parnay sat straight in his saddle. "Goddammit, old man, do you want the job or not?"

"Sure, Mr. Parnay, I'll sign on as foreman for your cows. When do we start?'

He hunched himself up bigger than he really was. "I don't want you and your boys fucking up, José Jesús. The damn bank will hang me by the balls if I can't pay off for these critters."

"I know all about banks, Mr. Parnay, so don't worry. I've got a good bunch of vaqueros here."

"A good bunch of thieves is what I've been told."

"That too, Mr. Parnay."

✳ ✳ ✳

My blood cleaned out the whiskey that summer. My hands steadied, and I didn't want to die anymore. The days were good, with the smell of horse sweat and the yowling of cows from dawn to dark. The grass stayed green until early June, and Parnay's cows got nice and fat and they threw a nice mess of calves. We moved at a slow pace between Dudley and Buttonwillow, and it didn't take but a quarter of his herd to pay off the bank.

"You boys did real good work," he said.

"We could use some new pants and blankets," I said.

"I know that you have something due for your work, and that's a fact." Parnay looked off toward a little dust devil. "You boys been eating a god-awful lot of my beans, and I know there's been a few of my cows went down your throat."

"Gets awful cold at night sometimes," I said.

"They got lots of room for you boys over at the reservation if you don't take what I say," Parnay said.

"There's no beans left in any barrel," I said.

"I'm going up to Stockton tomorrow. You'll have some beans by the end of next week."

"There's two places in Stockton with pants and blankets that will serve," I said.

"I'll check one or the other for the best deal," said Parnay.

The days were good, but the nights were better. For one thing, there weren't many varmints in the southwestern part of the great valley, so the cows were placid enough. It was too dry for grizzlies and too poor for wolves. The few coyotes were nice to have around for the sleeping because there's nothing better for a sound sleep than listening to a coyote try to sweet-talk a mama deer out of her little fawn. The stars came down every night to nose level, and after the boys got finished with their talking and laughing, the God of all Spirits started whispering in my ear.

"Grab the pommel and hang on, old man," he'd say.

"Not much longer," I'd answer. "Beans for supper and a pair of pants beats ten mules loaded with gold by a long shot. Not much longer though. I can't handle any whiskey again or put up with some damn fool of a white man with a plan to use me like a slave or worse."

"The saddle and pommel always come together, José Jesús. It's okay to hang on with both hands when the horse bucks and twists and tries to throw you on the dirt."

"The boys would laugh at me if I hung on to the pommel."

"You must hang on, Tipne Man. You've got to endure this stretch of time, so go ahead and grab the pommel when the need arises. Hang on a while longer, old man."

It was the same every night, as if the God of all Spirits was a professional singer at a Lonewis, or something. Always the same, with the stars on my nose and the same whispers every night. "Endure," he said. "Endure."

❋ ❋ ❋

Parnay was an odd duck, but even for a white man he was one very ugly bird. I had to warn my vaqueros not to laugh in his face, and mostly they didn't, but at night while they were riding picket around the herd, or when they were drinking coffee around the campfire, Parnay got called lots of names. Woodpecker—El Pajaro Carpinteria—for his red hair and long pointed nose, was the best.

Agustín Hinio was the vaquero from the rancho south of San José Village, and for an old man he could always make the biggest fool of himself. He'd walk around the greasewood fire and imitate Parnay's jerky little walk. We all rolled in the dust, gagging with laughter, when Agustín made the bump on his throat move in rapid jerky probes, just like a woodpecker swallowing a big acorn. The men laughed so hard that some of them lost the braid in weaving their new *reatas*, and then they'd get mad and throw kindling wood at Agustín.

All my vaqueros—even the half-breeds—made their own reatas. No grass ropes for my crew—nothing but rawhide—and in a wet year like 1859 it was difficult to find good leather. Wet weather, bad leather—that was the rule. The truth was that a hide from an old skinny dried-up cow was best for a reata because a thin cow had lots of glue in her hide. Fat cows lost their glue and weren't good for much except when they're steamed under a layer of hot rocks or turned slowly on a spit over manzanita logs. The leather from a skinny cow made a long and strong reata, one that would outlast five grass ropes.

All my vaqueros—even the half-breeds—used a reata *larga*. When freshly braided, these lassos were longer than twelve men from head to toe, and all of my men could throw their loop the entire length to snare a cow by forefeet or hind feet or horns. Best of all, my vaqueros threw their reatas with the grace of a marsh hawk swooping down upon a little vole. They were beautiful to watch, my vaqueros.

It gave me great pleasure to ride with Agustín and Carlos and all the men, but I kept my smiles hidden when one or the other performed some graceful deed. I never paid them a compliment, of course, for there was no need to exhibit gratuitous gestures with men who respected one another. Men do what is expected of them, or they are not men. Nothing less is accepted, only the best of efforts, so compliments must be taken as sarcasm or an effort at humor or as an implied threat. Compliments serve no worthy function with men.

Uncle Podnow always told me to look for the truth in life, but even the greatest tipne doctor of the People had a blind eye in certain matters, like with his sonofabitch son, Hineh. But nevertheless, in the instance of my vaqueros, the truth was clear. Undeniable, in fact. All of my men were skillful with the reata, all served to protect the animals in their charge, and all gave honor to their horses. They were vaqueros, and none would behave in a thoughtless manner, and none would fail to give his life for the other. Also, none would accept a compliment.

"José Jesús!"

I ignored whoever was yelling and kept on with my thoughts. It was clear to my mind that compliments were dangerous weapons used by a few fools, most women, and all white folks. Of course a vaquero could usually ignore fools and white folks because they behaved in the same predictable fashion, but a man had to be exceedingly cautious when some woman or other granted him a compliment. I need to warn my vaqueros that a woman's smile and her subsequent compliment were like a spider's web to a greenback fly—soft and comfortable and deadly. When a man receives a compliment from a woman, he instinctively returns the thought in a like manner. Beware! A man must be exceedingly cautious in giving compliments to a woman because women have no sense of humor. They are like a she-bear with cubs, and a compliment to a woman becomes an unfailing promise to a woman, and therefore, the source of endless revenge if the man's unintended compliment is perceived as unfulfilled.

"José Jesús! Jose Jesus!"

Women know nothing of life, only of grubbing around for roots and taking care of their cubs and making a man uncomfortable. The God of all Spirits was not perfect in giving life to the People. Not by any stretch of the imagination. Women and mosquitoes serve as constant reminders of his imperfection.

"José Jesús! Pay attention to me!"

"Be quiet. I'm talking to myself and having a good time."

Brother Coyote said the God of all Spirits intended life as a big joke, and that is why men must seek the company of men and avoid women at any costs. See what I'm saying? Women can't tell a good joke, so why hang around them?

"José Jesús! There are some lightning clouds along the horizon. Where do we head the cows?"

"You got a head, Carlos. Use it. Just leave me alone."

The twins, of course, were exceptions to any set of rules. They were careful to give compliments only to other women who held lower status or women who gossiped with malicious intent or women who squawked like scrub jays when there were men about. My twins never gave me a compliment. They smiled with their stomachs and not their teeth. They moved with the grace of vaqueros. Vaqueros! All of my men could throw their reata loop crossways, from the left or right, underhand, overhand, or backward, and always with grace. The patient grace of unhurried perfection, so what was the need of foolish smiles and glib compliments for my vaqueros or my twins? Why demean them for behavior that was expected? A good foreman or a good husband must swallow his smiles and maintain their respect. Such was my experience.

"Carlos! You damn fool! Get those cows down into that little draw over there! Can't you see there's a damn storm coming!"

"Hey! That's no storm, Tipne Man. We've got a big bunch of ducks heading toward us, and that's all."

Wind and dust swirled like a lost banshee looking for a home.

"Hey, Tipne Man!" Agustín Hinio's voice whipped against me like a stream of thin splinters. "That big old cloud over there is nothing but a big herd of woodpeckers!"

Coyotes were the most difficult of animals to lasso, and elk were the easiest. A fat elk made a nice change from beef, so I always sent a few of the boys down to the swamp every week or so to bring back a hindquarter or two. Of course hog meat was good in a pot of beans. Whenever one of the ugly beasts happened to drift away from a white man's ranch, one of the boys would encourage it to move along with Parnay's cows for a while. We got so we thought that fried pig fat was real nice when there was a touch of frost to the night air. Twice Agustín captured a coyote, and when the others gathered around to tease him as if he was chasing the camp dog and not a genuine coyote, he blushed like a teenage virgin and said, "It was nothing. A lucky throw."

During the quiet green time of early summer, Parnay came out in his buckboard every full moon to bring us the beans, blankets, and canvas pants. He'd kick dust for a little bit, ask a few dumb questions, and then follow his track back to the ranch. As the summer progressed, we moved the herd farther south, and Parnay lost track of us and couldn't find us and provide our necessary provisions. I sent a few of the youngest vaqueros to grub some roots, and once Carlos swapped a shorthorn yearling for a barrel of potatoes from a rancher by the name of McKittrick.

"Who you boys riding for?" he asked.

"Parnay," I said.

"You going to tell him I bought this cow fair and square?"

"Nope."

McKittrick studied my crew, one by one. "Well now, I'd rather swap goods with you boys than to see some varmint bust into my barn."

"Lots of varmints hereabouts," I said.

"I can always use some more of those good shorthorns," McKittrick said.

"We'll keep you in mind," I said.

✵ ✵ ✵

The first break in the summer heat got the boys all excited, and they went hooting and howling through the scrub chasing after a coyote that had a sharp limp from his left rear leg. The lassos were singing like a bunch of cicadas, and no one was paying the least attention to the herd, not even me. Two explosions came like thunder from a clear sky and brought every vaquero to a dead-still stop. Woodpecker waved at us with his shotgun and then let off two more explosions. The entire herd took off at a full gallop directly toward a little cliff cut by the winter runoff. We did our best to turn and stop the crazy beasts, but it was dusk before they were settled and we could count the dead and injured.

"What in hell did you fire off that shotgun for? The herd was fine before you chased them off that cliff." I was real mad at the stupid white man.

Parnay's woodpecker's throat fluttered until two of the boys fell flat off their horses with laughing. He finally got his tongue working. "You damn Indians have got no sense of responsibility."

"You damn whites have got no sense in your heads to be shooting a shotgun near a bunch of cows." I was ready to let Parnay have his cows and beans both.

Woodpecker pecked for a bit, hauled off a barrel of beans and some blankets from the buckboard with nobody lending a hand, then drove away under a full moon and a trail of dust.

"Hey, boys!" Agustín yelled. "Let's go catch us a coyote. We've got plenty of light."

"We've got six heifers to butcher and a herd of jumpy squirrels to watch." I was still mad and ready to send somebody after Parnay to tell him we quit his damn job. "Agustín and Carlos, you two go on down to that gully to cut up those dead cows, then smoke up the lot of 'em for later on."

"Hey, Tipne Man! That's a big job. We need——"

"One more word from you, Agustín, and you're on your own. Move it, you two. Now!"

They reined their horses about and moved away, but not before Agustín hissed, "Damn white folks have no sense of humor, do they? Am I correct in this matter, Carlos?"

"Especially those damn white tipne doctors," Carlos answered.

We stayed with Parnay for the next two winters because the damn reservation was the only option we could figure. Beans and pants were better than whiskey and loafing around every day. Nobody would hire a digger for cash money when there were hungry white folks and hungry Mexicans or even yellow folks standing in line for jobs.

The winters were dry, with low fog at night and pale-blue sky during the day. There were a few piddling storms from the northwest each year and one gully washer from the south in April of 1861, but the pickings were very slim for Parnay's cows.

In early spring of '61 we moved the herd quickly down from Dudley to Buttonwillow, then farther south to the sink around Buena Vista Lake. But all in all, it was still hard to keep the cows in grass and water. The heat was like a hammer between the eyes, and I felt worse than after a three-month drunk. We lived in clouds of alkali dust all day and clouds of mosquitoes all night. The boys stopped with their jokes and chasing coyotes. Woodpecker never showed up all summer, so there were no beans or pig fat—just skinny cows and good reatas.

The spring after the second dry winter, 1862, I moved the herd lickety-split through the wetlands south of Tulare Lake, up the south side of White River, and into the high country above Hot Springs. We traveled through purple wildflowers and up into air that tasted like manzanita cider. The horse felt good between my knees, and the cattle got fat on juicy mountain grass. At night, while my vaqueros broiled cow ribs or elk ribs over chamiso root coals, I told stories of the old days—of Estanislao and Murrieta and José Jesús. They ate and spit and drank mint tea and listened. I told them about Sedit, my lovely wife, and Manuel, my lonely son. The cows listened along with the moon and stars. Fat cows and fat vaqueros.

After the first good rain in the fall of 1862, we retraced our steps down the mountain, across the great valley, and over to Dudley. We delivered the herd back to Woodpecker just after the first frost.

"They look good," he said.

"The grass was decent, and we didn't lose too many," I said.

"Looks like a good calf drop."

"Good enough," I said.

Parnay looked over his shoulder while he talked. "We'll trail half the herd over to San José in a week or so. I hear that the price of beef is sky high."

"Why's that?"

"There's a big war going on back in the States, and the soldiers need hides and bully beef both. We'll get top dollar for the cows, and I can buy up some more land."

"Who's doing the fighting?"

"The northern states are trying to keep the southern states from starting up their own country."

"White men are fighting white men?"

"Yup," Parnay said. "Mostly it's white men anyway."

I could feel Agustín about to fall off his horse again, so I turned in my saddle and shouted, "Let's get to work, you damn lazy coyotes!"

My vaqueros followed after me. We dashed past Parnay's little cabin and past his pathetic little orchard and over the first hill before I called a halt.

"The whites are fighting the whites!" I shouted, and we all fell to the ground like rifle-shot geese. We rolled on the ground in a delicious frenzy until one by one we went silent and stared quietly at the empty sky.

✳✳✳

Parnay was a Boston man, so naturally his face was red and pinched up like he had never in his entire life had a good shit. That's the way Boston men were—tight-assed and tight-lipped.

The day before we were going to trail his cattle over to San José Village, a bunch of fellows rode into Dudley. These were the kind of white men that had teeth sticking out of their mouths like a sick porcupine and eyes that were black empty pools. They appeared at Parnay's cabin just about at dusk, where I was mounted on a nice gentle black mare and Parnay was sitting a nearly white gelding. As usual, he was filling my ear with useless information about how to move cows over hills with heavy timber.

"How do?" one of the Missouri men said to Parnay.

"Well enough." Parnay gave me a little signal, and I nudged my mare a few steps backward.

"You ain't no abolitionist, is you?" the Missouri fellow asked.

"What do you boys want?" Parnay said.

"Well, now. We's kinda like sutlers, you know. We's makin' sure our Confederate boys get plenty to eat so's they can kill lots of damn Yankee sonsabitches."

"I've got nothing to sell," Parnay said. "All my cows are spoken for."

Two of the Missouri men moved behind me. There was just Parnay and me—all my vaqueros were out with the cows.

"I got no money to buy anyway," the spokesman said.

"Guess we haven't much to talk about," Parnay said.

At some signal that I didn't detect, the gang pulled pistols and rifles. "Fact of the matter," the Mizzoo fellow said, "we's looking for donations from every true son of the Confederacy. From every other sonofabitch too."

Parnay didn't say anything, but his face turned a poison-mushroom red.

"We's also looking to kill us a few sonsabitching damn Yankees."

Parnay just looked at the ground and shook his head with a real slow back and forth motion. The red disappeared from his face.

They killed Parnay. There were maybe ten shots, altogether in one massive explosion. His gelding did a quick twisting buck, then ran wild-eyed past the corral and the tiny cabin, and off through the buck brush and tall grass. Parnay's left foot stayed hooked into the stirrup, and his body bounced and skidded and stirred up a long trail of dust until man and horse disappeared off to the east.

The Missouri boys laughed and hooted and slapped knees at the amusing sight of Parnay's departure from life. "Did you ever see such a sight?" the spokesman said. "I do believe that damn Yankee sonofabitch did shit all over hisself before we killed him."

They all laughed.

The snaggle-toothed leader smiled at me. "Well now, my digger friend. I guess you and your boys is going for a little ride with us. Yessiree, Bob, a nice little ride."

CHAPTER NINETEEN

Fall, 1862

THE MOON CAME FULL THREE times before we got Parnay's cows to where they wanted them. The snaggletooth leader was the worst bastard of the lot with his whip to our backs and holding food back from us. On an early morning, just into Arizona over the Rio Grande River, I nodded to Agustín and watched as he threw a smooth little underhand throw of his reata over snaggletooth's head and yanked the sonofabitch into the dust without a whisper of protest from the sonofabitch. We left him in the open for the vultures to make quick work, and moved on with the herd.

There was nobody but me that saw Agustín's move, but it was beautiful to the eye and warm to my stomach. The rest of the Confederate Army boys got a little easier with us from that day forward, and when the herd was moved into a pen of barbed wire near that town of Santa Fe, the army boys disappeared with all the horses. Me and my vaqueros started walking toward the west.

I'm certain in my mind that if Carlos had been with us from the beginning we could have stayed together and made the trip back a simple task. But the story according to Agustín was that Carlos disappeared the morning before the Confederate Army arrived at

Parnay's little farm. Agustín thought he might have gone over to Fresno on some errand or other, but none of us vaqueros knew the true fact of the matter.

As it was, we all got split off one from the other within a few days after leaving Parnay's shorthorns in Santa Fe. I wore my moccasins to useless shreds and somehow lost my shirt, pants and by the time the great valley was underfoot, there was just an old rag to cover my balls. There were some white ladies at a farm in the middle of no-where in Western Arizona, and one handed over the rag for my balls, a cup of water and a tortilla filled with black beans. She was the only one of four ladies, one man and a passel of white kids that gave this old digger something to wear and something to eat. No smile from her or any of the others, but the black beans tooted me all the way from Arizona to the great valley.

Even in the great valley there weren't many farm wives or village wives that gave me much of anything, but there were always lots of half-breeds and quarter-breeds hanging around the little towns, and most would share their whiskey if I told them some amusing lies about the old days. Damn 'breeds—dumb and ugly both.

***

Palu shouted at me the very first thing out of her mouth. "You got no money for clothes, but you got money for whiskey!"

"Quiet," I said. "My head hurts with your yelling."

"I can tell that you've had lots of whiskey and see for a fact that you've got no horse or decent clothes." Palu put hands to her waist. "I've lost all my patience for the likes of you!"

"Leave me alone," I said.

It was only a day or two before Palu kicked me out of her lodge, and I moved onto the reservation near Visalia. It was that or nothing, and besides, there was plenty of whiskey to mooch around the reservation. White and Indian—everybody had lots of whiskey for the Tipne Man.

One morning, a couple of old Tachi ladies who lived on the reservation scurried around my mat like two black beetles. "Click, click, clack" was all that I heard from them until one shook me by the shoulders and touched her nose to mine while she yelled: "José Jesús, are you awake?"

I had a little lean-to under an oak tree, away from most Indios and all the damn white folks that ran the reservation. "Go away," I moaned.

"Hineh is here—Hineh, son of Podnow and nephew to your dead father. He's here in the valley," they whispered.

I had thought for a long time that the sonofabitch was dead from one disease or another, and anyway, I couldn't move my head up off my bed of stale tule reeds. "Where is the sonofabitch?" I whispered back to the old crones.

They moved closer to my ear. "Your cousin Hineh works for a white farmer on a big ranch near Lemoore."

My stomach churned, and red dots danced on both eyeballs. "Get me something to eat," I said to the old ladies. "Coffee too."

I couldn't do much about Hineh right off, of course. I ate a little more over the next few days, and drank a little less whiskey than usual. My dreams changed from black mud to violent red clouds, with Brother Coyote running all over and singing about Hineh as a traitor to the People, and Hineh as the white man's mercenary. "Let's go kill the sonofabitch," Coyote kept howling into my dreams.

The two old Tachi ladies turned out to be mostly quiet, but they were always quick to give me both food and little crumbs of gossip each day. It looked to me as if the reservation life had worn them down to a frazzle, and the taking care of me gave them a way to move through the day with something to keep them busy. Not busy like in the old days, but one little job that took more time than it was worth.

They told me that Hineh was a blacksmith and general mechanic for a white farmer not a day's walk from the Visalia Reservation. The Tachi ladies seemed to figure that because he had a bunch of white-man's skills with machines, and because he was a tipne doctor to the People, the white man gave Hineh the foreman's job for the entire farm. They told me that my cousin was paid cash money at the end of every month, and that Hineh also had his own lodge and permission to glean the leftovers from a big garden and a nice walnut orchard on the white man's farm. There were, they guessed, twenty Yokuts and a few half-breeds working for my cousin. All this information I received from the two old Tachi ladies over a period of three months or so. To top it all, there were two Tachi men who worked for Hineh and they came to the reservation for whiskey every pay day, so they also stopped by my lean-to and bragged about how mean Hineh treated the white man who owned the farm.

It didn't bother me that the two old ladies had nothing else to do on the sonofabitching reservation except wake me every day at sunrise to feed me atole and gossip. I noticed that their eyes got to sparkling a week into their new vocation as nurse to an old drunk, and that they also began to comb and braid their hair like when they were young girls. The two of them smiled and talked through their hands and told me that Hineh was a mean sonofabitch. Real mean, in fact, because he was the very worst kind of tipne doctor. The old ladies told me that Hineh was a poisoner.

The so-called chief of all the remaining Yokuts and half-breeds and quarter-breeds that were scattered in and around the reservation was an old man by the name of Chief Kanti. The old Tachi ladies told me that the chief was lying around on a white man's bed and that he was about to die, so when a *winatum* came to ask if I'd come and see Chief Kanti, I just rolled over and moaned. I was pretty drunk because of the pain in my fingers and arms and back, so it was Carlos, the chief's winatum, who kept throwing water on me until I said, "Stop with the damn water, you damn half-breed!"

Carlos fed me tobacco tea until my stomach was all puked out and the ringing sounds had left my ears. "Get some of that damn duck-grease soup from Palu," I said. "She's just up the hill from this damn reservation, just get me a little duck-grease soup and some of her atole and I'll be back on my horse." So it was that three days after he sent for me, I got to Chief Kanti's shack, which was mostly uphill and not more than five miles from the Visalia Reservation. Hineh was already there, sitting in a willow-wood chair next to the bed of Chief Kanti.

"Smells like a white man is here," I said.

"Smells like a stinking drunk Indian just came in." Hineh looked up at me from his seat. "Hey! My little cousin. So you're sucking whiskey bottles now. Whiskey's way-better 'n any teat, ain't that so, José Jesús?"

"Better a drunk than a white man's whore," I said. "You must have an asshole bigger than a man's head, Cousin Hineh."

"Quiet, the both of you." Chief Kanti struggled to sit upright. His old wife and Carlos propped pillows between the wall and his shoulders. "I'm about dead, you boys, so there's not much time."

"All the Yokuts are dead," I said. "There's nothing left but old men and drunks and a few dogs that lick at the white man's boots."

Hineh stood to face me, but Carlos and two men from the reservation forced us both to sit and pay attention to the chief. Hineh had the only chair, and the rest of us took spots on the dirt floor.

"My sons are dead." Chief Kanti began to cry real tears. "My brothers and cousins are all dead," he said. "All who were born of my Eagle clan are dead."

I clapped a slow beat with my hands. "All the People are dead," I said. "Even those who walk about among the white man are dead."

I put my hand on Chief Kanti's leg. "Go ahead, old man. Go ahead and die and pretty soon I'll come looking for you up in Tipiknits Pahn."

"We must have a chief for those who still live," Chief Kanti said.

"Not me," I said.

"Not me," said the two men from the reservation.

"I'll take over," Hineh said. "My mother was aunt to your mother's cousin."

Chief Kanti squinted at Hineh. "Yes, I do remember your mother. She was a squawking, complaining woman, wasn't she?" He slumped back against the wall. "There are so few of the People left," he whispered.

I stood and leaned against the door frame. "Let it go, Chief Kanti. There's no need for a chief, and there's damn-well no need to let Hineh cause trouble for a bunch of useless Indios."

Hineh made some nonsense motions toward me, so I let go a long smelly fart and chanted, "My magic is stronger than yours. My magic is stronger than yours."

The two men from the reservation laughed along with me until Chief Kanti began coughing and shaking as if he was on his last legs. "I'm going," he croaked.

His old wife began crying and moaning and clapping at a rapid pace.

"Listen now," Chief Kanti said. "You must all honor Hineh, for he is now the chief of the Tachi and Yaudanchi and all the mixed-up people on the reservation." A gentle sigh flowed from his mouth, and both eyes fluttered shut.

The reservation men joined with Chief Kanti's wife and Carlos in clapping and singing in honor of the dead man. After a bit I joined them, but Hineh simply sat and smiled at the dirt floor.

❊❊❊

Hineh took over Chief Kanti's shack, kicked out the old widow, and took a girl named Poiyuk as his wife. Hineh told Poiyuk's father to shut up or get poisoned.

The two old Tachi ladies fed me atole.

"He quit the white man," one said.

"Poisoned him too, and that white man can't hardly move around anymore," the other said. The fat old Tachi lady gave me her squinty smile. "He's a regular coyote with the women now, that Hineh."

The skinny old Tachi lady frowned. She was a Baptist Tachi lady now. Gertrude the Baptist Tachi lady. "He's a sinner, all right," she said. "Yup, a coyote; that Hineh's nothing but a gray-muzzled old coyote."

Maud smiled her fat, squinty smile again. She was of the true faith—Maud the Catholic Tachi lady. "Maybe he'll kill himself with all the fucking," said Maud the Catholic.

I was getting mad enough to almost get sober. Between the old Tachi ladies and all the visitors who kept lining up outside my reservation lean-to, there was hardly any time for serious drinking.

"His wife!" Poiyuk's father bugged his eyes at me. "There's nobody can get bride price for a woman under sixteen—eighteen is bad enough." Now he was pacing back and forth in front of my nose. "Most Yokuts women are twenty before they get married. This behavior of Hineh is an act of rape upon my daughter, not marriage! It is an insult to me and to all of the Yokuts."

"The Yokuts are dead," I said.

"Do something!" Poiyuk's father yelled. "You are the supreme tipne doctor of the Yokuts and the Miwok. Stop this rape of my daughter and the poisoning of the people. Stop this madness!"

The old Tachi ladies fed me atole mixed with toasted grasshoppers. Palu brought me her concoction of white alder bark and yerba buena and duck grease. One of those Jehovah Witness Tachi ladies put her hands on my shoulders and mumbled words I'd never heard before. She went on and on until I blasted her with one of my ear-splitting shouts.

"Hineh ruts with a twelve-year-old child," Gertrude whispered.

"Day and night," Maud said. "People line up outside the door to his shack for a chance to talk with the chief while he ruts with the child."

"We've got to do something," I said.

"What can you do?" Gertrude said.

"Hineh's a poisoner," Maud said.

"I'm the supreme tipne doctor of the People. I'll think of something."

"No whiskey," Palu said.

"Eat the atole," the old Tachi ladies said.

"Pray with me," the Jehovah's Witness said.

"Go to hell," I yelled. "Give me some peace and quiet!"

I was an invalid with an arm needed to help me walk a few paces to take a piss or shit. I had no place to flee because the old villages of the Yokuts were a distant memory. Now it was the white people who plowed our land and shot us dead if we trespassed on their land. It was also the truth of the matter that I couldn't pay attention to Hineh because I was an old drunk. An old drunken digger who could barely put one foot in front of another. The folks who lined up at my lean-to and begged me to take care of the biggest poisoner that they had ever suffered were in the same boat with me. None of us had any power, and we had no sheriff or lawyer or schoolteacher to plead our case. We were all diggers, and the written law of California allowed as how any white person with a gun could kill any digger for no reason or provocation whatsoever. The damn sonsabitches!

I tried my best to stay sober. The walks that Palu made me take were good, and staying away from the whiskey sellers was better. After I got hold of a horse, I did a little vaquero work down around Kettleman City, and also I took on a little doctoring. Mostly it was antu doctoring, not tipne doctoring. Broken arms, not broken spirits. When the first frost of 1872 hit the valley, it got harder to get my joints loose in the morning, and I couldn't work the reata like in the old days, so the white boss chased me off the job. The supreme tipne doctor of the Yokuts and Miwok chased off his own land.

"Get outta here, you old digger." That's what the white boss said to me.

The foreman of the outfit was a Sonoran fellow, so if the white man wasn't around, he'd give me few days' work and even let me belly up to the cook wagon for some good beef. Those Sonoran boys always remembered that Murrieta rode at my side against the white mushroom people, and they remembered the horse gangs and the days when the Yokuts and Miwok had the white sonsabitches on the run. It was lucky for me that the vaqueros on the white man's ranch were all Sonorans and Yokuts and Yaquis. There were no white vaqueros, only a white boss to yell at the diggers and tell the supreme tipne doctor to "get outta here!"

The poisoning spread through the Valley. Hineh was the biggest evildoer, but there were lots and lots of other folks who found that they could make others sick or dead with a few words and a little hocus-pocus bullshit. I guess the People were never meant to live mixed up with strangers. The God of all Spirits wanted the Tachi to live peacefully in their own domain, not scrambled with Wowol and Wukchimni and mixed blood and who-knows-what-all. Some of the old folks tried to keep the annual Lonewis going to appropriately celebrate the death of those who had become spirits during the year, but mostly the Indios and half-breeds hung around the Portuguese parties or the Mexican fiestas and did mean things to one another. Hineh was just the best at doing mean things to his own people.

CHAPTER TWENTY

Summer, 1865

"WHAT'S THE MATTER, YOU INDIO?" The little Mexican boy kicked me again in the ribs. "You dead or something?"

Yellow jacket wasps buzzed about my puke. They fussed and argued and secured small brown lumps to their undersides, then disappeared into the hot blue sky. I could see the boy and the yellow jackets and various flies scurrying up and down my arm, but I couldn't move. The inside of my head pulsed as if serving as the skin over a large drum, but I couldn't move a toe or finger. The boy disappeared, and with the sun higher and hotter, I could see the iridescent glints of handprints on my arm and upper thigh. The poison called *haiyenal*; the crushed powder of the beautiful iridescent rock haiyenal.

I chased my memory back to the time when Uncle Podnow led me on a two-day hike into the western mountains—the barren, witchy, evil mountains west of the great valley. He touched the rock with a stick and said, "This is my most dangerous poison. It is worse than the rattlesnake, for if you touch it, you will die." He demonstrated how to use tongs and supple leather to crush the rock into powder and to store it in a clay flask. "If you spill this poison on the clothes of your enemy, he will die a painful death."

"What is the poison called?" I asked.

"Haiyenal." Podnow stared into my eyes without a single blink. "You must keep this place a secret, for I will show it to only one other person in my life."

"Who else?" I asked.

"That is my secret," Podnow said.

Poiyuk's parents were from my Tachi village. Their little girl, this wife of Hineh's, was of the Dove clan and therefore always running around with messages for one person or another. She was not a gossip but more like a winatum who is assigned by those in power to deliver news or instructions or threats from one person to another.

After three days I could talk and eat, but I could not move my arms or legs. "Why are you here, Poiyuk?" I murmured.

She swallowed three times before answering. "I must," she whispered.

"Hineh?"

She nodded, then after a short silence, "He says I must clean the shit from your backside." Poiyuk swallowed again. "He says I must sing to you as I would to an infant—that I must sing to you as a child at his mother's teat."

I bit my tongue to draw blood. Hineh wanted me alive—an insect to torture before squashing.

Poiyuk pulled the putrid blanket from me and cast it from my tiny lodge. She dipped a rag into a basket of water and rubbed my crusty backside. She cleaned my ass and balls and hummed through thin lips. I watched as her sweat slipped down her nose and onto my stomach. After I was clean, her tears and sweat felt cool on my body.

She stopped humming, and I dozed far into the hot day. When I opened my eyes, she still sat next to me on the dust of my floor.

"What now?" I asked.

She didn't answer but cradled my head to tip a basket of chicken broth into my mouth. The greasy, salty flavor brought the juice of life into my mouth. "Thank you," I said.

Poiyuk whispered, "José Jesús. Can you hear me?"

"Certainly, Poiyuk. Tell me what my cousin wants me to know."

Poiyuk covered her mouth with her hand. "Do you know Kaiyetsawa?"

"He's a Chinuk man at Lemoore Ranch. A hardworking fellow with a nice fat wife."

"Solit is the wife," Poiyuk said. "She has an infant son."

"She has good hips and will give her husband many sons."

"My husband told Solit to join him in his lodge and to leave both her husband and her infant son." Poiyuk placed both hands into her mouth and muttered. "Solit refused my husband."

"Did Kaiyetsawa kill Hineh?"

"No. Kaiyetsawa took his family to a ranch near Hanford." Poiyuk made her face look old, maybe sixteen or seventeen. "Kaiyetsawa is a good sheep shearer, and the white rancher allowed him space for a small lodge."

I waited patiently for Poiyuk to continue, but she turned from me so that I could see the scabs behind her ear. Her tiny breast beat like that of a frightened quail.

"As you know, Tipne Man, the Portuguese people celebrate the death of their god with a great fiesta."

"Yes, Poiyuk, I know their god and their celebrations."

"All those of the Yokuts who could get permission from their masters joined together and walked to Hanford to view the rituals and eat the good food. We all showed great dignity and refrained from laughing at those Portuguese who carried large wooden crosses on their backs and whipped themselves with leather thongs."

"Tell me," I said.

"Toward the end of their journey, some of the Portuguese men crawled through dust on their hands and knees."

"You must not demean those white others who behave in this fashion, my little dove. They lust for passage to their Tipiknits Pahn, and mean no harm to others."

"The Yokuts hid their smiles and remained silent through the entire parade of whips and crosses."

"Their behavior serves to show how much they honor this spirit of theirs."

"Yes," said Poiyuk.

"The Portuguese people gave everyone food?"

"Solit and I were sitting at a table while Hineh stood beside us with one hand on my shoulder and the other on Solit's shoulder. We were eating the sweet, fatty lamb, and my husband said nothing for a very long time." Poiyuk licked her fingers as if cleaning away bits of grease.

"Was Hineh drunk?"

"No! Hineh never touches the whiskey."

"What happened?" I asked, only to help the poor girl finish her duty. The end was obvious.

"Kaiyetsawa stood and confronted Hineh and said, 'Drop your hands from my wife.'"

"How did Hineh respond to Kaiyetsawa's demand?"

My husband leaned forward until his nose was almost touching Kaiyetsawa's nose. 'Solit will soon enter the land of the dead if she does not obey me,' Hineh said."

Now the tears rolled down from Poiyuk's blackened eyes without pause. She clawed her ravaged face with both hands. "My husband put his gloved hands on Solit's shoulders again. He smiled at me, like I should be happy with his attention to Solit, then he turned and quickly disappeared into the crowd."

"What happened next?" I asked.

"Kaiyetsawa took his wife home, but she was sick before they reached their lodge. Solit tried to urinate, but could not. Her stomach swelled as if she were ten moons pregnant with twins. She kept screaming, "I'm going to die! I'm going to die!""

Poiyuk was breathing with the short, shallow gulps of a woman delivering a child. "Late in the night, Hineh appeared in the lodge of Kaiyetsawa and said, 'Let me rub the skin of Solit, and she will recover her health.' But Solit screamed, 'No! No!' and Kaiyetsawa pointed his shotgun at my husband."

"What happened next?" I asked.

"They sent for a white doctor, but it was too late. When Solit died, she had black spots all over her skin."

I tried to move some part of my body, but it felt as if I were covered with dried adobe mud from neck to toes. "The sonofabitch."

Poiyuk leaned down to whisper in my ear. "Can you hear me, José Jesús?"

"Yes," I whispered back.

"Hineh said you must live, not die. My husband said that he will not allow you to die until all of the People and all of the white men bow to his power."

"The sonofabitch."

Halhalis was a friend of mine of long standing, a Tachi fellow and chief of the Prairie Hawk clan. He was a real good man whose father had worked for me up at Sutter's Fort, and when Halhalis's father got married, I had Sutter set him up with a nice ranch over between Visalia and Lemon Cove. There weren't any white folks around in those days, so Halhalis's father had a bunch of Tachi and Wukchumni working for him. He ran sheep and a few cattle and put his bottomland in wheat, beans, and squash. Halhalis's father got shot and killed when he tried to shoo some white fellows off his land in 1852—early spring, as I recall. These white miners were irritated with the heavy rain that year, and they couldn't get up to work on any of the good rivers. According to my friend Halhalis, these white fellows didn't say a word to his father—they just pulled out a bunch of guns and shot him dead.

Well now, as anyone could have predicted if they knew Sutter for more than five beats of the heart, the sonofabitch had never taken the time to draw up a legal deed for the land of Halhalis's father. So it was that in early 1856, a man by the name of Hiram Williams turned up and told Halhalis and his mother and two sisters that the land they'd been working for nearly eight years was now a white man's land. This Williams fellow was a decent sort of person, so he let Halhalis set up a lodge near a little grove of oak trees, and he also let Halhalis and his mother and sisters do some work around the place. A little vaquero work—plowing with a team of bullock and chopping weeds—the same stuff they did when the land was Tachi land and not white man's land.

Here's the important part—it turned out that Halhalis grew into a big, handsome man, the kind of man that made folks just smile when his name was mentioned. Even the white folks gawked and kicked dirt when Halhalis was around. Williams put Halhalis to work when the boy was fifteen or so, and the Prairie Hawk Clan made him their chief a year or so later—that's the kind of man Halhalis was.

When Hiram Williams was out on his ranch chasing after a calf down at the creek bottom, he speared himself with a chokecherry snag. His widow made Halhalis the foreman of twenty or so Tachi and Wukchumni and a half-dozen Mexicans. She also entertained the young man on numerous evenings while they ordered seeds from the seed catalog or parts for the incubator from the farm implement catalog.

Neither Halhalis's young wife nor Halhalis's mother gave much thought to the widow lady and her affection for him because they both figured that a big and wealthy man like Halhalis could handle at least two women without any problem. The mother and first wife were correct as far as they could see, because Halhalis kept all three women happy—especially when his mother was able to show both wives how to cook both the Tachi way and the white man's way. The problems developed for Halhalis not from his women but from Hineh, who started to drop by the ranch for breakfast, lunch, and dinner.

I was still feeling bad in my bones and couldn't get around very much, but I heard all the details from Poiyuk and from Mrs. Williams and from the old Tachi ladies from the reservation. Palu tried to keep all those ladies away from me, but I told the old woman to shut up so I could hear some good gossip. It was bad enough to feel bad all the time without some busybody trying to ruin the few good things in life.

This is what happened.

Halhalis gave a dance for all the Tachi folks that he could contact with his winatum. It was an old-time dance, with Cuksa the clown and professional singers and lots of good food. Of course some of the Wukchumni and a few Mexicans and Mrs. Williams were also invited, and because there was no other polite option, so was Hineh. The dance started out just fine, with two cows and a horse steamed under hot rocks, and baskets and baskets of dried salmon and acorn mush, and a couple of big baskets of toasted grasshoppers. Lots and lots of good old-fashion food. That's the kind of fellow Halhalis was.

Hineh came over to the dance from that Lemoore Ranch of his in a buckboard wagon with three barrels of whiskey strapped to the rear end and each barrel rigged with a pull-down spigot. Halhalis tried to chase Hineh and his whiskey wagon away, but Hineh just laughed. "You want some poison on your back?" Hineh yelled. "You want the shit cleaned from your ass every day, like your friend José Jesús?"

When Halhalis turned his back on the threats, Hineh let everybody have their fill of the whiskey, and pretty soon the Tachi boys were fighting with the Wukchumni boys, and both of the Yokuts groups began teasing the Mexican fellows. Naturally, the Mexican boys took out their knives, and before the professional singers and Cuksa the clown could get people interested in dancing and singing and clapping to the old songs, all hell came down on Halhalis's party. Worse, while my friend Halhalis was putting bandages on stab wounds and chasing the Mexicans off his property before the white man's sheriff came around, Hineh grabbed Halhalis's young wife around her breasts and started pulling her toward the woods.

"You come with me, or I'll poison your husband," Hineh told the beautiful young Yokuts woman.

"Get your hands off that girl!" Mrs. Williams yelled.

Hineh threw eagle down at Mrs. Williams and hissed, "Stay away, white witch! Halhalis is a dead man if you interfere with my pleasure."

Mrs. Williams picked up a stout oak log, walked five paces to where Hineh held the pretty Yokuts woman, and bashed Hineh smack on the top of his head. "You damn troublemaker!" she yelled. "Get your damn whiskey off my property!"

Hineh sat in the dust and stared at Mrs. Williams. He threw another pinch of eagle feathers at her in a petulant, nearly effeminate, motion. Then Hineh crawled over to a bench next to a huge plank table and pulled himself up to the picnic. The Tachi people and Wukchumni people and Mrs. Williams stood around whispering while Hineh slowly consumed huge quantities of horse meat and acorn mush and grasshoppers and coffee.

Later, after Halhalis put an ax into each of the whiskey barrels, and after he got the singers doing what they were paid to be doing, he sat down at the table next to Hineh and he also started eating the good food. I had it from all three of my favorite gossip ladies that neither man spoke to the other, and none of the guests dared join them, not even Mrs. Williams.

Now, it was widely known that Halhalis's mother was a very good antu doctor. She could never dance in the Lonewis battle against the tipne doctors, but still, she could cure almost anyone who could pay her fee. She tried to save her only son with a poultice of yerba Inez leaves and a tea of miner's lettuce and by letting blood from every swollen joint, but Halhalis died anyway. They burned the Prairie Hawk clan chief with all of his money, and they burned his lodge, and his pretty Yokuts wife and Mrs. Williams both burned their hair short to honor his death and each woman held each other to cry as they shuffled around the mourning fire. That's the kind of fellow Halhalis was.

Soon after he killed Halhalis, Hineh went around to the house of Halhalis's mother, and while she slept in a white man's bed surrounded by a tent of mosquito netting, Hineh rubbed his hand across the netting, and the old woman began to cough. The next morning she started to vomit and was dead before sunset. Hineh was very pleased with killing two such important people, and now all the people in the southern great valley were afraid of him.

Mrs. Williams and the pretty Yokuts wife disappeared together; my gossips said Fresno or Sacramento, but they couldn't swear to either big city. Now Hineh could wave his arm toward any person— Indian, Mexican, or white—and they'd run fast in the opposite direction. Hineh always made a point of telling me all about who he poisoned and how rich he was. That's the kind of man Hineh was, the sonofabitch!

❋ ❋ ❋

I missed Brother Coyote. I missed his jokes and bad advice. Hineh wouldn't let go of Coyote Spirit, and my cousin let his big black teeth hang out of his mouth every time I even hinted how much I missed my spirit brother.

"You never did have any good luck," Hineh would always say. "A little teat sucker is better off without a tricky spirit brother around."

The problems of the People lay like tumors on my stomach. Every night sweat bubbled over my body as the beetles crawled through the tule thatch and the frogs complained with incessant monotony. Palu muttered about the lodge through each day as she did chores and fed my visitors, and then she snored like two cougars having a fight through each night.

"Old Coyote is having great fun hanging around me," Hineh cackled. "Best fun the scrawny sonofabitch has ever had—especially with toting my poison around and scaring the hell out of the Mexican folks. Yes sir! We are one helluva pair! Yes indeedy."

CHAPTER TWENTY-ONE

Summer, 1868

I WAS STILL ON THE RESERVATION in my little tule-thatch hut, and still missing Brother Coyote. It was already hot enough to fry acorn mush on a griddle, when the white man leaned over my bed. He wore pinched-on glasses and a useless black hat on his head. The sonofabitch was back again—the third or fifth time, I didn't know or care.

"You want to hear more?" I asked him.

"Yes."

"Why? What's a white man want with an old Tachi fellow?"

"You are one of the last Yokuts, José Jesús. Certainly the last full-blood Tipne Man in the valley, and I want to write down everything you remember from the old days."

"What do you want to hear? Tell me."

"Anything at all. Just keep talking about things that happened to you and the Tachi people."

I moved my bones to find a more comfortable alignment of back and butt. "Well, for one thing, those padre fellows were dumber than most of the old-time Tachi elders. For another, all those Spanish spirit doctors were just plain stupid compared to Podnow."

"Who's Podnow?"

"He was the elder brother of my father and supreme tipne of the People." I sucked in some air to keep talking. "Podnow was also my teacher."

"Okay, go ahead."

"Well now—it is an undeniable fact that most of the white people I've ever met were dumber than most of the Yokuts, yet those damn white invaders kept on living and multiplying while the People up and died."

"Interesting observation, old man."

"More interesting to me is that the invaders live and Hineh lives and the People die."

The white man rubbed his dark-brown beard with his left hand. "Tell me about Hineh."

"Well now, the latest I heard was just a few days ago from a young woman who visits me occasionally."

"Are you talking about something that recently happened to Hineh?"

"Certainly, I'm talking about a bunch of Wowol folks so scared of Hineh that they hired two of the best tipne doctors in the great valley to kill the sonofabitch."

The pinch-nosed white man sipped water from a glass bottle and wiped sweat from his forehead. "Who are these tipne doctors that you are talking about?"

"One was named Foster, and I knew him from past Lonewis dances. He was a real powerful doctor. A good doctor too, who could admit when he couldn't cure a person. He used the white name of Foster and got lots of work from Mexican folks and some white folks also. He was a good man and so was that friend of his named Kosewa."

"Go on. What happened with the Wowol?"

"These two good doctors called a dance at the Wowol village, and they sang some magic songs to kill Hineh, and they shot magic arrows into the night to pierce Hineh through the heart. Tipne doctor Foster and tipne doctor Kosewa called for help from their spirit guides, and while the Wowol beat the foot drum and clapped both sticks and hands and sang along with the paid singers, the two doctors screamed horrible threats of violence toward Hineh. The doctors drank baskets of tanai and floated among the red clouds of Tipiknits Pahn, and they drank tobacco tea and puked all over the ground. They turned the poison of Hineh into a wispy gray cloud that floated into the night to sneak into Hineh's lodge and into Hineh's nose and throat and mouth and ears. In the dreams of the two good doctors, Hineh died a slow, painful death, and all the Wowol were as happy as kids eating toasted grasshoppers. The Wowol paid Doctor Foster fifty dollars in gold money and Doctor Kosewa thirty dollars in gold money."

The ugly white man smiled. "Those two tipne doctors killed your cousin Hineh with their magic? Wow!"

"Just hold from speaking before I'm finished, you dumb sonofabitch."

He dropped his smile and sat upright on his little wooden stool. After rubbing at the sweat again, he waved for me to continue.

"It was a week after the big Wowol dance, and those two good doctors were over at Telweyit to cure an old man who had bumps all over his back. The doctors and the old man and the old man's two sons were in the sweat lodge when Hineh and some Tachi men came through the door and walls and shot Doctor Foster full of arrows. While those bad men were cutting off the head of the good doctor, Kosewa ran to the river and jumped into the deep water."

I let the silence spin for a while, just to put the white man in his proper place.

"That's it?" the white man finally asked.

"Oh, you want to hear the end of this story?"

"Certainly, old man, I'm a scientist from the University of California and must collect accurate information for my studies," said the white man.

"Tell me how my accurate information will be used by such an esteemed personage."

"I write books about the aboriginal cultures of our west coast, and give lectures to educated audiences throughout the world, old man."

"One gold coin," I said.

"I collect this information for science, not for a traveling circus."

"One gold coin."

He dug into a pocket and flipped the coin onto my lap.

"Well now, Mr. Smartass, it seems that Hineh walked calmly out of the wrecked sweat lodge, and when Kosewa emerged from the water to breathe, Hineh threw a magic arrow and struck the good doctor in the face. A bit later in the evening, Hineh's bad men found Kosewa's body wedged between two rocks, and Hineh also severed that good doctor's head and threw it back into the water."

The white man frowned but remained silent.

I rolled over onto my side to remove the sight of such an ugly face. He looked like a half-dead city rat, not a country rat with bright eyes and a nest full of treasures. "Maybe the padres were correct," I whispered to the wall. "Maybe the Yokuts and Miwok and all the others are mere children who have no ability to command God's beneficent good will. Maybe the Californios were right when they claimed the Yokuts as perpetually corrupted by the wild freedom of the old days. Maybe the Americans are correct when they kill the People like rabbits fit for the snare."

"Where did you get those big words, José Jesús?" He tapped his pencil on the pad of paper. "You sound like an educated white man."

I pulled a wool blanket over my shoulders. "Me forget," I said. "Me just a dumb digger, a no-good digger that can't talk good white man's talk."

The pencil tapping stopped. I heard the stool move over the packed dirt toward my bed, and the rat-faced American coughed. "I'm sorry, old man" he said. "Go ahead with your story."

I let him sit for a while until the noise of his breathing jangled my nerves, before spitting out the next part of Hineh's story.

"After the good doctors were killed, I was able to walk around for a short distance, and I could suddenly appreciate the taste of cold water in my mouth and the hot sun on my back. That damn half-breed, Carlos, came over to Palu's lodge to boost me up on an old horse and lead us around and around in circles. I could hear the ravens and see the magpie scooting from tree to tree."

"Hineh?" the white man said.

"Whatever he demanded of the People, he received. Money, a man's wife or daughter—whatever he wanted. Those who hesitated in complying with his request were killed by Hineh's gang of bad men or poisoned by Hineh himself. Two years after I lost my spirit brother and a year after I started wobbling around, Hineh sent his winatum around to the little villages and ranches and to the reservation to invite everyone to a big Lonewis at his Lemoore ranch. All the Yokuts were required to attend, and some were forced to leave their white bosses in the middle of harvesting the winter wheat or rounding up sheep from the swamps near the river. Nobody dared stay away from Hineh's Lonewis because they were all scared shitless, plus everybody had lots and lots of kin who had died since the last Lonewis."

"Tell me about this Lonewis. As I recall, a Lonewis is a ceremony to mourn the dead."

"The Lonewis celebrates the lives of those People who have died since the last Lonewis."

"Fine, go ahead."

"There were only two doctors who danced for those who were still alive, not like in the old days when dozens of doctors danced for the grievers." I turned back to face the white man. "Even during the gold rush there were a lot of doctors at the annual Lonewis."

"What happened to all the Yokuts?"

"The white farmers drained the beautiful tule marshes is what happened, so the Yokuts either died or moved."

"Beautiful tule marshes? How can you call a bunch of swampland beautiful? They're nothing but mosquito holes full of malaria."

"The malaria and the white men came at the same time. Before the white men, the tule marshes and lakes were beautiful. We caught fish larger than a man and collected tasty roots and green herbs. Herds of deer and elk and antelope filled our tule land. There were ducks and geese and shore birds without number, and the God of all Spirits gave his People the most beautiful and productive land in the world. He gave us the beautiful tule marshes and the bountiful lakes."

"Oh! Really? You are certain that there was no malaria before the white man?"

"None at all. About the time that Sutter started with his New Helvetia—that's when the malaria started to hit the People."

"My, that is very, very interesting data." He scrubbed his beard and made some notes. "Okay, let's get back to Hineh's Lonewis."

"Well, things started when Hineh stared at me from across the central fire while his winatum threw on more logs and even some pine stumps full of sap. Those flames jumped toward the stars and illuminated Hineh's feather headdress, eagle-down necklace, hand feathers, and magic arrow tray. The sonofabitch strutted about the central fire and slowly made his way about the six smaller fires, and he was always posturing, making evil threats toward me—always curling his lips back over his black teeth and spitting at me like a cornered cougar."

"So you were the other dancer?"

"Just me and Hineh."

"Tell me about your regalia."

"I wore no feathers or paint. I carried only Podnow's old basket tray, nothing more."

"How old were you and Hineh at his Lonewis?"

"Seventy or so for me, and Hineh was a bit older."

"Okay, go ahead."

"I stood near the central fire and watched Hineh, but I listened for whispers from the spirit world. There were twelve professional singers who clapped and sang, but the People remained silent as stone. Cuksa the clown did not appear. The owls were silent, but the spirits whispered to me with soft *coos*. Hineh finally dashed toward me, screaming his ghost scream and slashing the night air with his Spanish knife. I threw a handful of eagle down toward him, and he stopped short, as if frozen cold."

"My goodness!" the white man said. "What happened?"

"Well, Palu stood from her seat and came to my side. Then the old Tachi ladies gimped over and stood between Hineh and me, and next came Carlos and the eldest of the elders from the reservation, along with many of the older women. They made a circle around me to stare silently into the dark. They made no threat to the bad boys or to Hineh, and soon the only sound we could hear was a coyote howling at the blood-slashed moon."

"Have you ever observed such an intervention by the audience at any previous Lonewis?"

"Never."

"Hmmm. I believe I've read of a similar mediation of good people and evil opportunists with other indigenous tribes. I'm pretty sure that it was with the Onondaga Nation, shortly before our war with Great Britain."

"I've heard good things about those Iroquois people—but don't mistake an eastern tribe with a valley village."

"Of course not. I studied at Harvard University and have an intimate understanding of the differences."

"I'm tired. Go away."

"Just finish the Lonewis. And I'll leave for the day."

I let him squirm for a while on his three-legged stool.

"Let's see," I said, "it was about the time the coyote commenced howling that Hineh dropped his Spanish dagger, and he seemed to wilt just like a plant with its root chewed off by a gopher. His eyes turned dull and rheumy."

"I yelled into the silence. 'Coyote! Where have you been? Do you remember when we were brothers?' Coyote came trotting down the moonlit path and flopped at my feet. 'I've been messing with that cousin of yours for a long time,' he said."

"You and the coyote spirit had a conversation that everyone gathered could hear?"

"Certainly."

"They could hear both you and the spirit?"

"Certainly."

"I see." The white man went to his pencil-tapping for a while, then, "Please continue with the Lonewis, sir."

"'How can you stay with Hineh? He's a poisoner,' I asked.

"Coyote sat in the dust at my feet, all floppy-jointed and relaxed. 'Hineh's chief of all the People in this part of the great valley, and he's a tipne doctor to boot.'

"'Does he make you laugh?' I asked.

"Coyote scratched his left ear, then sat looking at me with a vacant expression. 'Nope. That cousin of yours is one mean sonofabitch.' Coyote shook the dust from his coat. 'Hineh's meaner than a badger with his foot in a metal snare.'

"You going to stay around Hineh?"

"Nope, I'm all finished with Hineh."

"The Lonewis singers started singing to the slow, steady beat of the foot drum. A pine stump flared with exuberant tongues of flame. I walked over to Hineh and dribbled a pinch of eagle feathers over his shoulders—then I started my slow dance around the center fire. Palu joined me, and then the Christian ladies and the elders and honored younger men and women filed into line in neat, quiet progression. Finally the half-breeds and quarter-breeds and strangers among us joined the others who followed my lead. We danced and sang and cried for those who had died since the last Lonewis, until the moon changed place with the sun."

"What happened to Hineh?"

"One of the Tachi bad boys put a blanket over Hineh and tried to give him some water, but Hineh turned his head away and started to stuff dirt into his mouth."

"Then what?"

"The People celebrated the death of their kin for the next four nights. They repeated jokes performed by the dead, and they burned tule mannequins of the dead, and everyone cried. The People laughed and they cried at Hineh's Lonewis, and at the end Hineh was so thin that his bones showed through the skin. On the fifth day of his Lonewis, Hineh died, and I walked back to Palu's lodge to sit and think about why the People were all still dying."

"What happened next?"

I turned to face the wall again. "Go away, white man. I'm tired."

"Please! Just one more story."

"Go away."

"I'll come back again, or maybe I'll send one of my assistants to write down more of your stories."

"I'll be dead. I'm an old man."

CHAPTER TWENTY-TWO

Summer, 1870

IT TOOK TWO, THREE MONTHS, I don't know exactly how long. Palu was dead, so time didn't matter. The old ladies were dead, and the reservation was full of dead people and drunks, so I got up out of bed and started walking. I didn't know where, just someplace away from that miserable place. Folks along the way—white and red both—gave me enough to eat, and at night I'd crawl into a bunch of leaves, and my dried-up skin always shook hard enough to keep the dreams from coming on too bad. No sense in hurrying a sack of old bones, so maybe it was six moons. I didn't know and didn't care a rat's ass one way or the other.

Chief Takac of the Waksachi people let me live in a small lodge in his village. He was younger than me by twenty years or so, but we made a good pair with our gossip about the old days and complaints about the new days. We drank a little tanai tea from some nice Pomo baskets that he had, and we stared into the fire for most of every night and day.

"You want me to get you a woman, José Jesús? The nights get cold pretty soon."

"You got one that doesn't talk very much—a nice fat old lady who's always quiet and respectful?"

Takac shook his head. "We've some fat ladies, but they'll talk your ear off, and we've got some old quiet ladies, but stones in the river have more wit."

"I could use another blanket. Just keep the women and white folks away from me." I sipped the tea. "I'll just watch Coyote brother mess around and maybe drink a little whiskey now and then."

Chief Takac laughed. "Is that coyote friend of yours still a randy sonofabitch?"

"He'd screw rolling tumbleweed if it slowed down just a bit."

"No whiskey, José Jesús. Not in my valley."

"Two blankets then." I wagged a finger in his face. "And keep those damn white folks off my neck. They're nothing but scrub jay busybodies with their questions and insults."

Takac filled my basket. "Two things you've got to know, José Jesús. I can't stop the weather, and I can't tell white folks what to do."

"Three blankets then—got no fat on these bones at all. Damn sonsabitches white people."

❋❋❋

The busybodies found me again—not the man with the black hat but a tall black-haired woman. She had a black man who toted her notebooks and writing desk and drove the fancy phaeton up from Fresno. She wore a veil over her face, and I could never make out her eyes or the lines over her eyes, but I still knew that she was a liar.

The sourpuss bitch said, "Here's the twenty pounds of beans and ten pounds of rice that I promised the last time we talked."

The black man dumped both burlap bags next to my fire pit.

"I've got nobody to cook for me, and my fingers don't work anymore," I said. "Give me dollars to pay some old woman to cook my meals."

"You'd just go buy whiskey if I gave you any money," she said.

"None of your damned business what I buy or don't buy."

"Hear now!" The black man moved between the woman and me. "Don't you go messing with this here lady." He shook long black fingers in my face. "She's trying her best to be nice to you damn diggers."

"We're not diggers, you black sonofabitch! Yokuts!"

"Clarence!" The white woman raised her voice. "I have business with José Jesús. He's the last full-blood medicine man of the Yokuts, and we need his stories."

"He's a mean-mouthed old man," Clarence said.

"Bring my desk here to my side, and then please wait outside this shack until I call," she said.

"Gladly," Clarence said. "It stinks like a digger skunk in here."

When he returned with the desk and after he set it up, I waved my clay pipe in his direction. "Damned nigger," I said.

"Digger fool," Clarence said. "Digger drunk!"

"Out, Clarence, get out of here right now!" She watched her servant pass through the blanket door of my shack, and then settled on her three-legged stool. "Let's see now, the last time that we talked, you were going to tell me about the Dream Dance Ceremony."

"Ten dollars, gold coin," I said.

"I do not negotiate with Indians over matters within the boundaries of my professional expertise," she said.

"Well now." I leaned forward and stirred some smoke from my little fire. "Then you can just go straight to hell, you skinny mushroom bitch!"

"Apologize, Mr. Jesús. You must apologize for your rude words to me, or I'll be forced to have a word with the sheriff of this county."

"The damn sheriff has no business with me or anyone else in this valley." The smoke was getting nice and thick. "This here place is Chief Takac's village."

She opened the left drawer of her desk, pulled out a black Spanish fan, and set it flashing back and forth. "You and the chief both know that the whole lot of you are trespassing on a white gentleman's property. He's been very patient with Takac and the rest of his diggers, but he most assuredly has plans for this pleasant little valley."

"Look, lady, on your way to hell you can go fuck your white gentleman." My blood was going at a good boil now. "But if you really want a good fuck, skinny bitch, I'll give my coyote friend a whistle, and he'll give some real good service."

"Clarence!"

✳ ✳ ✳

A month after the skinny white bitch hightailed it down the hill and away from Takac's village, an old Wowol trader plopped his butt down in Takac's lodge. After three cups of tea and more silence than words, he pulled a small bundle of jimson weed from his pack. "I got this from some Paiute fellows," he said. "They say it's the best dream medicine they've ever found."

I took a big smell of the bundle and kept my mouth in a big frown. "Smells like dried horseshit," I said.

The old Wowol trader smiled. "Three ounces of gold for the bundle."

"One ounce is too much," I said.

"For you, José Jesús, it is two ounces of gold. I always save some Paiute tanai for important tipne doctors."

"Name another tipne doctor, you half-breed thief. Who's left besides me?" I waved my old arm in his old face. "Keep your dried-up old horseshit."

Chief Takac coughed, like a small animal deep in the woods. "Tell me, sir. I keep hearing strange reports coming over the mountain about the Paiute people. What's going on over there in the desert?"

The trader put the tanai bundle back into his pack with slow, discrete movements. "They're all going crazy over there."

"The Paiute going crazy?" I could feel my heart thump and a sheen of sweat build on my face. "Crazy! I'm going crazy with no whiskey around here and this old Wowol trader is charging white-man's prices for dried-up horseshit." I leaned forward to bug my eyes at the fellow. "Don't tell me about any crazy Paiute—just keep your damn mouth shut if you can't give a good deal to the greatest tipne doctor of all the Yokuts in the great valley."

Chief Takac never raised his voice. "Steady down now, José Jesús. If you want some whiskey, just go down the hill to the reservation. If you want a nice quiet place to die, then stay here in my little village. Just remember, no whiskey and no drunks around here."

I turned from both those useless old men. Damn busybodies messing with a tipne doctor who needed just one bottle of gin to cut the pain in his arms and back. Damn reservation was nothing but drunks and dead people like Palu and the old Christian ladies, that's what the reservation was. Damn white sonsabitches.

"Here's some tobacco tea." Takac had a voice that brought hummingbirds to his lips. "This here is brewed from Yankee tobacco, and you'll never have anything nicer or sweeter."

I took his basket without saying a word.

Takac gave a similar basket filled with steaming tea to the Wowol trader. "Tell me about the Paiute people," he said.

"They're dancing around every night from dusk to dawn." He lowered his voice to a whisper. "They're trying to get all their dead spirits to come alive again."

"Why is that, do you think?" Takac could easily be talking about the weather or the clover crop.

"They want to kill all the white people," the trader whispered.

"That little bunch of Paiute say they can kill all the whites?" I chuckled a little into my tobacco tea. "Those Paiute fellows are good fighters all right, but they'll get their asses kicked going up against white soldiers."

The trader joined us in some soft laughter. "They aren't too smart, those Paiute folks. They figure to bring back all their dead ancestors from the time when Eagle created the world. Those Paiute are dancing and singing almost every night, and that's a fact."

"Bunch of bullshit," I said.

"They've got their tipne doctors traveling up to Tipiknits Pahn to argue with the dead ancestors. They figure if all the dead ancestors return, then they'll have an army big enough to drive the white folks out of their desert."

"Nonsense," Takac said.

"Bullshit," I said.

The trader turned his fox-colored eyes toward me. "You want the tanai or not?"

"I'll give you an ounce of gold dust next time you come through the valley. You know damn well it'll just get all moldy in that pack of yours."

The trader stood and hauled the pack onto his shoulders. "Looks like a tough winter coming along. I didn't see a single leaf on any maple tree from the ridgeline down to the first valley oak."

"We've got wood stacked up past the eaves," Takac said.

"You'll just waste that damn tanai of yours," I said.

The trader gave us both a nice smile and stooped down through the deerskin blanket hanging over the entrance of Takac's lodge.

※※※

The messenger appeared while snow still covered the sheltered spots. He smiled at Chief Takac and at me and drank two cups of tea before he finally got down to his message. "Chief Joijoi invites all the Waksachi to a big dance at Saganiu."

"Ah, we will have a Lonewis dance?" Takac asked.

The messenger smiled with the middle part of his lips. "There's no need for the Lonewis celebration anymore, and there's no need to burn your hair short for the dead folks." He smiled to the last tooth in his mouth. "There's no need to cry or stop eating meat or stop taking a morning bath like we did in the old days."

"You drunk or something?" I asked.

"No need to get drunk either. All the ancestors back to the time when Spotted Cat made the earth are coming back to us."

"Who's this Spotted Cat, and what in hell are you talking about?" I shook my head. "The man's crazy, Takac. Give him some atole and get him out of here."

The winatum continued with his idiot smile. "Chief Joijoi went to the desert country and met with a Paiute tipne named Mohman. Now you must come to our dance and listen to Chief Joijoi. Come to the dance and visit with your old ancestors."

Chief Takac raised up his chin. "What's the harm in it, José Jesús? We'll listen to what Joijoi has to say and talk with our friends who are still alive. The dead ancestors can show up or not; we'll still have a good time."

"Nope, I can't see any part of travel this time of year. There's still a bunch of snow up in the mountains, and these old bones can't walk through any snow or cold water." I pulled the old blanket up over my shoulders. "I'll just stay here and sit by the fire."

Takac turned to the messenger. "Tell my friend Chief Joijoi that the Waksachi will attend the dance." He gave a big wink. "Tell him that José Jesús, Tipne Man for all Yokuts and Miwok, will also attend the celebration."

"Good, very good." The man reached into his carry pack. "Here's the time string. Come to the Saganiu Valley in twenty-one days. Don't burn your hair short, like for a Lonewis, but please arrive with kind thoughts in your head."

"Pshaw!" I said.

Every river that we had to cross roared over the banks and through fragile stands of willow, alder, and cottonwood trees. At the south fork of the San Joaquin, we walked up and down the hills looking for a likely spot to ford the river. Takac settled on a spot at a northerly bend and then collected every scrap of rope from his villagers. Some of the strands were white man's hemp—most were good old-fashioned milkweed rope. Bit was tied to bit, and three young men charged into the green froth to carry rope from one side to the other. They were driven against rocks, pummeled with logs, but emerged on the other side to puke and moan and rub blood from their bodies.

Twice I thought Coyote was waiting for me in Tipiknits Pahn. Water colder than ice filled my mouth and nose. The young man holding the rope sang his song and I sang mine, but he was strong and I desired life more than death, so finally we crawled over rocks and let the warm sun seep into our bones.

Infants were tied into waterproof baskets and pulled across the river with no loss of life. Only two old women and one of the brave young men were carried away in the floodwaters. The remainder of Chief Takac's Waksachi village struggled over two more sharp hills and through two precipitous canyons before arriving at the flat-topped hill overlooking Saganiu River.

Chief Joijoi stretched his arms to embrace the crowd. I could see a few scraggly remnants from Yokuts and Miwok villages, and they smiled at me and cheered their charismatic leader. The other folks in attendance? I didn't know or care why they were here. There were maybe two hundred and fifty folks, all in all.

"This is why we are assembled atop this beautiful hill," Joijoi shouted.

Mothers hushed rambunctious children; men stopped telling lies, and all turned to their host. "This is why we are assembled," he repeated in a more moderate voice. "The Eagle—our creator—will soon reveal himself to us."

"*Ahh*," the crowd sighed in a hiss of excitement.

"Six of our dead ancestors will return from Tipiknits Pahn, and they will be followed by six more and six more, and each will whisper instructions for us through our tipne doctors."

A group of six Monache Paiute made loud yodeling, otherworldly screams. They whirled around and around, like water falling through a hole, then collapsed in whimpering ecstasy. Others from the Paiute villages joined in this demonstration of joy and smiled through the entire disruption. Chief Joijoi stood silently with his arms outstretched and maintained a smile of benevolent patience. When all was quiet, he spoke again.

"José Jesús, supreme tipne of the Yokuts and our own Miwok, will sit at my side. Many lesser tipne of the Yokuts and Miwok and Paiute will surround me. They will listen for Eagle. They will listen to the ranks of dead ancestors—six after six after six—to reveal their secrets."

Screams and laughter and weeping and fainting swept through the crowd. "This is what you must do," Chief Joijoi finally said. "First you must paint your totemic patterns on your body as a welcome to the dead ancestors of your village. Next you must listen to the singers and follow their instructions. No sleeping! No fooling around! Any who disobey the singers will turn instantly into a log of wood!"

"*Oooo*," the crowd said.

I sat under a screen of tule thatch mounted on four stout branches. The shade was pleasant. An old Wukchumni woman brought me a lamb joint, a bowl of atole, and a basket of water. "Your mother and I were cousins," she whispered.

"Are you ready to join my mother in Tipiknits Pahn?" I asked.

"Certainly not, José Jesús, I believe that soon your mother will join us here in this village." The old lady moved about as if she had recently walked through a thicket of poison oak. "Your mother will return to us very soon—maybe today, but certainly tomorrow." She paused with the wiggling. "All the dead will follow Eagle back to the great valley. I will embrace my husband and your mother—all the dead ancestors will return to us." Tears dribbled from her eyes and down off her nose.

"Thank you for the water," I said. "It is cool on the tongue."

She nodded toward a tall Tulamni man who walked slowly about the circle of spectators until all stood still to listen. "I have danced with the ghosts of my ancestors," he said.

"Yes! Yes!" the crowd responded.

"I have danced with the Eastern Paiute beyond the mountains, and I have danced with the Washoe people. In both villages, the ghosts joined me to circle around the fire to sing of their return to your villages. The ghosts sing of blissful days in your company, and they rejoice in your happiness."

The crowd exploded with screams of excitement. "Begin the dance," they shouted. "Begin the dance!"

Two teams of six dancers stepped forward, and two sets of six singers started shaking their elderberry clap-sticks. They sang, *"Hai' na na ni na' na ni. Hai' na na na' na ni."* Everyone joined in circling the fire. *"Hai' na na ni na' na ni,"* they sang. No one saw the moon rise or heard the owls hoot. They sang and danced around and around the fire. *"Hai' na na ni na' na ni."*

Every once in a while, one of Joijoi's winatum scooted over to my side and whispered, "What do you hear, greatest tipne doctor of the People?"

"Nothing," I said.

"Give us a signal when the spirits speak to you," the winatum said.

"Tell the old Wukchumni lady to bring me some tobacco tea," I said.

"I will do as you ask, José Jesús."

When the first rosy blush eased over the eastern mountains, the tall Tulamni man stepped forward and the dancing stopped. After a long moment, the professional dancers led everyone in one circuit to the right, then three turns of the circle to the left.

"We are finished," the tall Tulamni man shouted.

Men and women and children ran to the river. Boys tackled girls and laughed as they held them under frigid water. Wives soaped husbands and whispered promises of delight to come. Young children cried from up and down the shore, "I'm hungry! I'm cold! Hold me, Mama! I'm hungry!"

"Come!" called the husbands, and they led their families back to the assigned campsites. Everyone scrounged dry wood for cook fires, and they waited for Chief Joijoi to demonstrate his hospitality. They watched the slaughter of live steers, and well past the noon hour each received a small portion of beef for their use. The young children cried, "I'm hungry, Mama. Give me some bread or mush or atole. I'm hungry!"

The headmen and elders of the various villages gave Chief Joijoi hard looks while the women searched along the river for roots and greens. All were embarrassed that their host was unable to provide sufficient food for his guests. At dusk the dancing and singing started again. *"Hai' na na ni na' na ni,"* they sang. Always to the left—step with the left foot and drag the right. Step and drag and sing, around and around the huge central fire. *"Hai' na na ni na' na ni."*

"Heard anything, tipne?"

"No."

"Heard anything, tipne?"

"No."

The sixth night was different.

"Men of the Yokuts and Miwok and Paiute," the tall Tulamni man called. "Bring your horses to the dance tonight. Some will ride, and the rest will dance. Tonight Eagle will listen. Tonight our ancestors will speak with the tipne. Tonight our ancestors will return from the dead and tell us what we must do to rid our land of the white invaders."

The crowd stared at the tall Tulamni man with large tired eyes and empty guts, but at dusk the dancers moved to the left—step and drag—while the owners of horses rode to the right. Dancers and riders sang a new song: *"Ya a ya e hai'ya kawai' yo. Ya a ya c hai'ya kawai' yo."*

"What do you hear, José Jesús?"

"I haven't heard a damn thing tonight and nothing from the last six nights." I gave the winatum a mean look. "Stop with the same question all the time. Just bring this old man something to eat."

"There is nothing to eat, José Jesús." The old woman bent to whisper in my ear. "Chief Joijoi says a troop of white men are coming toward our hill."

"Why?" I asked.

"Maybe they think that we will cause trouble."

I looked into the eyes of this woman. "Are you saying that the damn white folks around hereabouts think that this bunch of women and children and old men will cause them trouble?"

"Maybe they are afraid we will bring back our dead and chase them from our land."

"Pshaw! Forget the damn white men and bring me a pipe and tobacco."

The old woman looked down at the dirt as she spoke to me. "Chief Joijoi wants no trouble with the white people, and he wants you to tell all the Yokuts and Miwok and Paiute to return to their homes."

I tried to stand but collapsed on my butt. "Now? Joijoi wants us to go running off in the dark?" I shook one hand in the woman's face. "Are you mad? Chief Joijoi wants women and children and old people running down hills and through flooded rivers in the dark?"

She held up both hands. "Listen, José Jesús." The old woman stood and turned toward the main fire and screamed, "Listen to me."

The cousin of my mother watched as the dancers bumped to a halt. The singers also stopped and horses were reined still.

"The white soldiers are coming!" the old woman screamed. "They have guns and dogs and long knives!" Her voice was the winter wind through bare oak trees. "They will shoot the men and rape the young woman. The white men will slit the bellies of children and pull out your intestines for their dogs! Run!" she screamed. "Run for your lives!"

My chair collapsed under the charge of a horse. I rolled into a protective shell, but bare feet kicked and rolled my body until a tree diverted the stream of horses and people from my bag of bones. Men screamed as they were impaled on sharp willow branches. Women called, "Child! Child! Where are you?" Sparks exploded from the fire and drifted toward the dead ancestors. Gunshots echoed from canyon walls with the thunder of a huge foot drum. Screams and gunshots tore through my ears to gather in a jagged rock under my heart.

"José Jesús!"

I opened my eyes to see Chief Joijoi pull on my arm.

"Run!" he said. "The dawn is nearly upon us. Run! There is light enough to see the way!"

I sat and looked into his eyes. "You sorry sonofabitch! You're worse than any white man!"

Joijoi sat in the dust at my side. "The spirits wouldn't come," he whispered.

"You damn sonofabitch!" I yelled. "You called the white soldiers, didn't you?"

"There is no food." Tears flooded both his eyes. "There are no spirits for the People." He grabbed my shoulder. "The Paiute promised food and spirits."

I struggled to stand and made a feeble kick at Joijoi's leg.

"I'm sorry," he said. "What could I do?"

"You damn well better start running yourself, Joijoi. A bunch of your own people are going to come after you. Run, Joijoi, run!"

❅ ❅ ❅

In the fall of 1870, Takac organized another ghost dance in his own Eshom Valley village. "Just give it one more try, José Jesús. I've talked with some Paiute singers who guarantee that they've talked with dead people."

"Drunks or liars," I said.

"C'mon, José Jesús, just sit on a chair, and we'll feed you all the food you can eat. You don't have to say a thing."

"Feed me some steamed horse and a big bottle of gin, and I'll sit wherever you want."

"No gin! No whiskey!" Takac said.

"What's the matter with you, Takac? I thought you had some good sense in your head." I shook an old finger at his old head. "What do you want? Another slaughter like up at Saganiu Hill?"

Takac shut his old eyes and kept talking at me like he was an old wife of mine. "There were no white soldiers with dogs."

"Damn right, just that stupid Joijoi caught in his lies about ghosts and lots of food. Damn murderer, that sonofabitch, to send old women over cliffs and into rivers. A damn slaughter, that's all his ghost dance amounted to."

"We need you, José Jesús. The People are eating dirt. They all want to die."

I stood, even though my knees were clattering and my throat felt clogged with vomit. "They've got no reason to live, Chief Takac. Not one good reason, so why shouldn't the People eat dirt and die?"

His voice went up a notch, as if his throat was running short of air. "The ghost dance will give the People the inspiration to live, Tipne Man. If we can get them to join together and dance and sing and smile, then maybe they can make it through these hard times."

"I'm finished with this land, my friend, and so are the spirits." My cane was leaning up against the door frame of Takac's shack. "I'm going to find myself a place to die."

"Don't go. There is no one else to help the People, José Jesús."

I ignored Takac and gathered my little carry sack of mementos.

Chapter Twenty-three

Summer, 1872

IT TOOK ME ABOUT TWO weeks. I put one foot in front of the other until I walked into the white man's town of Porterville and made myself a little lean-to up on a hill away from any trouble. The white folks didn't care about any old digger, and they pretty much left me alone. The children yelled names at me and tripped me with sticks between my legs, but that's the way of all white children. That half-breed sonofabitch Carlos stopped by my little lean-to a few months after I moved to Porterville. He gave me some food and gossip and told me about Takac's ghost dance. There was no Eagle and no dead people, of course—just a bunch of drunks flopping around in the dust. It was another complete fiasco—not another slaughter. Just a big waste of time.

I got myself a regular route in that town of Porterville, just like an old beagle dog. One woman gave me bread every day, and I got a cup of bean soup from another. That's the way it was for José Jesús, the supreme tipne doctor of the People. So the days passed with no laughter but without too much pain. The moons and seasons passed, and the only bother I had was from the snoops who kept coming to me with their questions. Questions, always questions, but I always insulted them, and they eventually disappeared. I cackled at them as they drove their two-wheeled carts and buckboards down off my hill—the damn busybodies, the sonsabitches!

I had to admit that Carlos was my only pleasure. He started to show up every week and sit at my side while we both listened to the silence. He didn't ask any stupid questions, and when the fire went cold, I'd curl up on my tule-reed mat and fall asleep. In the morning there was always a blanket over my shoulders and a big pot of beans sitting on the burned-out fire. Even better than the beans were the chunks of pig meat scattered through them, and both the beans and meat were real tender. I could always gum the mess down with no trouble at all.

Gin was the best substitute for tanai. Especially the rainwater-clear gin, with juniper berries floating around in the bottle. This English gin brought to mind a tiny soft meadow, hidden among some scraggly foxtail pine and lots and lots of juniper trees. When I drank juniper gin my twins ran toward me with their smiles and jiggling breasts. "Roll over, old man," they shouted, and after I put my head down on my sweaty arms, one wife massaged my shoulders and the other rubbed my feet and kissed each toe. They rubbed and kissed and rolled me over to slip Kalu's breast in my mouth and my stiff rod into Hainan's moist vagina. Later we slept together in a tangle of arms and legs, like puppies after a delicious romp. The English gin always brought Kalu with her soft laughter and Hainan with her whispered songs.

On the nights that Carlos was with his family over in the white man's town of Fresno, I thought of those two white fellows that killed my twins. I thought of their ugly toadstool faces and imagined the pleasure of filling them with thunder and lead pellets. Maybe the ten-gauge shotgun was a better choice than obsidian-tipped arrows. I imagined easing the trigger slowly toward my nose until the black cloud erupted in an ear-splitting concussion, and the cloud changed from black to blood red, and those two Missouri-men floated effortlessly away over a mountain-spiked horizon.

Lately I'd been telling the busybodies that I was a hundred and five years old. They rode their horses from Porterville right up to where I was sitting in front of my lean-to, and then they let their beasts shit all over my yard.

"Twenty dollars gold coin," I yelled at them.

"Listen, old man," the snoops always said, "I'll give you twenty dollars cash money after we've finished talking."

They were all big liars, because after I talked to the sonsabitches so long that dust dribbled in my mouth, they would say, "Listen, old man. I'm broke today, but next time you can tell me about the spirit dancers, and I'll give you thirty dollars cash money."

They lied worse than I did. Anybody could watch their eyes and the wrinkles over their eyes and figure out what they wanted to hear. I always told them what they thought they already knew, the stupid sonsabitches. I never told the truth about anything that was important to the People. That was my guiding rule—never tell the truth to those pompous know-it-alls. Kroeber and his ugly, skinny women—they all preferred lies to the truth. I would have liked to see Kroeber run around in his bare ass. I couldn't believe that he was a real man with all his talk, talk, talk—just like those women of his with their skinny teats and skinny little moustaches. Kroeber with his big hairy moustache and his flock of women with their skinny little moustaches—they were all the same.

"Now, Mr. Jesús"—Kroeber always wore a tiny bowler hat and talked as if he hadn't had a good shit in a long time—"wasn't it true that the Yokuts lacked any belief in a single deity? They all worshiped a group of animal spirits who were designated as creators of the universe, right?"

"Twenty dollars gold coin—this old man can't remember much until he has twenty dollars in his pocket."

"Later," Kroeber always said. "At the end of the interview I'll give you some money. Now, let's get back . . ."

His women were the most fun. Whenever we got around to sex, they'd start chewing on their pencils. They'd eat erasers and get black marks on their cheeks and chin. "Please, Mr. Jesús, tell me about the Yokuts marriage rituals."

"The biggest cock got the most women," I'd say.

"Oh dear," she'd say. "I don't understand. Could you explain what you mean?" Beads of sweat mixed with the silken hair of her mustache.

"Us Indians never wore any clothes, right? You know that for a fact, lady. Since the women of our tribe always made all the rules, then it just stands to reason that the man with the biggest cock got as many wives as he could handle. I had eight wives. Do you want to see why I had eight wives, lady?"

"Uh, no, Mr. Jesús, that will not be necessary. I've never heard of such a ritual."

"Maybe that Kroeber fellow would like to see why I had eight wives. He seems real interested in cocks."

"No, do not disturb Dr. Kroeber with such trivial nonsense, and please do not insult our dedication to science. You must realize, after our many interviews, Mr. Jesús, that we're trying our very best to help you people before you're all gone."

"Well, if you want science, lady, then you'd better keep talking with José Jesús, the greatest tipne doctor of the People." I leaned closer to blow bean breath all over the ugly woman. "You people have been paying good money to those half-breeds and quarter-breeds. Liars and fools—that's who you science people are talking to, not real Indians like me."

✳ ✳ ✳

The juniper berry sat on my tongue and rolled slowly in slippery slides down my throat and chest. It could rest for days in my stomach. The juniper berry brought dreams of sorrel horses and golden eagles and my beautiful twins. Two dollars bought a bottle of the water-clear gin with juniper berries, and one dollar bought gin with no berries. The dollar gin exploded in my head and brought dreams of burning funeral pyres filled with scabby, worm-filled spirits who had no one to cry for them. These long-dead people of my cheap gin dreams screamed at me to grieve for them. They screamed for someone to lead them to Tipiknits Pahn. They screamed and screamed but no one listened—not even me.

My second favorite was muscatel brandy for ten cents. This Mexican guy by the name of Fernando sold me a mason jar full of muscatel brandy, and at the halfway mark down the jar, Brother Coyote trotted down the road and flopped at my feet. He didn't say anything until I was near the bottom of the jar—then old Coyote got up and started acting playful with his bark-barking to get me into some chase game. When the jar was flat-out empty, the two of us curled up and talked about the best way to kill gophers. We always started with gophers, and then moved along to larger varmints, such as rabbits and skunks and white people. That old Coyote fellow could get pretty mean when it came to dispatching varmints.

Of course there weren't a lot of anthropologists, so it always got down to pennies. Outside the dry-goods store in Porterville was the best place to beg pennies. I stayed away from the saloons because there were a bunch of mean, tight-fisted sonsabitches in the Porterville saloons. When I had three cents and my own mason jar, this Missouri fellow would sell me his white lightning. I always added a handful of cigar butts to the white lighting to give it some flavor. Outside the Gold Dust was the best place for cigar butts, as long as you didn't ask for any spare pennies. It took an hour or so to age the mixture until it was a nice mellow amber color.

There were two good reasons for the cigar butts. First, the white lightning tasted better when it got to about the color of my arm. Second is the fact that the moochers couldn't stand any part of lightning and cigars.

"Wha'cha got?" they always asked.

"Yokuts tea," I always told them. "Here, take a sip and tell me what you think. It'll put some hair on your balls."

The lady moochers always got a kick about the hairy balls, but the truth of the matter was that none of them could stand the taste or smell or any part of my Yokuts tea, so there was all the more for me, if you understand what I'm telling you. Oh, there were a few of the half-blood old-timers who pretended to take a drink, but I was the only one who could drink the stuff without puking all over the dirt. I'll tell you, though—a few slugs of lightning and cigars, and I felt like I was about twenty months pregnant. My stomach kicked out and the gorge pushed right up to the base of my tongue.

The good part of the Yokuts tea was the fact that it didn't take long for the dreams to start, and pretty soon I saw boiling red clouds with my dead father riding his winged sorrel horse all over the sky. Uncle Podnow would start dancing, and the People would begin clapping and singing and laughing and crying. Podnow's big belly bounced in perfect time with the beat of the foot drum, and sweat poured down, down, down until I'd be drenched with his sweat. Not a bad deal—three cents and my own jar, then the red clouds and Brother Coyote and Podnow's big belly.

"Now listen to that, will you? Who's flying around in a zigzag pattern through the red clouds and green trees? How about that! Look! Pokook, the little burrowing owl, our winatum from the spirit world—there he goes, flap, flap, and glide! Flap, flap, and glide!

"Hey! Pokook! Here—over here. Just one more sip and I'm ready. Hold still for a moment, Pokook, while I sip this last swallow of Yokuts tea. There. *Ah!* Now I'm ready."

Flap, flap, and glide.

"I'm ready, Pokook. Let's you and me and Brother Coyote fly around for a while. We'll study all the beautiful tule marshes up in Tipiknits Pahn. We'll sing and dance and cry with all the beautiful dead people, like in the old days."

Flap, flap, glide. "Nothing to worry about, Pokook—the People have Chief Carlos, so don't worry. Let's go."

Flap, flap, and glide.

www.ingramcontent.com/pod-product-compliance
Lightning Source LLC
Chambersburg PA
CBHW020357210626
46816CB00006BB/2013